Beyond Borders

Book Two

The Lone Star Series

D1621856

by
Bobby Akart

Other Works by Bestselling Author Bobby Akart

The Lone Star Series

Axis of Evil

Beyond Borders

Lines in the Sand

Texas Strong

Fifth Column

Suicide Six

The Pandemic Series

Beginnings

The Innocents

Level 6

Quietus

The Blackout Series

36 Hours

Zero Hour

Turning Point

Shiloh Ranch

Hornet's Nest

Devil's Homecoming

The Boston Brahmin Series

The Loyal Nine

Cyber Attack

Martial Law

False Flag

The Mechanics

Choose Freedom

Patriot's Farewell

Seeds of Liberty (Companion Guide)

The Prepping for Tomorrow Series

Cyber Warfare

EMP: Electromagnetic Pulse

Economic Collapse

Dedications

Every day, I wake up to a beautiful world filled with the undying love of my wife and the loyalty of our pups. Without them, none of my books would be possible. I wish every family could have what we have.

The Lone Star Series is dedicated to the love and support of my family. I will always protect you from anything that would disrupt our happiness.

ACKNOWLEDGEMENTS

Writing a book that is both informative and entertaining requires a tremendous team effort. Writing is the easy part. For their efforts in making *Beyond Borders*, book two in the Lone Star series, a reality, I would like to thank Hristo Argirov Kovatliev for his incredible cover art, Pauline Nolet for her editorial prowess, Stef Mcdaid for making this manuscript decipherable in so many formats, Christian Rummell and the folks at Audible Studios for producing the incredible narration, and the Team—Shirley, Denise, Joe, and Jim, whose advice, friendship and attention to detail is priceless.

A special thank-you to Kevin Baron and the team at *Defense One* for providing invaluable insight into the North Korean threat and how we'd defend against it. Also, thank you to Michaela Dodge, senior policy analyst at the Heritage Foundation, Center for National Defense, for their extensive background material on missile defense, nuclear weapons modernization and arms control.

Thank you all!
Choose Freedom!

FOREWORD

by Dr. Peter Vincent Pry
Chief of Staff,
Congressional EMP Commission

Executive Director, Task Force
on National and Homeland Security

The recent escalating war of words and actions with rogue nations like North Korea and Iran has given rise to a new sense of urgency about threats we face—especially the existential threat that is nuclear electromagnetic pulse (EMP) attack. I am pleased to write this foreword for author Bobby Akart as he continues to inform his readers, through his works of fiction, about the EMP threat, both man-made and naturally occurring.

With the Lone Star Series, you will learn about the potential of nuclear-armed satellites flying over America daily in low-earth orbit, positioned to collapse our power grid, destroy our way of life, and possibly kill up to ninety percent of Americans.

The Congressional EMP Commission warns North Korea may already pose a worldwide threat, not only by ICBM, but by satellites, two of which presently orbit over the United States and every country on Earth.

A single satellite, if nuclear-armed, detonated at high-altitude would generate an EMP capable of blacking out power grids and life-sustaining critical infrastructure.

Yet, after massive intelligence failures grossly underestimating North Korea's nuclear capabilities, their biggest threat to the U.S. and the world remains unacknowledged — nuclear EMP attack.

The EMP threat continues to be low-priority and largely ignored, even though on September 2, 2017, North Korea confirmed the

EMP Commission's assessment by testing an H-Bomb that could make a devastating EMP attack.

Two days after their H-Bomb test, on September 4, Pyongyang also released a technical report "The EMP Might of Nuclear Weapons" accurately describing a "super-EMP" weapon generating 100,000 volts/meter.

North Korea's development of a Super-EMP weapon that generates 100,000 volts/meter is a technological watershed more threatening than development of an H-Bomb and ICBM because even the U.S. nuclear deterrent, the best protected U.S. military forces, are EMP hardened to survive only 50,000 volts/meter.

My colleague, EMP Commission Chairman William Robert Graham warned Congress in 2008 that Russia had developed Super-EMP weapons and most likely transferred that technology to North Korea allegedly *by accident*, according to Russian generals.

The results of this newly discovered relationship between Russia and North Korea was that the DPRK now has the technology to win a nuclear war. At the very least, a North Korean EMP attack could paralyze the U.S. nuclear deterrent and prevent U.S. retaliation, perhaps even by U.S. submarines at sea that cannot launch missiles without receiving an Emergency Action Message from the president.

However, the warning signs have gone largely ignored. Although North Korea, Russia, and China have all made nuclear threats against the United States recently, in the case of North Korea and Russia repeatedly, most analysts dismiss the war of words as *mere bluster* and *nuclear sabre rattling*, not to be taken seriously.

In the West, generations of leaders and citizens have been educated that use of nuclear weapons is unthinkable and the ultimate horror. Not so in Russia, China, and North Korea where their nuclear capabilities are publicly paraded — missile launches and exercises are televised as a show of strength, an important part of national pride.

Then, there is the issue of an EMP attack. An electromagnetic pulse attack would be perfect for implementing Russia's strategy of "de-escalation," where a conflict with the U.S. and its allies would be won by limited nuclear use. It's their version of "shock and awe" to cow the U.S. into submission. The same kind of attack is viewed as an acceptable option by China and North Korea as well.

An EMP attack would be the most militarily effective use of one or a few nuclear weapons, while also being the most acceptable nuclear option in world opinion, the option most likely to be construed in the U.S. and internationally as "restrained" and a "warning shot" without direct loss of life.

Because an electromagnetic pulse destroys electronics instead of blasting cities, even some analysts in Germany and Japan, among the most anti-nuclear nations, regard EMP attacks as an acceptable use of nuclear weapons. A high-altitude EMP ("HEMP") attack entails detonating a nuclear weapon at 30-400 kilometers altitude — above the atmosphere, in outer space, so high that no nuclear effects, not even the sound of the explosion, would be experienced on the ground, except the resulting EMP.

An EMP attack will kill far more people than nuclear blasting a city through indirect effects — by blacking out electric grids and destroying life-sustaining critical infrastructures like communications, transportation, food and water — in the long run. But the millions of fatalities likely to eventually result from EMP will take months to develop, as slow as starvation.

Thus, a nation hit with an EMP attack will have powerful incentives to cease hostilities, focus on repairing their critical infrastructures while there is still time and opportunity to recover, and avert national extinction.

Indeed, an EMP attack or demonstration made to "de-escalate" a crisis or conflict is very likely to raise a chorus of voices in the West against nuclear escalation and send Western leaders in a panicked search for the first "off ramp."

Axis of Evil, and the entire Lone Star Series, are books of fiction which are based upon historical fact. The geopolitical factors in this series leading up to a potentially catastrophic collapse of America's power grid are based upon real-world scenarios.

Author Bobby Akart has written several fiction and non-fiction books with the intent to raise awareness about the threats we face from an EMP, whether via a massive solar storm or delivered by a nuclear warhead. While many books have been written about the results of nuclear war and EMPs, few have tackled the subject of using satellites as a means of delivering the fatal blow, until now.

The Lone Star Series is written to be thought-provoking. It will be a reminder to us all that you never know when the day before is the day before. Prepare for tomorrow.

Dr. Peter Vincent Pry
Chief of Staff
Congressional EMP Commission
Executive Director
Task Force on National and Homeland Security

About Dr. Peter Vincent Pry

Dr. Peter Vincent Pry served as Chief of Staff of Congressional Electromagnetic Pulse (EMP) Commission (2001-2017), and is currently the Executive Director of the Task Force on National and Homeland Security, a Congressional Advisory Board dedicated to achieving protection of the United States from electromagnetic pulse (EMP), Cyber Warfare, mass destruction terrorism and other threats to civilian critical infrastructures, on an accelerated basis. Dr. Pry also is Director of the United States Nuclear Strategy Forum, an advisory board to Congress on policies to counter Weapons of Mass Destruction. Foreign governments, including the United Kingdom, Israel, Canada, and Kazakhstan consult with Dr. Pry on EMP, Cyber, and other strategic threats.

Dr. Pry served on the staffs of the Congressional Commission on the Strategic Posture of the United States (2008-2009); the Commission on the New Strategic Posture of the United States (2006-2008); and the Commission to Assess the Threat to the United States from Electromagnetic Pulse (EMP) Attack (2001-2008).

Dr. Pry served as Professional Staff on the House Armed Services Committee (HASC) of the U.S. Congress, with portfolios in nuclear strategy, WMD, Russia, China, NATO, the Middle East, Intelligence, and Terrorism (1995-2001). While serving on the HASC, Dr. Pry was chief advisor to the Vice Chairman of the House Armed Services Committee and the Vice Chairman of the House Homeland Security Committee, and to the Chairman of the Terrorism Panel. Dr. Pry played a key role: running hearings in Congress that warned terrorists and rogue states could pose EMP and Cyber threats, establishing the Congressional EMP Commission, helping the Commission develop plans to protect the United States from EMP and Cyber Warfare, and working closely with senior scientists and the nation's top experts on critical infrastructures, EMP and Cyber Warfare.

Dr. Pry was an Intelligence Officer with the Central Intelligence Agency responsible for analyzing Soviet and Russian nuclear strategy, operational plans, military doctrine, threat perceptions, and developing U.S. paradigms for strategic warning (1985-1995). He also served as a Verification Analyst at the U.S. Arms Control and Disarmament Agency responsible for assessing Soviet arms control treaty compliance (1984-1985).

Dr. Pry has written numerous books on national security issues, including:

Blackout Wars; Apocalypse Unknown: The Struggle To Protect America From An Electromagnetic Pulse Catastrophe; Electric Armageddon: Civil-Military Preparedness For An Electromagnetic Pulse Catastrophe; War Scare: Russia and America on the Nuclear Brink; Nuclear Wars: Exchanges and Outcomes; The Strategic Nuclear Balance: And Why It Matters; and Israel's Nuclear Arsenal.

You may view his canon of work by visiting his Amazon Author page.

Dr. Pry often appears on TV and radio as an expert on national security issues. The BBC made his book War Scare into a two-hour TV documentary Soviet War Scare 1983 and his book Electric Armageddon was the basis for another TV documentary Electronic Armageddon made by the National Geographic.

ABOUT THE AUTHOR

Bobby Akart

Bestselling author Bobby Akart has been ranked by Amazon as the #3 Bestselling Religion & Spirituality Author, the #5 Bestselling Science Fiction Author, and the #7 Bestselling Historical Author. He has written sixteen international bestsellers, in thirty-nine different fiction and nonfiction genres, including the critically acclaimed Boston Brahmin series, the bestselling Blackout series, his highly cited nonfiction Prepping for Tomorrow series and his latest project—the Pandemic series, which has produced four #1 bestsellers.

Bobby has provided his readers a diverse range of topics that are both informative and entertaining. His attention to detail and impeccable research have allowed him to capture the imaginations of his readers through his fictional works, and bring them valuable knowledge through his nonfiction books.

SIGN UP for email updates and receive free advance reading copies, updates on new releases, special offers, and bonus content. You can contact Bobby directly by email (BobbyAkart@gmail.com) or through his website:

BobbyAkart.com

Epigraph

EMP: A threat from above to America's soft underbelly below.
The clock is ticking.
~ Bobby Akart

*****

Another weapon which has been getting increasing attention could be delivered via the kind of nuclear-armed ballistic missile that Iran and North Korea have been developing—a strategic electromagnetic pulse attack.
~ Frank Gaffney, Center for Security Policy

*****

We may be the generation that sees Armageddon.
~ President Ronald Reagan

*****

Preparedness is the key to success and victory.
~ General Douglas MacArthur

*****

Secession is a deeply American principle.
This country was born through secession.
~ former U.S. Congressman Ron Paul

*****

You may all go to Hell, and I will go to Texas.
~ Davy Crockett, former Tennessean

PROLOGUE

October 12, 2017
Committee on Homeland Security
2154 Rayburn House Office Building
Washington, DC

On October 12, 2017, congressional members of the House Committee on Homeland Security met to hear testimony from five witnesses ranging from senior fellows for policy institutes to the chief of staff for the Commission to Assess the Threat to the United States from an Electromagnetic Pulse Attack, or EMP. The hearing was titled "Empty Threat or Serious Danger."

Since the founding of the EMP Commission at the insistence of former Speaker of the House Newt Gingrich, scientists, sociologists, and infrastructure specialists have warned Congress of the threat America faces from an electromagnetic pulse, whether naturally occurring in the form of a coronal mass ejection, or man-made, delivered by a nuclear warhead.

In 2008, the EMP Commission Report made national headlines and began to raise awareness as to the threats our wired society, wholly dependent on electronics and electricity, faced in the event the power grid collapsed due to the massive pulse of energy generated by an EMP.

Report after report documented the potential destruction that could be caused by the detonation of a nuclear warhead above Earth's surface. A nuclear explosion would send high-energy particles cascading down to Earth, interacting with the planet's magnetic field and destroying the electronic systems below. The resulting pulse of energy would destroy millions of transformers in America's power grid as the pulse travelled along power lines, terrestrial and undersea communications lines, and through wired electronic systems.

The chairman of the committee began to wind up his initial remarks. "While the international community and the mainstream media has concentrated its attention on North Korean missile tests and the country's nuclear program, a new threat has emerged. The EMP Commission has brought to our attention new technology that, if true, would castrate our missile defense capabilities completely. Doctor, would you care to expand upon this premise?"

Dr. Peter Vincent Pry had been at the forefront of the efforts to alert the U.S. government of the threats faced from an EMP attack. One of the early sounders of the proverbial clarion bell, Dr. Pry was now in a position of prominence as chief of staff of the commission and a frequent speaker on Capitol Hill.

"Quite frankly," he began, "it's been said an *EMP is a threat from above to America's soft underbelly below.* North Korea appears to have pursued a satellite warfare program along the lines of the Soviet Union's Fractional Orbital Bombardment System, or FOBS. Dating back to the sixties, the concept involved launching an intercontinental ballistic missile into low Earth orbit. Later, the ICBM would de-orbit for an attack, effectively bypassing the weapon-detection systems in the U.S."

"Wasn't this type of weaponry prohibited decades ago?" asked the chairman of the committee.

"It was, by the Strategic Arms Limitations Treaty of 1979, otherwise known as SALT II. However, despite the agreement, in the early parts of this decade, we believe the Russians began testing their RS-28 Sarmat ICBM with a super-heavy thermonuclear warhead as part of their satellite reconnaissance program."

"And what evidence do you have of this?" asked a skeptical congressman.

"Congressman, the Russians heralded the RS-28 Sarmat as an effective response to our Prompt Global Strike program. Months after the initial tests were declared to be successful, the Russian

Academy of Missile and Artillery Sciences announced they would be building a variant capable of deployment via satellite by the year 2020."

The congressman pressed Dr. Pry further. "What does this have to do with North Korea?"

"Sir, in '04, two former Russian generals and EMP experts from their former country warned the EMP Commission that the technical details for developing a super-EMP were, quote, *accidentally* transferred to the DPRK. Several months later, Russian scientists had been dispatched to Pyongyang to help with their satellite and nuclear missile program. This was confirmed by South Korean intelligence."

Another member of the skeptical congressman's party entered the questioning. "Wouldn't this whole satellite deployment scheme be too inaccurate to be effective? I mean, how would they guide it to their target?"

"An electromagnetic pulse attack doesn't require an accurate guidance system because the area of impact, depending upon the altitude of detonation, is so large. For example, studies have shown that North Korea or Iran could initiate an EMP attack against our country from a freighter or submarine by lofting a warhead to twenty miles above the Earth's surface. Upon detonation over Washington, for example, the Eastern Interconnection grid would be destroyed, which supports most of the U.S. population and generates seventy-five percent of our electricity."

The chairman followed up with a question. "So what you're telling us is it's not the target below that matters as much as the height above the Earth's surface when the warhead is detonated. Correct?"

"You're correct, Mr. Chairman. If the Earth did not have a magnetic field, a large vertical pulse of electric current like this would strike the area immediately below the point of detonation. But in reality, the Earth's magnetic field deflects the flow of electrons across the surface of the planet to create a very large, brief burst of energy— an EMP. This is why there is an inverse relationship between the height of the detonation and the surface area affected; the lower the detonation altitude—the smaller the affected area. A height burst of three hundred miles over, say, St. Louis would affect the U.S. from coast to coast."

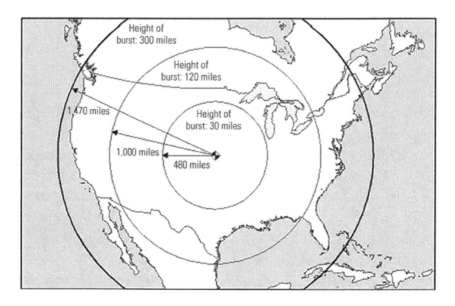

"I understand the nature of nuclear EMPs," began the skeptical congressman, "but Kim Jong-un has not proven that he has miniaturized a nuke to travel on an ICBM, much less a satellite. Our reports indicate that his ICBMs routinely break apart on re-entry."

"Congressman, with all due respect, delivery of the warhead via satellite is far different from an ICBM. Think of the weapon as being dropped from a hot-air balloon, using a minimum amount of thrust to insure its descent to a general target area. Our media and, quite frankly, Congress continually provide the American people a false sense of security that, as you say, North Korea has not demonstrated the ability to miniaturize a warhead. The fact is both the road-mobile KN-08 and KN-14 ICBMs could be easily adapted for space deployment. If the North Koreans deployed this weapon to detonate, our nation would be thrust into darkness without warning. To say otherwise is irresponsible."

The congressman shot back, clearly annoyed by the witness's challenge. He became animated, waving his arms above his head in feigned mockery. "Fearmongering is considered irresponsible too, sir.

For decades, this EMP Commission has screamed *the sky is falling, the sky is falling*, yet nothing has materialized. To me, this is just another attempt to expand an already bloated defense budget. Or worse, force higher utility bills upon the American people to pay for unnecessary modifications to a perfectly capable power grid. Our country has enough realistic threats to address without fabricating fictional ones."

Dr. Pry shook his head in disbelief and stared at each of the committee members. He'd devoted his life to raising awareness about the devastating impact an EMP would have on American society. He knew.

The threat is real.

PART ONE

Black Friday, November 25

CHAPTER 1

November 25, 2022
Black Friday
The Calgary Stampede
Calgary, Alberta, Canada

In the blink of an eye. The human brain processes external stimuli faster than imaginable. Thirteen milliseconds is all it takes for the brain to process and assess everything the human eye can see. For now, that's about twenty times faster than the world's most powerful supercomputers. It was also the amount of time Cooper Armstrong had to react when the lights went out on his final ride on top of One-Night Stand.

Cooper heard the buzzer indicating he'd beaten the bull. He'd stayed on for the requisite eight seconds. He was going to Las Vegas!

But then, the buzzer abruptly stopped, and he was thrust into darkness. In those milliseconds before the power grid collapsed, Cooper's brain processed his location in relation to the arena's stands. His body also processed the predicament he was in.

Ordinarily, at the end of a successful bull ride, the rodeo clowns arrive on the scene to distract the bull while the rider safely dismounts. This time was different. Nobody within the arena could see, except for maybe One-Night Stand, a bull that seemed to possess some type of demonic superpowers.

Cooper's body reacted much quicker than his normal decision-making process allowed. There were four stress responses to imminent danger, hardwired into human beings after thousands of years in which we learned to adapt and survive.

One is known as *tend and befriend*, a threat response found in humans who recognize danger and immediately move to protect their young by putting their own life on the line. Innate in mothers, one might call this the *Mama Grizzly* response.

The other three, known as *freeze, fight, or flight*, are responses based upon circumstances. Freeze responses are commonly associated with possums, deer, and myotonic goats—playing possum, deer in the headlights, and fainting.

Fight and flight have common biological effects on the human body, such as increased blood pressure, dizziness, shortness of breath, and increased adrenalin. When a person's brain instructs the body to flee, the hands and feet become cold. With a fight response, the hands become hot.

These responses are not calculated. The decision is made within milliseconds, designed by nature to force the human brain to take sudden action to protect the person from danger.

Cooper's training at the ranch, as well as his experience in the arena atop a bull, served him well to supplement his body's natural responses. As the light disappeared, in a split-second lapse of focus, Cooper closed his eyes and visualized one of those giant transformer robots slumping over as their power plug was pulled.

He quickly gathered himself and followed his normal routine as he slid off the side of the bull. His brain reminded him of which direction the arena railing was from his position near the center of the ring, and he stumbled in that direction, fully aware of the snorts and thundering hooves of One-Night Stand close behind him.

He opened his eyes gradually, allowing them to adjust and provide him the best possible night vision. He could make out the dim flickering of cigarette lighters in the stands, held high in the air by the fans. He was racing toward the light when he collided with something, sending him tumbling to the dirt floor of the ring.

A grunt and groan indicated the obstacle was another person, most likely a wayward, temporarily blinded rodeo clown. Cooper didn't hesitate as he gathered himself onto all fours and began crawling toward the rails. He made his way toward the stands and the half-cheering, half-laughing crowd.

I'm glad they're amused.

Cooper found his footing and stumbled toward the rails, crashing into them in the darkness. He heard the sound of hooves beating against the dirt behind him. One-Night Stand was charging after him. He grabbed the rail and hoisted himself up. His first step was solid, but his left leg slipped off the rail and dangled as the bull raced closer.

Instinctively, Cooper turned to assess the threat, but he couldn't see. He ignored his frequent lamenting of the pursued in a horror flick who constantly turned to see the killer closing the distance on them.

Run! he'd shout at the television. *Don't turn around!* he'd said on more than one occasion.

Fortunately, strong powerful arms intervened to overcome his hesitation. He was grabbed by his shirt and pulled over the rail before being dropped unceremoniously to the dusty concrete floor of the stands.

"I've got ya," said his brother Riley amidst the chants of *Coop, Coop, Coop.* "I've got ya, brother."

CHAPTER 2

November 25
Black Friday
The Calgary Stampede
Calgary, Alberta, Canada

"Whadya think happened?" asked Cooper as he stood up. He dusted himself off and closed his eyelids slightly to observe One-Night Stand stomping around the ring, circling like a shark on a mission.

"The lights went out," replied Riley.

Cooper looked at his brother and laughed. "Ya think?"

The people in the stands began to stomp their feet on the aluminum flooring of the stands surrounding the arena. They chanted in unison.

"Turn on the lights! Turn on the lights!"

The sound was deafening as cigarette lighters illuminated the interior of the Calgary Stampede as if they were waiting for Kenny Chesney to appear on stage. Cooper could barely hear his sister as she spoke.

"Guys, I'm not sure the lights are coming back on," said Palmer as she joined her brothers. She showed them the display on her cell phone. "See, it's dead."

Riley searched through his jeans pockets and pulled out his phone. He attempted to power on the display. Nothing.

"Come on, y'all," started Cooper. "Don't mess with me."

"Seriously, Coop," said Palmer as she thrust the phone in his direction. "See for yourself."

Cooper took the phone and tried to turn it on. Then he reached his hand out to Riley, who turned over his cell phone as well. They were both dead. Coop looked around the arena, the dim lights emanating from lighters providing enough of a glow to confirm his suspicions.

"Nobody's phone is working. Look around, you guys."

Riley and Palmer circled around to survey the people in the arena. Many were trying to access their phone service and couldn't. The chanting began to quieten down and was replaced by the murmur of private conversations regarding their phones.

Palmer grabbed them by the arms. "It's just like Daddy said. If the power goes out, check your electronics, like cell phones or radios. If they don't work either, we've been hit with an EMP."

"You've got to be kidding me," Riley protested. "I never thought that would actually happen. If this is an EMP, we're screwed."

"Everybody will be screwed," added Cooper in a hushed voice. He leaned into his younger siblings and whispered, "These people may not realize what this means, but we do. We've got to get out of here now and protect the horses. If Daddy's right, the cars won't work and it's the eighteen hundreds all over again."

Palmer grabbed Riley's hand without saying a word. Cooper placed his hand on Riley's shoulder as the three made a human train through the crowd toward the exits. Cooper looked around for indications of illuminated exit signs or emergency lighting. There was none. Just as they began to descend the ramp to the outside, he paused to turn and look behind him. He'd just performed the ride of his life, and only a handful of people knew it.

Palmer and Riley pushed open the doors to the parking lot in unison, allowing a burst of cold air to smack the trio in the face. The dampness and cold air was a reminder of the impending snowstorm forecast for the Rocky Mountains tomorrow. The barely visible crescent moon on that Black Friday wouldn't have been much help anyway.

"Come on," Cooper instructed as he took the lead. They began to dart through the gathering crowd outside the arena. As the number of people diminished, their fast-paced walk turned into a jog in the direction of the rodeo participants' trucks and trailers parked by the south entrance to the sprawling complex.

"Hey, my car won't start!" shouted a man in the distance.

"I can't even unlock mine!" exclaimed another.

"How can everything be broken?" asked a girl just to their left as they picked up the pace.

A couple of minutes later and slightly out of breath from breathing the cold, damp air, the rodeo kids arrived at their father's Ford F-450 truck and the trailer holding their three horses. Palmer pulled the truck's key fob out of her jean's pocket and began pressing the button. The truck didn't respond.

"How are we supposed to open this thing? There isn't a key. Just this stupid remote."

Riley grabbed the fob from his sister and pushed the button repeatedly, expecting a different result. He began to fiddle with the device, hoping an actual key was hidden inside it. He was unsuccessful and frustrated.

"Forget what's happening right now; what if the car battery was dead? You couldn't get in the dang thing with this stupid remote."

Riley threw it against the side of the truck, and the fob fell to the ground in two pieces. Cooper shrugged off Riley's outburst, as the fob, and most likely his daddy's truck, were worthless now anyway.

"Come on, dudes, let's party! Beer's on me!" shouted a cowboy as he and his female companion raced by Cooper.

The girl turned her head and shouted back as they skipped past the front of the truck. "Yeah, the space aliens are coming! It's like, you know, the end of the world!"

Cooper sighed and surveyed his surroundings. There were no signs of light anywhere. There were a couple of bonfires started near the parked cars as people began to look for ways to stay warm. He thought for a moment and then was reminded of the horses, who were restless from all the commotion outside their trailer.

"Palmer, let's calm the horses down," said Cooper. "We need to make a decision."

The three Armstrongs walked to the rear of the trailer and began to nuzzle their horses through the windows. This had an immediate calming effect on the animals, who'd grown up with the rodeo kids for years. For all intents and purposes, they were part of the family, not just a critical part of their rodeo activities.

For the first time, Palmer was starting to show concern for their circumstances. "Coop, if this was an EMP, that means somebody is attacking us. They may have started a nuclear war with the North Koreans. Heck, Russia and China may be shooting at us too."

"It's possible," said Cooper. "It could be a solar flare, but either way, we're seventeen hundred miles from home."

"We could ride the horses back," interjected Riley. "It would take forever and a day, but we could do it."

"I don't know, Riley," said Palmer. "Realistically, in the dead of winter and through the Rockies, it might take months. Where would we sleep? How would we eat?"

Cooper moved in to take charge and calm his siblings' nerves. "Listen up, y'all. Let's not get overwhelmed right away. First off, we're ahead of ninety-nine percent of these people because we have an idea of what has happened and the long-term impact. Let's take advantage of what Momma and Daddy taught us and get secured for the night. Chances are, this coming snowstorm will force us to hunker down until it passes anyway. That'll give us time to come up with a plan."

"A lot of our gear is at the hotel," said Riley.

"Yeah, so we need to get movin'," Cooper suggested. "Palmer, you and Riley saddle up the horses. I'm gonna get our stuff out of the truck."

"Are you gonna bust out the windows?" asked Riley before adding, "Daddy'll tan your hide."

"My guess is they'll be pretty happy to see us," said Cooper with a laugh. "Besides, the truck's insured."

"Very funny, a lot of good that'll do ya," said Palmer with a chuckle. "C'mon, Riley. This leather's gonna be cold and stiff to work with. It'll help if we do it together."

Riley opened up the twin gates as the hinges squeaked their

complaint over the cold air. "After six months in the saddle goin' home, we'll loosen up that leather."

CHAPTER 3

November 25
Black Friday
The Executive Residence
The White House
Washington, DC

President Harman took some time to adjust to life within the Executive Residence of the White House. She and her husband, well-known intellectual property and media attorney David Huff, had lived in a multimillion-dollar home in Brentwood, California, a suburb of Los Angeles.

The Oakland native, who had resided in a nine-hundred-thirty-eight-foot condominium in San Francisco during her career as the city's district attorney, found that marriage suited her, and she'd adjusted to life with a wealthy attorney with ease.

However, in their new home within the most famous building on earth, she was surrounded by over one hundred maids, butlers, chefs, and florists, who maintain the first family's four levels of luxury known as the Executive Residence.

1600 Pennsylvania Avenue, America's most prestigious address, was more than a working residence for the president and the First Husband. It was also their place of refuge. David transferred his practice to his law firm's DC office and quickly embraced the Washington way of life when his wife became the junior senator from California.

After her sudden thrust into the position of President of the United States following the demise of her original running mate, President Joe Billings, President Harman became overwhelmed at the immense power and responsibility she was afforded. Oftentimes, she would retreat to the Executive Residence to seek solace. She was known to block out the staff and sit alone in the West Sitting Hall, enjoying a glass or two of wine.

On some evenings, when David was travelling back to LA, she'd partake of an extra glass just to calm her nerves. Her drinking was not a problem, as her husband assured her. However, he suggested she really should limit her intake to just two glasses.

President Harman took another sip of a California red wine from a large Bordeaux glass that she had the staff maintain in her bar. It held four more ounces than the standard red wine stem glass.

She'd parted the drapes adorning the large arched window of the West Sitting Hall where it overlooked the West Wing of the White House. This particular day's presidential activities were unremarkable in most respects. Much of the staff was given a long weekend off to be with their families. The maintenance personnel were frantically readying the White House with Christmas decorations. All in all, she was pleased, as the world seemed to be behaving itself.

"Hi, dear," said her husband as he announced himself. He'd been working late at the office on a defamation suit concerning a high-profile client. He tossed his briefcase and coat on the seat of a wing chair and wrapped his arms around the president. "I hate that you have to wait for me to get home. I'm sorry."

She laughed and ran her hands across his. After taking another sip of wine, she said, "David, trust me. I'm not lonely. Sometimes, I need an opportunity to be alone with my thoughts. After all these months, I still have to pinch myself from time to time to remember it's real."

A light rain started to fall, leaving trails of water on the bulletproof windows. As their view outside became obscured, they broke their embrace and walked to the sitting area. David poured himself a glass of wine, eased into a side chair, and crossed his legs.

The curtains were still pulled open, and as David told her about his day, she stared mindlessly at the Washington skyline. Her mind wandered as David went on about his client's case and the viciousness found on social media.

Then something changed. Her mind was too slow to process it at first. She slowly leaned forward on the edge of the chair and stared. *What is it? What's different?*

Ignoring her husband, President Harman stood and walked toward the arched, lunette window. She was at the end of her second glass of wine, but her senses weren't dulled too much to comprehend what had just happened.

There were no lights throughout Washington except for the White House. Traffic wasn't moving on Pennsylvania Avenue or in the distance on the Whitehurst Freeway. In fact, none of the headlights on the vehicles were working either.

Buildings weren't producing any light, including government structures like Blair House and the Eisenhower Executive Office Building. As far as her eyes could see, to the Potomac river and beyond, it was pitch black. Total darkness. Then a siren began to wail.

CHAPTER 4

November 25
Home of Secretary of Defense Montgomery Gregg
Georgetown
Washington, DC

Secretary Montgomery Gregg and his wife hosted the Yanceys for dinner on that Friday evening. The ladies, who had been friends before Billy Yancey and Secretary Gregg began working together, had enjoyed a day of shopping together at Tyson's Corner in McLean, Virginia. Full of excitement as the Christmas shopping season was launched, they suggested an impromptu dinner at the Greggs' Georgetown home.

Secretary Gregg, still reeling from the North Korean Mother's Day appearance of Dear Leader, Kim Jong-un, was in no mood for entertaining. However, he indulged his wife because he enjoyed Billy's company, and it gave them the opportunity to speak in private without Carl Braun, the director of the Special Activities Division of the National Clandestine Service, being present.

While Braun, Yancey, and Secretary Gregg shared *common interests*, he and Billy were old friends and fellow Texans. That made them practically family.

"How did North Korea and Russia become aligned?" asked Mrs. Gregg. "I always thought it was China who was joined at the hip with North Korea."

"Their relationship goes back to the late eighteen hundreds," started Billy. "It wasn't until the last few decades that Moscow began to assist in advancing North Korea's technology toward a viable nuclear weapons program."

"Billy's right," said Secretary Gregg. "In essence, the old Soviet Union helped create and prop up the Kim regimes. While Russia's economic leverage over the North is not as substantial as China's, their military support is invaluable to Kim."

"Plus, there is the energy connection," interjected Billy. "When we imposed sanctions on Moscow restricting their energy exports to Europe because of their invasion of Ukraine and Crimea, Putin laughed and upped his economic ante with Kim Jong-un. He tripled Russia's energy exports to the North, together with communications and military technology."

"Today, Russia along with China are the only two countries that provide Kim Jong-un with permanent transportation and telecommunications links connecting the Hermit Kingdom to the outside world."

Mrs. Gregg cleared the dishes and returned with a variety of holiday-adorned delicacies from Georgetown Cupcakes. She made an astute comment that impressed her husband, who rarely discussed shop with his wife.

"I don't trust Putin, and it sounds like the Chinese shouldn't either. The man smiles while he stabs you in the front. If he's helping North Korea with weapons and such, there has to be some kind of quid pro quo."

"Well said, dear," said Secretary Gregg. "You're right. The Kremlin may not be Kim's biggest defender, but their insertion into the stalemate between our country and Pyongyang complicates matters. Like China, he doesn't want North Korea to fall into Seoul's hands and under our thumb. It also sends a message to Beijing that Kim has more than one friend."

Everyone chose a cupcake and a dessert fork. The delectable cupcake melted in Secretary Gregg's mouth as the conversation slowed for a moment.

After Mrs. Yancey commented on the delicious treat, she added, "Monty, this whole situation has the country on edge. Virtually every one of my friends asks me this question, so, if I may, I'll pose it to you. What happens next?"

Before Secretary Gregg could answer, a series of loud popping sounds could be heard, and then the Gregg home was consumed by darkness. The heating units stopped. The steady hum of appliances from the nearby kitchen ceased. All the lights shut off, leaving only the glow of two candlesticks flickering in the center of the table.

"Oh my!" exclaimed Mrs. Gregg. "I didn't know we were having a storm this evening. I saw the drizzle, but that's it."

"Wait here," Secretary Gregg said brusquely as he pushed away from the table. Instinctively, he walked directly to the dining room window and pulled the curtains open. The lights were out in all of the surrounding homes. He looked up and down the street. Nothing was moving.

Nothing.

"Monty?" asked Billy.

"Billy, this is not good. Go outside and fetch my security—"

Secretary Gregg was unable to complete his sentence when a loud rap was heard against the front door. He rushed to answer it.

"Sir, we have a situation," said one member of his security detail.

His wife called for him from the dining room. "Monty? What is it? Has something happened?"

He ignored her and turned his attention back to the uniformed members of the Defense Security Service. The DSS was an agency within the Department of Defense tasked with protecting the secretary and his family.

"Do you have comms? Can you get in touch with Stanley?" Secretary Gregg was referring to Stanley Sims, the longtime director of the DSS and a hands-on manager.

"No, sir."

Secretary Gregg shook his head in disbelief as he surveyed his surroundings. The evidence before him had all the earmarks of an EMP attack.

I can't believe he's done it. Touché, Kim.

"Okay, hold your position. I have satcoms in my safe. We'll see if it survived the pulse."

He turned and returned to the dining room, where the dinner

party stood at the window, staring into the darkness.

"Everyone, please. Let's get away from the window. Perhaps you should follow me into the study."

Mrs. Gregg became visibly upset. "Monty, get away from the window? Why?"

"This may be part of a broader military operation," he replied. "I don't know yet. Please follow me."

He led them into the study, where a fire was beginning to burn out. Billy reached for a couple of logs and placed them on the flames. He stoked the coals, and the increased flame immediately warmed the room. He calmly turned to Secretary Gregg.

"EMP?"

"Most likely," Secretary Gregg replied. "I hope that's all it is, for all of our sakes."

Mrs. Gregg slumped into a chair and wiped the tears off her face. "Monty! You're frightening me. Please explain. Are we under attack?"

Secretary Gregg dropped to his hands and knees and rolled back a corner of the Persian rug in front of the fireplace, revealing a safe. Installed prior to their ownership of the home in Georgetown, it still opened by using a combination lock rather than an electronically controlled lock.

He spun the dial and removed a government-issue Inmarsat satellite phone. Along with cash, important documents, and his beloved 1911 handgun, the safe worked to store electronics for protection from an EMP.

"How can you be so calm?" Mrs. Yancey asked her husband, but Secretary Gregg provided the answer.

"Panic is our greatest enemy," he mumbled in response as the satphone powered up. "In fact, Kim's counting on it."

CHAPTER 5

November 25
Black Friday
The Armstrong Ranch
Borden County, Texas

Major and Lucy paused the DVR while they cleared the dishes from the living room. Major had spent a lot of time on the ranch with Preacher that day, assessing their fences and discussing the final sales of cattle before winter set in.

When the kids were away, their evening meals together were far more casual. Each of them had their spot on the sofa and a place to prop up their feet to soak in the warmth of the fire. Supper was their chance to catch up on the day's events regarding the ranch and news from around the world.

The paused screen showed a picture of Cooper hung up on One-Night Stand during that fateful ride a month ago. The chyron generated by the CBS Sports Network read *Cooper Armstrong Returns*. Their son, who was already well-known on the rodeo circuit, was now catching the attention of major sports networks. Cooper's good looks, down-home attitude, and drive to be the best was a winning combination for sports networks looking for American heroes rather than focusing on athletes who disrespected their country and profession.

"Honey, let's skip dessert tonight," said Major as he piled his plate and the empty pots into the sink. "In fact, leave these dishes for me. I'll knock 'em out after Coop rides. Right now, I'm nervous as a—"

"All right, I get it," said his wife with a chuckle. "I'm anxious too. These can wait."

The married couple of nearly thirty years scampered back into the family room like two kids ready to watch their favorite cartoon.

Major settled in next to Lucy and pressed play on the remote. The screen remained frozen. He banged the remote on the palm of his hand, a typical man technique, hoping to jar the device into working. Once again, he pressed play.

Same result. Nothing happened.

"Did the batteries die?" asked Lucy.

"I reckon." Major dashed back to the kitchen and pulled open the junk drawer, their name for a designated drawer filled with everything from pens and paper to nuts, bolts, batteries, and loose change. You know, *necessary junk*.

Within a minute, Major had returned and was already pushing play, frantically pointing the remote at the television rather than at the DirecTV box well below it. He tried rewind, fast-forward, and pause again. Nothing.

"Honey, I don't know what's wrong. It's not responding."

Major looked at the grandfather clock, which had stood near the dining room entrance for generations. He decided to take a chance that Cooper hadn't started his ride yet. He changed the channels rapidly and then returned to CBS Sports. All of the channels returned a staticky, snow-filled screen.

Major dropped the remote and unplugged the DVR box. In the past, temporary glitches in the operations of their satellite system could be resolved by a reset. By unplugging the unit, allowing it time to get its act together, and then plugging it in again, the device would suddenly function properly.

He fumbled with the cords as the pressure of time weighed upon him. Major silently cursed himself for relying upon this electronic device to preserve his son's most important bull ride of his career to date.

"Major," said Lucy as she jumped off the couch, "there's something wrong. I can't access our cell phone service. I mean, the phone powers up, but there's no internet connection, and I even tried dialing your phone. None of the phone lines are working."

"Let me see," he said, abandoning the remote.

Major plugged the DVR in again and reached for Lucy's phone. Longtime married couples don't doubt one another, they just simply want to *see for themselves*. Lucy willingly handed over her iPhone and fumbled through the sofa cushions in search of her iPad.

"Major, this is an awful time for DirecTV to quit on us," Lucy lamented. "Let me see if I can pull it up online at ProRodeoTV.com."

The iPad display illuminated, but there was no internet connection. She then picked up the cordless phone, hit speaker, and pressed Preacher's number on speed dial. The annoying fast busy signal sound filled the room. She held it in the air in disbelief.

"I have an idea," said Major as he calmly dropped the iPhone onto the coffee table. "Let me try something. Miss Lucy, go in the kitchen and find the weather radio. You know, the crank-up kind we got from the Red Cross. I think it's in the cabinet above the fridge."

"No, it's in the steel trash can in the pantry, but I'll get it," she said as she quickly exited the room in search of one of the many Faraday cages they maintained.

He navigated to the guide on DirecTV and scrolled through to the Spanish-language channels. The same static appeared. Then he found his way to channel two-sixty-four, BBC America. The expression on the dour-looking Brit said it all. As he turned up the volume, the screen changed to a graphic.

BREAKING NEWS ... MASSIVE POWER OUTAGE STRIKES U.S., CANADA

"Hey, it's working!" exclaimed Lucy gleefully as she dropped the radio on the side table. "Wait? This is the BBC channel. Have you tried—?"

Major reached for his wife's hand and replied, "Hang on. This is bad."

Kurt Barling, a thirty-year veteran journalist with the BBC, was reporting from their London bureau.

"Thus far, the only report we've received is a brief statement from Secretary of

State Damian Williamson from his residence at Carlton Gardens in Chevening. It appears that much of the United States and Canada, from coast to coast, has been thrust into darkness by a cascading failure of the nation's power grid. There are no reports emanating from the States at this time, and our attempts to reach reporters in our Washington bureau have failed."

"Major," started Lucy as she clutched her husband's arm, "he said Canada, too. The kids are gonna be—"

Major put his arm around Lucy and pulled her head against his shoulder. "Let's not jump to conclusions. At least we have a source of information."

Major stopped talking as Barling's face suddenly grew serious. He was holding his hand to his earpiece and shaking his head from side to side. He grimaced and looked into the camera.

"We have now received further word that the Ministry of Defence has placed the Royal Navy, Air Force and the British Army on their highest levels of alert. Although a formal statement will be forthcoming from Air Chief Marshal Sir Stuart Lovegrove, our sources have told us that it is likely the United States has come under attack, and this may be the beginnings of a broader military conflict. In just a few minutes, we will be taking you to—"

Major's mind began to race as he tuned out the rest of Barling's report.

United States has come under attack. Beginnings.

He turned to Lucy. "Listen to me, honey. Now is not the time to panic, but we've got to move quickly. This has to be a nuclear EMP attack; otherwise Texas would be in the dark too. It could be the start of all-out nuclear war, I don't know. We have to get everybody to safety."

"The phones don't work."

"I know. Preacher and I have worked out a system for this. It's kinda like Paul Revere's ride to warn the patriots."

"Okay, what do you want me to do?" she asked as she wiped the tears off her cheeks.

"Get the shelter opened up and the power running. As the families show up, get the women and children settled. Keep them calm. Send the ranch hands here to load up food out of the pantry."

Lucy nodded her head and fought back the tears. "The kids. They're all alone."

Major gently put his fingers to Lucy's lips. "And they're levelheaded, practical, and most importantly, they're Armstrongs. They'll be fine."

CHAPTER 6

November 25
Black Friday
The Armstrong Ranch
Borden County, Texas

Major bolted out the front door and skipped the steps as he hit the mulched walkway leading to the barn. His adrenaline was pumping, raising his body temperature as he entered the near-freezing temperatures outside. In his haste, he never considered grabbing his jacket and gloves hanging on the wall by the front door.

He was in the process of saddling his horse, cursing his suddenly cold, stiff fingers, when he heard the sound of horses racing toward the barn. He reached for a flashlight mounted on the outside of the stall and went by the water troughs to investigate.

"Who's that?" he shouted into the darkness as the light from his flashlight scanned the field to find the riders.

Preacher shouted his response as his horse closed on the barn. "Major! It's me and Antonio. Something's happened!"

"Yeah, huge power outage." His voice lowered somewhat as the riders came toward the barn at a full gallop.

"Whoa," the riders said in unison, encouraging their horses to a stop. Dust and a few rocks were kicked up onto Major's jeans as they arrived.

"Antonio, do you know something?" asked Major.

"*Si, señor,*" began Antonio, who had arrived at Armstrong Ranch alone when he was sixteen. He had snuck across the border with his mother and sister through Terrell County, with the assistance of human traffickers. Once they'd arrived in America, the traffickers

29

demanded additional payment or the family would not be allowed to go free. When his family gave them the seventy-three dollars in their possession, the traffickers raped and murdered his mother and sister. Antonio received a beating but managed to escape. Preacher had found him on the banks of the river, drinking the muddy water. He'd lived and worked on the ranch since.

Antonio continued. "I was listening to radio from Coahuila— XHRF." XHRF, one of the original border blaster radio stations on the Mexican side of the border outside Laredo, was known for its traditional Mexican music and lack of political commentary.

"No power in Tamaulipas, Nuevo León, and Chihuahua. *Transformadors* explode. Power poles on fire. *Oscuridad*, all dark, everywhere."

Preacher held the young man's horse as Antonio dismounted. "San Diego and Tucson, too?"

"*Si*, Preacher. No power in America."

Preacher handed the reins to the young man and pointed toward the fence rail next to the barn. Antonio led the horses away and tied them off where they could drink water for a moment.

"Major, did they hit us?"

"I think so, Preach. We were trying to watch Coop's ride and the screen went blank. We found the British station. They think we were attacked."

"EMP?" asked Preacher.

"Most likely," said Major. "You guys need to saddle up again and bring everyone to the shelter. Miss Lucy's getting it ready out back now. I'll take the houses by the river and near the barnyard. Send Antonio out to the back forty. You've got the south side of the ranch."

"We're on it," said Preacher as he turned toward Antonio and the horses.

Major added more instructions. "Tell everyone don't pack much. Kids' favorite toys. Grab only the clothing they can carry. If they have vehicles, and they're still running, tell them to park them in front of the entry gates to the ranch. I want everyone back here within the hour!"

"Hah!" shouted Preacher as he dug his heels into his horse. "We're on it, boss!"

Major stood in silence for a moment and gazed at the cold, clear sky. A meteor shower was providing a show as a comet, designated SW-3, made its appearance following its fracturing in 1995. He watched in awe as the comet's debris painted a broad stripe of glowing pebbles and dust in the sky.

Living on a ranch in a desolate part of Texas, the night skies stood out in a brilliant illumination of stars, planets, and space debris. It was a peaceful experience.

With a chuckle, Major mused at the irony. Now the rest of the country, as it experienced total darkness, devoid of the constant barrage of artificial lighting from vehicles and buildings, would be able to view the beauty of SW-3 as it crossed the horizon. For them, however, there would be no peace—for years to come.

CHAPTER 7

November 25
Black Friday
Presidential Emergency Operations Center
The White House
Washington, DC

The Bush administration, under the guidance of Vice President Dick Cheney and Secretary of Defense Donald Rumsfeld, made substantial changes to the nation's continuity-of-government plan. During their tenure in office, they ran catastrophe drills in which they were taken to Andrews Air Force Base by their Secret Service details.

Once there, they joined a team of forty to sixty security personnel and high-ranking government officials, along with other cabinet members. Each was transported to remote locations across the country to underground bunkers and secured military facilities.

The plan, designed to keep the U.S. government fully operational in a time of attack, dated back to the early Cold War-era of the fifties when duck-and-cover scenarios were considered sufficient. Now, state-of-the-art technology was utilized to deliver warnings, updates, and directives wirelessly to key personnel.

However, in the case of an electromagnetic pulse attack, communication lapses for a period of time were to be expected until the president, vice president, the Speaker of the House, and the cabinet were protected within the secured bunkers.

While federal budget constraints prevented each key player in the continuity-of-government plan from having their own fallout shelter, the facility within the White House for the president was the next best thing to Cheyenne Mountain and Raven Rock.

The Presidential Emergency Operations Center, or PEOC, was a recently expanded and updated underground facility beneath the East Wing of the White House. Initially constructed under President Franklin Roosevelt during World War II, the PEOC had undergone substantial changes to make it impenetrable to any form of ICBM nuclear attack, enemy invasion, or terrorist operation.

President Harman and her husband moved quickly through the tile-covered hallways, instinctively ducking under the pipes suspended from the low ceiling, which contained hardened wiring for mechanical equipment and communications networks.

Several armed military guards greeted them at the thick, solid steel door, which resembled a bank vault's door. Past a reception area, the president entered a large conference room adjacent to the PEOC's nerve center.

The conference room was small, but it contained comfortable sofas, a kitchenette with drinks and snacks, and a few magazines. It resembled an upscale physician's waiting room.

"Madam President, the First Husband will be required to wait here," stated a lieutenant commander in the Navy, who was in command of the facility at the moment.

She nodded and embraced her husband. They exchanged a brief kiss, and he smiled as he whispered to her, "You've got this, Alani."

Warmed by his brief words of encouragement, President Harman left him alone and followed her escort to the PEOC's situation room, which was different from the one located under the West Wing in one respect, it was twice the size.

In 2010, tall fences were installed near the West Wing and a massive construction project was undertaken. Officially, the renovations to the White House complex were described as an update to the facilities' infrastructure system. Unofficially, the contractors were using tunnels to greatly expand the East Wing PEOC facility, gaining access from behind the West Wing.

A sprawling, multiroom structure was built, which required many truckloads of heavy-duty concrete and steel beams. Additional tunnels were installed to connect the West Wing to the PEOC to allow faster evacuation of the president to the nuclear-proof facility. It was also expanded to provide for better long-term sleeping quarters for the First Family and the president's staff and essential security detail.

President Harman entered the PEOC situation room and was greeted by her chief of staff, Charles Acton, as well as Deputy Secretary of Defense Harold Cummings.

"Charles, talk to me," ordered the president.

"Madam President, thirteen minutes ago, two nuclear warheads were detonated approximately two hundred fifty miles above the Earth's surface in the area of Oregon and Virginia."

The president walked through the PEOC's nerve center and studied the screens mounted in a semicircular shape around the room. Every computer station was manned by uniformed military personnel with telephone headsets. They were busy speaking with American government facilities around the globe and constantly updated the monitors with data.

She had a thousand questions, but these were the first that came out. "Why didn't our missile defense systems shoot them down? I mean, were there more than two? How could this happen?"

"Madam President," started Deputy Secretary Cummings, a former Air Force general, "we've monitored North Korea as well as the usual nuclear threats on our highest state of alert for many months. These—"

"How could we miss ICBMs launched from North Korea?" She shouted the question, drawing the attention of some of the military personnel.

"They did not come from the Korean peninsula, Madam President," he nervously responded. "It is our belief they were dropped on us from above, via satellite."

"What? Why didn't we take them out?" The president was incredulous.

"Madam President," responded Deputy Secretary Cummings, "the response time is practically nil. By the time our global reconnaissance picks up the incoming nuke, it's too late to shoot it down. The satellites are in low Earth orbit to begin with, and the flight time to the point of detonation takes under three minutes."

President Harman began walking back and forth along the upper level of the theater-style situation room. She rubbed her temples as a headache began to set in, partly from stress and the histamine effects of the red wine she had drunk earlier.

"How widespread is the power outage?" she asked.

"Madam President," Acton began to respond, "our information is still coming in, but based upon initial reports, both the Eastern and Western Interconnection grids have suffered a catastrophic, cascading failure. If my memory serves me, that would impact much of Canada and parts of Northern Mexico."

President Harman ran her fingers through her dark hair and continued to massage her temples. *This is a nightmare.*

"Charles, please find me a bottled water and Excedrin," ordered the president before she turned her attention back to Deputy Secretary Cummings. "Where is Monty?"

"Per continuity-of-government protocols, Secretary Gregg, the Secretary of Homeland Security, and other cabinet members are en route to Raven Rock, ma'am," he replied. "The vice president is being taken to Cheyenne Mountain."

Acton returned with an Evian and three Excedrin. President Harman didn't hesitate to take the painkillers and drink three long gulps of water. The prospect of the medication taking hold and a deep breath combined to calm her nerves somewhat. It was time to become Commander-in-Chief.

"Okay, gentlemen. What else do we know? Any indication of who initiated this?"

The deputy secretary responded, "Nothing confirmed at this time although our intelligence and knowledge of the North Korean advancements in satellite technology would point to them. The CIA has provided us nothing to believe either the Russians or Chinese are involved in this."

"Has there been any other activity, militarily or diplomatically, that provides us an indication of their intentions?" asked the president.

"Militarily, no," replied Acton. "Diplomatically, our information is still incomplete. State is sending their people to Raven Rock now. It will take a little time to gather our entire emergency team."

"Where is Homeland Security?"

"The director is also being transported to Raven Rock," replied Acton.

"Am I to remain here?" she asked.

"At some point, you will be moved there via Air Force One."

"When?" asked the president.

"As soon as we're comfortable that the missiles have stopped falling," replied Acton dryly.

CHAPTER 8

November 25
Military Air Transport
Near Frederick, Maryland

Secretary Gregg and his wife joined other members of the cabinet on a Boeing C-40 Clipper, which departed from Andrews Air Force Base to a military-protected landing strip at the Defense Threat Reduction Agency in Pennsylvania at the base of Raven Rock Mountain. Billy Yancey and his wife were not authorized to travel on the transport because he was not considered essential personnel, but Secretary Gregg arranged a ride for them to Lackland Air Force Base near San Antonio, where the Senate president pro tempore was awaiting pickup. After the Speaker of the House, the president pro tempore was next in the line of succession pursuant to the continuity-of-government plan. The Yanceys and Greggs said their goodbyes and exchanged promises to stay safe.

Secretary Gregg had never flown on the C-40, and after the flight was airborne for the short flight into the mountains of Pennsylvania, he took a brief tour with his top aide, Assistant Secretary of Defense Jackson Waller.

"How many of these aircraft did they harden for this purpose, Jackson?"

"A dozen, I believe. In addition to Andrews, they're at Scott Air Force Base in Illinois, Hickam in Hawaii, NAS Jacksonville, and even Ramstein in Germany."

"We could've driven and gotten to Raven Rock quicker," quipped Secretary Gregg. "Except I'm sure the highways are crammed full of stranded motorists. Lot of people out shopping and traveling this weekend."

They moved through the cabin and found a couple of seats over the wings that were out of earshot from the other passengers, especially the director of Homeland Security, who was now able to make contact with the president. They were able to hear bits and pieces of his conversation, as the director was slightly hard of hearing, which caused him to speak loudly.

"You notice she's speaking to him first?" said Secretary Gregg in a questioning tone. "Do you think she blames me for this? After all, it's my job to defend."

"Monty, there is no defense to what most likely happened," replied Waller. "Reagan began warning the Congress back in the eighties of this possibility, and he was ridiculed by the media as promoting Star Wars as a military doctrine."

"I've been aware of the possibilities, though. Thanks to Dr. Peter Pry and Admiral James Woolsey, the EMP Commission kept the conversation active in the halls of Congress. As is typical, Congress paid lip service to the issue but didn't take adequate steps to protect us from the threat."

Waller raised his hand slightly so they would stop talking. They listened to the Homeland Security director as he completed his phone call with the president.

"Monty, this isn't on you. If anything, you've been begging the president to take the fight to Kim on his soil before it came to a moment like this. Whether the nuke was launched from Kim's backyard, dropped from a satellite, or tethered to a damn balloon, all of this could've been avoided if she'd followed your advice."

Secretary Gregg pointed his finger toward the front of the aircraft as the director of Homeland Security headed in their direction. As he walked past, he avoided eye contact. This didn't go unnoticed by either of the men.

"Well, there you have it, Jackson," started Secretary Gregg. "She's back in the PEOC getting an earful from her man Cummings. This whole thing is gonna be hung around my neck like a ten-ton albatross. I'm surprised I was even allowed on the plane."

"There's no way she'd replace you during a time of crisis, Monty. Don't sweat it. Besides, you're the best she's got when it comes to military strategy and she knows it."

Secretary Gregg adjusted his position in his seat. He looked behind them to see if anyone else had suddenly appeared. They were still alone, as the majority of the passengers had congregated at the rear gallery to commiserate about the demise of America. He, for one, was not ready to throw in the towel.

"Jackson, nobody blindsides me and gets away with it, including Kim Jong-un. But this president no longer has the media watching over her. She can kick me out of Raven Rock into a snowdrift and nobody would know about it."

"Monty, that's not going to happen," interjected Waller reassuringly.

"It might. She could undermine my authority within the cabinet and the Defense Department. Most of them are lifelong politicians. Who's gonna stand up to defend a Secretary of Defense who allowed the power grid to collapse across America while on his watch, hmm?"

Waller sat up in his chair and tried to console his friend and superior. "Of course, that's not totally accurate, so there might be a silver lining."

"What do you mean?" asked the secretary, who was having a rare moment of self-pity.

With a puzzled look, Waller turned to look his friend in the eyes. "Monty, have you not heard? Texas is still under full power. Their grid stood strong."

CHAPTER 9

November 25
Black Friday
Texas Governor's Mansion
1010 Colorado Street
Austin, Texas

The Mansion, as residents of Austin often referred to it, had been the official residence of Texas governors and their families since 1856. It was the oldest governor's mansion west of the Mississippi River and the fourth oldest that had been continuously occupied. Tonight, Governor Marion Burnett was hosting her annual kick-off-the-holiday-season gala with the unveiling of the Christmas tree and décor within the massive Greek Revival-style structure.

Most dinners at the governor's mansion were intimate affairs, with the guest list ranging up to a dozen attendees. For this dinner, donors were invited, but so were the chairmen and CEOs representing banking, transportation, and, naturally, oil and gas.

"Marion, I must say, this is your finest Christmas kickoff yet," said Mickey DeWitt, president of Midland-based WestTex Oil and Gas. At just under four hundred thousand dollars, the DeWitt family was one of the largest donors to Governor Burnett's coffers over the years. Make no mistake, this was the way politics worked. The annual event was about stroking the egos of donors as well as putting movers and shakers together to make deals. Needless to say, everyone was looking to get the governor's ear.

"Why, thank you, Mickey," said Governor Burnett with a smile as she accepted a peck on the cheek from DeWitt. Marion reached out and provided a gentle squeeze of Mrs. DeWitt's hand. "You know, old friends, I could not have done this without both of you. You've been loyal supporters and dear friends throughout my career."

"Well, now, Marion," began Mrs. Dewitt, "not to mention we're practically neighbors. The only large ranch between our place and yours belongs to Major Armstrong, and he's practically family to us all."

"He sure is," said Mr. DeWitt as he joined his wife's side. A waiter with a tray of champagne glasses strolled past the group, and both DeWitts eagerly grabbed a glass. Governor Burnett raised her hand and declined. *This is a working dinner.*

"Y'all know Major," she began. "He's not much for rubbin' elbows. He and Lucy always have a standing invitation to join us, but they're not up for puttin' on the Ritz, as they say."

"That's quite all right. We love them dearly," said Mrs. DeWitt with a chuckle. Then she raised her glass. "Besides, there's more bubbly for us, right?"

"Marion, while we have a moment," started the oil man, "I'd like to talk with you about my permit application to drill in the Guadalupe Mountains National Park. The Interior Secretary said the application is moving forward, but I still need the state to sign off on the water-reclamation permit."

Governor Burnett smiled and held her hand up to stop him from talking. "Say no more, old friend. We signed off on it Wednesday afternoon before everyone left for the Thanksgiving weekend. I wanted to tell you the good news in person."

"We're good to go?" asked Mr. DeWitt.

"You betcha. Drill, baby, drill!" The governor found her campaign voice momentarily as she channeled close friend and ally Sarah Palin.

As the threesome finished up their small talk, a commotion began toward the rear of the room. Two members of the governor's security detail were sticking their heads above the nearly two hundred guests in search of the governor.

When they made contact, they quickly approached her, gently shoving their way through the crowd. They were followed by her trusted chief of security, Ryan Long, a former Texas Ranger and friend of Major's.

"Excuse us. Madam Governor, may we have a word?" said Long.

"Um, sure, Ryan. Excuse me, folks."

Long pulled the governor away from her curious guests and spoke directly into her ear. "There's been some sort of attack on the country. Our information is incomplete, but about ten minutes ago, the Eastern and Western Interconnection power grids collapsed. Most of Canada is impacted by this, as well as parts of Mexico."

Governor Burnett instinctively looked at the well-lit ballroom. "Nukes?"

"We're unsure, Governor. From our best information, it doesn't appear to be H-bombs. Most likely an electromagnetic detonation."

"Washington, too?" she asked.

"As far as we can tell, yes. All of our information is coming from news broadcasts from Europe. This literally happened in the last ten to fifteen minutes."

Governor Burnett looked around the room and saw some of her guests appeared worried as they looked at their cell phones. "I should make an announcement, don't you think?"

"Yes, ma'am," replied Long. "So you know, we've alerted the Texas Fusion Center. They are coordinating actions between Texas Homeland Security, the Infrastructure Protection Unit, and other field operations."

"Last question. Is there any indication that the attack is ongoing?"

"No, ma'am. However, out of an abundance of precaution, we'll need to get you into the shelter. We can always travel through the tunnels to the Fusion Center."

The governor nodded and made her way to the stage, where a string quartet and a harpist had been playing Christmas music. She walked up the steps to the side of the stage and approached the microphone.

"Good evening, everyone," she began before being interrupted by thunderous applause. Then the chants made famous on the campaign trail began.

"Texas strong! Texas free!"

"Texas strong! Texas free!"

Governor Burnett raised her hands and lowered them to quieten the crowd. "Thank you, everyone. I must notify you of some very disturbing news."

The crowd's chant quickly died down and was replaced by nervous chatter amongst the guests.

"The information we have is sketchy, but it's being reported by foreign news sources that our nation, and much of Canada, is experiencing a massive blackout."

The crowd erupted in murmur and conversation. It became so loud that the governor tapped the microphone, releasing a series of loud thumps through the speakers.

"Please, folks, listen up. We don't know what has caused this or if there is something more nefarious afoot. However, as you can see, the power is still on in Texas. That means we can all get to our homes and safe places until more information can be gathered. I'm sorry, but everyone needs to leave quickly, but safely. As word of this spreads, the streets may become chaotic."

Someone in the crowd shouted a question. "What are you gonna do?"

She responded with authority. "Texas has prepared for this possibility for decades. We have Texas Homeland Security already taking measures to dispatch all available law enforcement, first responders, and guardsmen to control those opportunists who try to take advantage of this situation."

"Will we be attacked, too?" asked a distraught woman from the rear of the room.

"We don't have any indication of that," she responded. Then she exhibited her command of the situation. "My friends, we sleep well at night because we've taken the steps to be ready for this eventuality. Now, do your part, get home safely, and let our Homeland Security team do its job. Also, turn on those emergency radios I gave you my first Christmas in office!"

CHAPTER 10

November 25
Black Friday
Deerfoot Inn & Casino
Calgary, Alberta, Canada

It took Cooper, Riley, and Palmer less than an hour to traverse the city streets of Calgary and make their way to the Deerfoot Inn & Casino on the south side of town. All three of them were loaded down with gear, as they left very little behind in the truck. As they ambled along, dodging pedestrians and stalled vehicles, they discussed the realities of travelling to the Armstrong ranch on horseback. They'd have to be selective on what they carried with them. The additional weight would be hard on the horses.

The first challenge they faced upon arrival at the hotel was securing their horses. They all agreed their rides were more valuable than all the disabled vehicles in Calgary. Not only would they have to take extraordinary care of their horses' health, but they'd need to constantly stand guard to prevent someone from stealing them.

By acting decisively, they were the first three to leave the Calgary Stampede and therefore were the first cowboys to arrive on horseback. On a vacant lot next to the hotel, which was used for overflow parking, a wood and aluminum lean-to shed stood alone in the darkness.

They got their horses settled in and walked into a nearby stand of trees in search of tall grasses to pull for the horses to feed on. It wasn't the best setup, but it would do for the night. Like people, a horse's well-being would deteriorate rapidly from dehydration in just three days. Food was important for good digestion due to the rapid buildup of acids in a horse's stomach, as well as for their mental health.

They decided to take shifts staying with the horses and, while remaining vigilant, make every effort to gather grasses for feed. Riley took the first shift, and Cooper handed him a rifle.

"A lot of good this thing will do me," said Riley. "It's empty, remember?"

"I know, no ammo," replied Cooper. "But the bad guys won't know that. You point it at 'em, they'll tuck tail and run."

"What if I need backup?" asked Riley. He turned toward the hotel, which was nearly a thousand yards away, and pointed. "I can see our room from here. Are y'all gonna watch out the window in case of trouble?"

"No, we'll use these," replied Palmer. "Daddy kept a few things under the backseat. You know, to be used with our get-home bags."

Palmer opened her backpack and pulled out a Christmas cookie tin that was sealed with aluminum duct tape.

"Great, Momma baked cookies in case we got hungry," said Riley sarcastically.

Cooper opened his pocketknife and handed it to Palmer. She ran the blade around the opening and then popped the lid off. A piece of one-inch foam fell out and blew across the vacant lot with the increasing wind. She closed the knife and returned it to her brother.

She handed an aluminum foil rectangle to each of them. Riley eagerly unwrapped his, most likely hoping Momma's cookies were inside. Instead they revealed three matching handheld Uniden MHS126 radios. Palmer pressed the power button and the display illuminated.

"Great, they work," exclaimed Palmer as Cooper and Riley followed suit. "Mine has almost a full battery charge."

"Unbelievable! Why isn't it fried like the rest of this stuff?" said Riley as he pointed to the graveyard of automobiles in the Deerfoot Inn parking lot.

"Riley, you really should pay attention to our parents sometimes," admonished Palmer. "This cookie tin acted like a Faraday cage."

"Who?" he asked.

"Faraday was this scientist guy who figured out a way to protect electronics from massive blasts of energy, like an EMP. By taking these radios, wrapping them in heavy-duty aluminum foil, and securing them in this metal container lined with foam, the EMP went around the cookie tin instead of inside it."

"Check it out," said Cooper. "It's got a GPS compass, it's submersible in water, and has dozens of channels to choose from."

Riley studied the display and held the radio in the air. "Will it reach Texas?"

"No, the range isn't that good, but we can use it to communicate for situations like this one," said Palmer. She reached into the cookie tin and pulled out another aluminum-foil-wrapped device. She opened it and showed her brothers the contents.

Cooper asked, "Is that a solar charger?"

"Sure is," she replied. "Daddy tried to think of everything. This will soak up the sun and recharge any device we have with a USB cable. The radios last around ten to twelve hours, but we can recharge them as we ride using this solar charger."

She handed the device to Cooper and he pressed a button. Five green lights illuminated near the top of the cell-phone-sized device. "Amazin'," he mumbled.

Shouts from near the front of the hotel grabbed their attention, and Cooper swung around. "Something's goin' on. Palmer, grab what you can, and let's see if we can get into our rooms. Riley, monitor channel eleven but don't use it unless it's an emergency. We need to conserve our battery life. I don't think it'll be very sunny tomorrow to help us recharge."

"Ten-four," said Riley with a laugh, using CB jargon.

Cooper and Palmer slung their rifles over their shoulders, picked up what they could, and headed for the hotel's side entrance. The door was propped open, and a couple of guests were standing outside with drinks in their hands.

One of the drunks addressed Cooper and Palmer. "Well, hey there, wayward travelers. Did your horse and wagon break down?"

"Come on, Palmer," said Cooper as he ignored the men and pushed his way past.

"That's pretty rude, buck-a-roooo," said the other man to Cooper. He was far more inebriated than his friend, so he didn't hesitate to address Palmer. "Aren't you gonna introduce us to your lady friend. Whadya call yourselves? Buggle bunnies or some such?"

The men, focused on Palmer, never saw what hit them. Cooper had dropped his gear on the carpeted floor of the hallway and quickly shoved both men off balance until they fell backwards out the door. Their drinks flew out of their hands, dousing one another, which generated more complaints than the act of landing on their backsides.

Cooper pulled the door shut and heard the lock snap shut. "Let 'em chew on that awhile."

Palmer laughed hysterically. "I could've taken those two, you know."

Cooper grinned as he gathered his gear. "I know, but I had a little frustration to let out. Let's stop by the front desk and see if our keycards will work."

A crowd was gathered in the lobby around the bar, where drinks were being served for cash only. Cooper chuckled to himself as he thought about how worthless money was at this point. Tomorrow, after the liquor wore off, these people were going to wake up to some harsh realities.

Before they approached the counter, which was illuminated with a dozen candles, he removed his coat and dropped his duffels on the floor. He covered his rifle with his coat. "Watch my stuff and keep the rifles undercover. I don't want people to freak out."

"Got it," replied Palmer as she removed her gun and jacket.

After a few minutes, Cooper returned with a bellman, who had a skeleton key to open the doors in the event of a power outage. He escorted them to their room and unlocked the door.

"Don't let this close while you're gone," he said as he turned the bolt lock to prevent the door from closing. "We won't always have time to do this in the future."

Cooper scowled at the man in the dark and pulled a twenty-dollar bill out of his pocket. "Will this twenty get you back up here if necessary?"

"Oh, yes, sir, it sure will," said the bellman as he stuffed the Canadian bill into his pocket. "Thank you!"

Cooper locked the door behind them and felt his way along the wall until he could open the curtains, allowing ambient light to provide some relief from the darkness.

Suddenly, the room was lit up as Palmer found her SureFire tactical flashlight. "This will help us get organized. Can you see Riley from here?"

"Yeah, I can barely make out the lean-to. Once we get settled, I'll go back down there and keep him company for a while. Maybe we can start a fire to help stay warm. It'll draw attention, but that's a might better than freezing to death in this cold."

"Tomorrow and especially tomorrow night will be brutal," said Palmer.

"I agree. We may go to double duty down there to stay alert. As the sun rises and people figure out what's happened, it will be more dangerous for anyone guarding the horses."

Palmer patted her brother on the back and slung her bug-out bag on one of the beds. "Let's see what Daddy has packed for us. Open yours up, too. Maybe we can consolidate some things."

"Palmer, we're gonna have to ride seventeen hundred miles to get home. Have you thought about what that means? It'll be hard on us and the horses. Not to mention the fact that people will be trying to take what we've got."

"I get it. We've got a lot to work with here, but one of our first priorities needs to be ammo for our rifles. We'll have to find a way to pick some up while on the road home."

"Okay," said Cooper. "Let's get organized, and you catch some sleep. You'll have the morning shift at first light."

PART TWO

Saturday, November 26

CHAPTER 11

November 26
Raven Rock Mountain Complex
Liberty Township, Pennsylvania

Since the advent of the hydrogen bomb and the revelation of its destructive capability, leaders within the United States government began to take measures to protect themselves. The Constitution laid out the basics of continuity of government as it related to lines of succession to the presidency. Our Founding Fathers never imagined a weapon so lethal that the entire government could be wiped out in seconds.

One of the early bunkers was built underground in the basement of the Greenbrier Hotel in West Virginia. As communications technology became more advanced and the size of the government grew, the need for more complex facilities arose.

The Raven Rock Mountain Complex, located near the Maryland-Pennsylvania border, dated back to the late nineteen forties when the U.S. government began to think about the consequences of their weapons technology. In essence, it was a freestanding city consisting of multiple three-story buildings tucked inside a mountain.

Like any small town, it had a basic infrastructure of utilities, first responders, and dining facilities, which operated twenty-four hours a day. Sleeping quarters were tight, but they had all the amenities of a studio apartment.

As the Cold War ended during the nineteen eighties, expansion and updating of the facility was set aside in favor of other forms of government spending. But then came 9/11, a wake-up call for all Americans and those within the government. Over the past twenty years, the Raven Rock complex had been rapidly expanded and could now protect over five thousand people.

Secretary Gregg had toured the facility many times. Raven Rock, also known as *Site R,* had become an underground Pentagon because of its formal designation as the Alternate National Military Command Center.

As Secretary of Defense, he maintained a permanent unescorted entry clearance. His wife was restricted to certain parts of the complex. After taking a moment to get her settled in, Secretary Gregg and his aide, Jackson Waller, immediately entered the command center, where they were greeted by Lieutenant Colonel Baker, the commander of the 1111th Signal Battalion, the so-called *Signal Masters of the Rock.* He was responsible for maintaining communications with the outside world and, as such, was privy to all communiques between the various intelligence agencies.

Colonel Baker was a permanent fixture at Raven Rock and had met Secretary Gregg on numerous occasions. He might have worked deep within a mountain, but he was also firmly entrenched within the deep state. He quickly pulled Secretary Gregg and Waller aside.

"Mr. Secretary, we've established full comms with all DOD facilities worldwide. You're the first to arrive, and I'll give you the latest intel rumor. This was a coordinated attack between Iran and North Korea."

"Iran, too?" asked Secretary Gregg. "Is this coming from the *agency*?"

"Yes, sir, via Israeli intelligence," replied Colonel Baker. "They apparently picked up postattack chatter from their resources in Tehran."

Secretary Gregg frowned and shook his head. "I warned everyone who'd listen that Iran was an existential threat on par with North Korea. When we entered into that ridiculous deal with Iran to give them back billions of dollars in exchange for empty promises, they raised the ante because they could afford it."

"Sir, Iran has been dealing directly with Pyongyang ever since," added Waller. "There's a reason they're referred to as rogue states—

they can't be controlled."

The voices of several other members of the cabinet were heard as the command center began to fill up with key members of the U.S. government. The three men abruptly halted their conversation.

"Thanks for the heads-up, Colonel," said Secretary Gregg. "I trust you'll come to me first in the future."

"Absolutely, sir," replied the colonel. He began to walk away to greet the new arrivals when Secretary Gregg grabbed him by the arm.

"Colonel, one more thing. Well, two, actually. Have you set up a line of communication to the Texas State House or their emergency operations there?"

"It's on my list for this morning," Colonel Baker replied.

Secretary Gregg leaned in to whisper, "Do you have someone you can trust to monitor their communication activity with the president and her staff?"

Colonel Baker thought for a moment and nodded. "I do. They'll only report to me, of course, and it's best you not be seen having direct conversations with the communications team. It would appear out of sorts."

"Understood. In addition, are communications between my personal office and others monitored or logged in any way?"

"They're not monitored, but they are logged per protocol. Every call is, including the president's."

Secretary Gregg leaned in closer. "If I need you to turn off my call logs, can you do that?"

"I can, but in order to avoid scrutiny, may I suggest you tell me in advance a block of time so that it doesn't appear that you haven't used your phone at all. The call activity can still be recovered from the internal servers of the communications system if curious minds choose to look into it."

"Thank you, Colonel. I'll keep that in mind."

After Baker left them alone, Waller whispered to Secretary Gregg, "What was that all about?"

Secretary Gregg's answer was simple, yet vague. "Possibly, our future."

CHAPTER 12

November 26
Raven Rock Mountain Complex
Liberty Township, Pennsylvania

President Harman addressed those members of her cabinet who were in attendance. Pursuant to continuity-of-government protocols, other members who were in the line of succession were moved throughout the country to protected bunkers. Within the command center of Raven Rock, a large conference room was constructed to act as a situation room for the president when she was within the complex. It bore the presidential seal on the wall and contained several monitors designed for face-to-face communications with other facilities like Cheyenne Mountain in Colorado and Mount Weather in Virginia.

"For decades, our biggest fear within the halls of government has been an all-out nuclear war with the Russians that blankets our entire country with radiation, destruction, and death. But after 9/11, our focus shifted to terrorist groups like al-Qaeda and ISIL, and rogue nations like Iran and North Korea. Now, it appears that an *Axis of Evil* has been formed between those nations, and they are the ones responsible for this heinous attack."

"Madam President," interjected the director of the CIA, "we have not yet confirmed the Israeli intelligence, and no country has claimed responsibility for the act. That said, NORAD has confirmed the proximate trajectory of the satellites to be consistent with the low Earth orbits of Iran's and the North Korean's."

"Thank you, but attribution will be determined soon enough," continued the president. "First, I want to hear Homeland Security's report on the impact this is having on the American people. Then we'll turn to the Secretary of Defense to discuss what to expect next militarily. Carla?"

Carla Pickering was the new director of Homeland Security appointed by the president last summer. Her predecessor, a highly respected former police chief from New York City, had resigned suddenly amid allegations of sexual misconduct. Pickering had been California's Homeland Security advisor during the president's tenure as a prosecutor in San Francisco. The two had successfully fought the challenges to San Francisco's sanctuary city status by the prior administration.

Before she was appointed California's head of Homeland Security, Pickering was formally trained as a community psychologist and focused on integrating social, cultural, economic, and political influences into communities and organizations. In California, her expertise was deemed invaluable in dealing with the challenges faced by undocumented workers.

"Thank you, Madam President," Pickering began, leaving her seat and standing in front of a single monitor showing a satellite image of the country. "This image was taken last night by the International Space Station. It clearly depicts the magnitude of the outage. As you can see, one state shines bright—Texas. We'll get to them in a moment. First, I'd like to address our options for the rest of the nation."

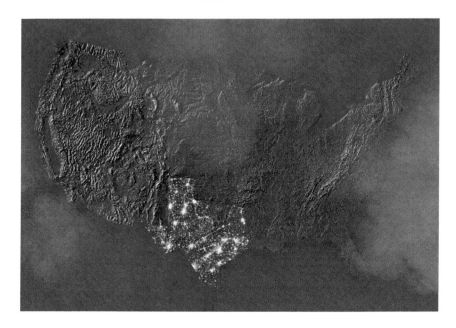

After everyone had a moment to study the image, Pickering continued. "Without trying to be flippant, this couldn't have happened at a worse time for the American people. Thanksgiving weekend has traditionally been the biggest travel time of the year. Thirty percent of the population is away from home right now. For some, their natural inclination will be to begin traveling home by whatever means of transportation is available. Others will rely upon friends and families to house them until their resources run out."

"What happens when those resources run out?" asked the president.

"America will become a dangerous place to live," replied Pickering. "Most people are creatures of habit and will move only if they're forced to. Just like livestock that are allowed to overgraze a field, they'll continue to consume until the food supply is gone; then they'll move on. Competition for resources and groups becoming territorial will force displaced Americans to find their way home, or they'll seek perceived sources of food and shelter."

"Away from the cities," added Secretary Gregg. "They'll naturally migrate to where they think they can hunt, fish, and eat crops and farm animals."

"Makes sense," said the president.

Secretary Gregg disagreed. "Not to the farmers and ranchers who own the land. I know the rural mindset having grown up in Texas and with people who came from rural communities. They're not going to open their resources up to outsiders. They have their own to protect and feed."

"With all due respect, Secretary Gregg," interrupted Pickering, "I have an advanced degree in community psychology. Our studies have shown that people will come together and help one another. Our role in government is to make this temporary setback manageable and fair. The best approach is to pool the nation's resources and help those in need the most—the elderly, women, children, and those who live in impoverished communities who don't have access to farms and stocked fishing ponds or cattle that can be butchered."

Secretary Gregg smiled and chose to remain silent. *Yeah, good luck with that approach.*

The president changed the subject. "Carla, how are people dealing with this? We're entering the throes of winter now. Proper shelter will become an issue."

"You're correct, Madam President," Pickering responded. "We're in the early hours of the crisis. Reports are coming to us via satellite radio hookups with our field offices. There have been reports of looting in retail stores in the major cities. Local law enforcement is doing an admirable job of bringing calm to the streets. However, as always, when nighttime comes, frustrations seem to boil over. Police and fire departments will have their hands full."

President Harman continued to gather information. "What can we do to help?"

"We're still trying to establish communications with our FEMA field offices in order to deploy our operating assets around the country. Our warehouses have meals ready-to-eat and bottled water to distribute. FEMA also has military transport vehicles that were hardened against an electromagnetic pulse."

"What kind of time frame are we talking about?" asked the president.

"Our communications linkups are the biggest issue—" began Pickering before being interrupted by the president.

"No, I'm sorry, let me clarify. Studies have always shown that society will begin to collapse within seventy-two hours. Does that hold true in our situation?"

"In my opinion," started Pickering, "there will be a period of time when Americans will stop to assess their situation—a transition period, if you will. People will gather together seeking information and pledging to help one another. Throughout their lives, they've experienced power outages or a lack of water pressure for brief periods of time. However, their actions in response to this temporary inconvenience was dictated by the rapid response of government to restore the utility at issue. Under the present circumstances, the question is when will society realize this blackout is long term in nature. As days turn into weeks and then months, a survive-at-all-costs mindset will overtake most people. A nation without rule of law is very dangerous considering there are more guns than citizens in the United States."

"Are we going to be able to stave off this downfall?" asked the president.

"For a while, yes. People will consume their refrigerated goods first and then deplete their pantries. The average American household has less than a week's worth of food in their kitchens. We've become dependent on the close proximity of grocery stores and mega-retailers like Walmart to feed us on a moment's notice. Without trucks restocking the shelves at the grocery stores, the food will be gone in a matter of days, if not hours."

The president leaned back in her chair. Secretary Gregg watched her mind work. She was rightfully concerned about helping Americans through this, but his mind was preoccupied with when the nukes would start flying.

"It appears we have three days at most to begin delivering relief supplies to three hundred million Americans. How can this be accomplished?"

Pickering responded, "Admittedly, we're not prepared for

something of this magnitude. However, by stroke of luck, Texas was spared from the effects of the EMP. I suggest we enlist their help."

"In what way?" asked the president's chief of staff. He had been taking copious notes during the meeting.

"Mr. Acton, we need to fly a team from Andrews to Lackland to learn the impact the EMP had on Texas. We know their grid was spared, but we need to determine if their communications and transportation systems were adversely effected."

"Let's assume they're in good working order. What will you need from them?" asked Acton.

"I believe we should use all of their mass transit buses, including school buses, to carry their available emergency food and water supplies to other parts of the country. As the buses return to Texas, they can carry Americans who are in most need of food, shelter, and medical attention. We'll focus on the largest population centers like Los Angeles, Atlanta, Chicago, Detroit, and New York. These are the cities in which our limited resources can have the greatest impact. Plus, by reducing their populations and redistributing the citizens to housing in Texas, the burden on first responders in these populated areas will be reduced."

The president nodded her head in agreement. "I agree with your assessment and the proposal. Put together your team and have them ready to travel by this evening or morning at the latest. I'll plan a phone call to Governor Burnett this afternoon and pave the way for their arrival."

Good luck with that, Secretary Gregg mused to himself as he imagined the governor's response. He was sure it would be coupled with the words *put it where the sun don't shine* in some form.

"Monty, let's hear from you," started the president, which shook Secretary Gregg back to the present. "Now is not the time to address what has happened in terms of the EMP. I'm most interested in how to protect our nation from the next wave of attack if one is planned."

"Madam President, we're ready for a follow-up attack in the form of a full-on nuclear assault. As to whether this is part of their overall strategy, time will tell. North Korea is highly secretive, and predictions of what they'll do next is conjecture. Our intelligence has found them on the same war footing for many years. Quite simply, they are ready to attack us on a moment's notice."

"Obviously," grumbled Acton.

"If the Iranians and North Koreans have used the EMP attacks as a precursor to a broader war, then it is my opinion the nuclear-equipped ICBMs would already be en route to our mainland. They would've hit us while we were scrambling to react to the power outage."

"So you don't anticipate a follow-up strike?" said the president.

"I anticipate everything, Madam President."

"Except satellites, right?" sniped Acton.

The hackles rose on the back of Secretary Gregg's neck. He bristled as he stared down the president's chief of staff. "Yes, we did anticipate a nuke delivered by satellite. But such an attack is indefensible. The only way to prevent it was to take out the DPRK's command and control apparatus, which we've never been green-lighted to do. Secondly, we should never have allowed Iran the financial wherewithal to expand its nuclear program. We should have undertaken preemptive measures—"

President Harman raised her hands and shouted, "Enough! Both of you. This is counterproductive. The purpose of this meeting is not to rehash the politics of the past or to cast blame for what has happened to our great nation. Monty, please, what additional actions are you taking to protect us in the event matters escalate?"

Secretary Gregg took a deep breath to calm his nerves. He broke the death stare he was exchanging with Acton and continued. "Madam President, we have done several things in the hours since the attack. First, we sent fourteen F-22 Raptors to South Korea to join our other stealth fighters in the event you order an air assault upon the North.

"Second, we have deployed our nuclear launch tracker, Constant Phoenix, to the Korean Peninsula. In the past, the newly redesigned Boeing WC-135 was used to monitor testing activities. With its capability to fly forty thousand feet above the North, it will provide us instant notification of an ICBM launch. The data received from the reconnaissance will be fed into our computers, and we can pinpoint within minutes the trajectory and likely target. This gives us a huge jump on preparing our defenses, which I've briefed you on in the past.

"Finally, and the following has only been performed in an experimental environment, we have specially designed F-35 Joint Strike Fighters that could intercept North Korean missiles in mid-flight."

"Let me interrupt you there, Monty," said the president. "Northup Grumman executives were not able to confirm to Congress that the F-35 aircraft could perform as required."

"I recall the testimony from four years ago, Madam President, but much has changed in both technology and training. Additional sensors were added, including the distributed aperture system consisting of two dozen electro-optical and infrared sensors. As we've discussed, there is no guaranteed method to shoot down an ICBM. Our best opportunity comes during the boost phase as the rocket leaves the launchpad. With the constant monitoring of Constant Phoenix and a dozen DAS-equipped F35s buzzing the coast of North Korea, we can detect when the rockets lift off. The maneuverability of the F-35s could have them in North Korea and out again before they knew what hit 'em."

"And if you miss?" asked Acton with a tone of sarcasm that, once again, Secretary Gregg didn't appreciate.

"Then we have our traditional means of defense. Constant Phoenix, working in concert with the F-35s, provides us another line of defense."

President Harman referred to her notes and then spoke. "Thank you, Monty. I have a number of phone calls to make to world leaders. I need to express outrage over what has happened, but more importantly, I need our allies to work with us to pressure North Korea to cease further hostilities. We can recover from an EMP attack. I'm not sure we can from an all-out nuclear war. No nation on the planet wants to experience that."

CHAPTER 13

November 26
Deerfoot Inn & Casino
Calgary, Alberta, Canada

It was just before dawn when the snow began to fall in Calgary. The winds that preceded the cold front froze Cooper and Riley to their core throughout the night. As the weather system began to pass across Alberta, frigid arctic winds dropped temperatures to below freezing, with a windchill factor into the teens. Commonly referred to as an Alberta Clipper, a weather phenomenon that affects central North America, the fast-moving low-pressure system moved quickly across the region, causing sharp winds and sudden temperature drops.

During the night, Cooper and Riley recalled the horrific spring storm that had crossed the high plains of the Texas Panhandle six years prior. The raging blizzard, which occurred the last weekend of April, caused downed power lines and snowdrifts up to eight feet. Texans called it *snowpocalypse*.

Preparing for the worst, the guys spent most of the night gathering up things to burn. Soon, cardboard boxes, trash, and discarded furniture from a nearby strip shopping center became acceptable combustible material.

Just after midnight, other rodeo participants began to arrive on horses, woefully underdressed for the rapidly dropping temperatures. Unlike Cooper and Riley, who'd found shelter for their horses, the majority of the new arrivals tied their rides off near the entrance to the hotel and scampered inside. Only their Brazilian friends from San Antonio, Adriano Morales and Eduardo Pacheco, noticed the fire and approached the Armstrong brothers.

After a few minutes of conversation, which included an update on the chaos that had ensued in the arena after the rodeo kids left, the Brazilians headed inside to sleep with the promise to return after sunrise to relieve Cooper and Riley.

"Coop, before the boys show up, tell me honestly," started Riley. "We've got nothing to work with, really. I mean, we've got get-home backpacks that Daddy has kept packed for us all. We've got rifles with no ammo. When we hit the road, we'll have no food and no idea of where to sleep at night. Do you think maybe we oughta hunker down here and see what happens? Maybe they'll fix the power or somethin'?"

Cooper removed his hat and knocked the snow that had accumulated off the brim. He scrubbed his head and wiped the sweat off his brow. The constant activity of gathering hay and fuel for the fire kept his body temperature up. "We'll talk about it some more inside with Palmer, who, by the way, is plenty tough enough to make a decision and carry it through."

Riley nodded and stuck his hands over the fire. "I know. Little sis knows more about this prepper stuff than I do. But you and I know about survival on the trail. Pops taught us a lot when we were little."

Their grandfather had grown up during the Great Depression and during a time when traveling long distances across West Texas was done on horseback. Fuel was scarce for their vehicles, and money was even harder to come by.

As the boys grew up, they were taught the importance of finding a water supply, adequate shelter, and how to find food sources by hunting, trapping, and fishing. Although the boys didn't practice the survival skills they'd learned as kids, the knowledge was still within them.

Cooper was about to add to Riley's thought when he noticed Pacheco and Morales coming in the distance. "Here comes the next shift."

"Should we talk to them about riding back together?" asked Riley.

"Let's feel 'em out first and then make the decision with Palmer," replied Cooper. "I like these guys, but I wanna make sure they're not gonna be a burden first."

*****

Twenty minutes later, after they had a conversation with their Brazilian friends, the guys fought through the thickening snowfall and returned to their hotel room. They were greeted by Palmer with two beds covered with extra blankets.

The inside of the room was illuminated with a bright white glow. The rising sun was obscured by the blowing white snow, which reflected to a nearly blinding level inside the hotel.

"I was trying to watch for you guys, but as you can see, visibility is less than thirty feet. I've never seen anything like it."

"Yeah, it's getting worse," said Coop, who removed his boots and coat at the door. "Pacheco told me he tried to check on you last night. You must've been asleep."

"Zonked out," replied Palmer. "When I woke up, I found the maid's station down the hall and gathered up some goodies. Extra wool blankets, soaps, shampoos, towels, and just for Riley, extra toilet paper."

"Good, thanks for looking out for me, sis!" he said as he slung his hat in her direction like it was a frisbee.

"Come on, y'all," started Palmer. "Get under the covers, warm up, and enjoy a protein bar each. There's also bottled water on the nightstands."

"Where'd you get those?" asked Cooper.

She pulled her spring-assisted knife out of her jeans pocket and opened it like a switchblade. "I popped the lock on the maid's utility closet. I found a case of water. See?" She pointed at the corner of the room near the window where their gear was stacked up.

"Dang, sis," said Riley with a chuckle. "I told Coop you weren't sittin' up here eatin' bonbons and sippin' champagne while we were freezin' our tails off. He wouldn't believe me."

"Shut up," said Cooper jokingly as he pushed his brother onto the bed and slid under the covers of the other bed. "Before I crash, let's talk about our options."

"I've been thinkin' about it, too," said Palmer. "This is exactly the scenario that Daddy always talked about. An EMP attack. Electronics fried. Months or years to fix. We gotta get home, and waitin' around here will only allow the country to fall apart more. We need to get a head start on the rest of 'em."

"I agree," said Cooper. "This is not gonna fix itself. Plus, who knows why this happened. If it was the North Koreans, like Daddy warned about, then they may have fired off nukes too. We've got to get to the ranch."

Riley crawled under the covers into his bed and propped up against the headboard. "Momma and Daddy might need us."

Cooper shrugged. "Emotionally, yes. But to protect the ranch, they're in good shape. Daddy and Preacher have been planning for years. They've talked about different scenarios. Defense of the ranch. Heck, they even discussed whether to shoot someone trying to steal eggs out of the henhouse."

"Momma, too, you guys," interjected Palmer. "Here's the way she put it. You do what it takes to survive during TEOTWAWKI. You know, the end of the world as we know it. Normal rules don't apply when it comes to personal survival and protecting your own."

"Yeah, but there are still certain morals," added Cooper. "We all have to make a decision as to how to act when threatened. There has to be a line in the sand that shouldn't be crossed."

"I agree," said Palmer. "We'll have plenty of time to talk about that when we hit the trail. For now, do we all agree to hit the road when the storm clears out?"

"Yup," said Cooper. "Next question. Normally, there's strength in numbers. Do we gather up some other riders who are returning to Texas? Or do we go it alone? You know, travel light so to speak."

Palmer wandered toward the window and pressed her hand against the cold glass. The heavy snow had created whiteout conditions. Then she looked on the floor at all their gear and the things she'd procured the night before.

"We can't handle all of this," she said as she gently kicked a duffel bag. "More riders will help us spread out the load. Plus, while you guys are sleeping, I'm gonna roam around the hotel and see what else I can rustle up, especially food."

Cooper slid down under the covers as a chill came over his body. "Okay, I can sign off on more riders. That way, we can sleep in shifts. Riley and I are comfortable with the Brazilians. They don't have anything to offer compared to our things, but they're loyal."

"We can trust them," said Riley. "They kept me from killin' that idiot in Fort Worth. I think they'd have our backs."

"Should we try to find anyone else?" asked Palmer. "Most of these guys are from Colorado and Texas. We'll all be headed in the same direction."

Cooper shook his head. "I've thought about that. Here's the thing. You can have too many chiefs, and eventually the group starts to pull against each other. Morales and Pacheco are pretty down to earth. Neither one of them would try some kind of power trip on us."

"Yeah," interjected Riley. "And with them, we don't have to sleep with one eye open at night."

"Then it's agreed," said Palmer. "As soon as the storm clears, the five of us head for Texas. Y'all get some shut-eye while I roam around the hotel looking for anything useful. I've gotta leave this door cracked to get back in. I'll pull Coop's boots behind it as I slip out so you'll be alerted to anyone coming inside."

"All right, sis," said Riley. "See if you can learn anything, too. Sure would be nice to know what we're dealing with here. I hate being in the dark."

"Literally," added Cooper with a chuckle.

CHAPTER 14

November 26
The Armstrong Ranch
Borden County, Texas

It had been less than twenty-four hours since Major and Preacher rounded up all the ranch hands and their families to head into the bunker. Lucy was there to greet everyone as they entered, working diligently to make them feel comfortable and safe.

Fear was one of man's strongest emotions, and fear of the unknown was considered one of the biggest mental obstacles to overcome in an uncertain situation. Every time a person encounters an unfamiliar situation, especially one fraught with danger, fear will manifest itself, oftentimes resulting in bad decision-making.

Lucy wasn't a psychologist, but she'd studied the men and women within her employ enough to understand their mindset and emotional responses. The Armstrongs and those who lived on their ranch were very much like a large extended family. As a result, Lucy knew who she could rely upon to keep this unusual situation under control.

After everyone was safely in the bunker, Major addressed the adults and explained what had happened beyond the Texas borders. Antonio helped with the language barrier, as did Lucy, who had learned some basic Spanish over the years.

They took baby steps in explaining what to expect and then combined humor to put the group at ease. It resulted in a relatively peaceful night within their crowded bunker; however, the next morning, as the group's biological clocks began to cause them to wake up, Lucy found herself having to convince several of the group that they were safe.

Preacher pulled Lucy aside and whispered in her ear, "Lack of information is frightening, too."

"I know," she replied. "I've stayed up much of the night with Antonio's wife, scanning AM band radio stations, but the news keeps repeating itself. There haven't been any official statements from the president or the military. Although stations around Texas give us updates on conditions in our state, they don't have anything new to report about the rest of the country. Now that it's daylight, maybe that will change."

"I snaked the AM/FM antenna wiring through the conduit to the top of the barn," said Preacher. "How's your reception?"

"Excellent," she replied. "I guess the airwaves are clearer without the radio signals from outside Texas. WBAP and KRLD in Dallas/Fort Worth are very strong. I can even pick up the Spanish stations out of San Antonio."

"Do you have folks lined up to help you feed breakfast to everyone? If not, I'll round up some helpers."

"No, I'm good, Preacher. Thank you. This morning, we're gonna eat cereal to use up the milk that everyone brought. It will go bad first. I don't know how long we'll have to stay down here, but I wanna eat up the perishable food first before we get to the stuff in storage."

"Good thinking," said Preacher. "Where's Major?"

"Still sleepin'," she replied. "He stayed up all night fiddlin' with the satellite internet system through HughesNet. Well, mainly he was cursin' it. He finally drifted off with the laptop tipping over on the bed between us."

"All right, I won't disturb him. It's just that I was thinkin' about going topside. I'm feelin' a little closed in, you know. Claustrophobic. I don't see how those astronauts do it. There's no way I could float around up there and not be able to step on solid ground. It ain't natural."

"No, it's not," added Lucy. "Would you like something to keep you busy? It might take the edge off."

"Yeah, please," Preacher replied eagerly.

Lucy pushed past Preacher and pulled a three-ring binder off the kitchen counter. She thumbed through the tabs until she reached the one labeled *food stores*.

"The families carried what food they could from their homes when they arrived," she started as she looked around the first bunker. "As you can see, it's stacked everywhere. The other bunker too."

Preacher chuckled. "In the chaos last night, I didn't pay attention, but folks were puttin' stuff in every nook and cranny. It's quite a mess."

"Yes, it is," added Lucy. "I need to put the food away and, just as importantly, add it to my food storage inventory. I don't know how long we'll be down here, but I've got to keep up with our inventory levels or things could get out of hand."

He took the binder and pencil from Lucy. "You've always been well organized."

"Thanks. When Major and I first embraced this prepping concept, we analyzed what it meant to be a prepper. It kinda came down to taking the best of my experience as a homesteader and Major's survivalist training over the years. A prepper is a well-organized hybrid of homesteading and survivalism. To me, that was all about keeping a detailed checklist of every aspect of preparedness."

Preacher laughed. "I know, beans, Band-Aids, and bullets. I've heard Major say it a thousand times."

Lucy chuckled with her longtime employee and friend. "You can only live three days without water and three weeks without food— the *beans* part of the equation. When doctors and hospitals aren't available, a simple cut could result in an infection that could kill ya, which is why we stock so many medical supplies. Where there is no doctor, you gotta take care of yourself. Finally, *bullets*, which includes weaponry, are used to defend yourself. If you can't defend it, it isn't yours."

"Dang straight. That's my department," said Preacher. He looked upward and ran his hand along the wall next to him until he almost reached the ceiling. "We've set up a pretty good plan, but I hate not knowin' what's goin' on out there. That's one of the reasons why I'm itchin' to sneak a peek. What if they're out there stealin' our horses or ravaging our chickens?"

Lucy patted him on the chest and laughed. "Don't worry, Preach. I think it's a little early for roving bands of marauders."

Chapter 15

November 26
Texas Homeland Security Operations Center
Austin, Texas

Governor Burnett was under siege. Not from an invading army, but from the local media. Once she was given clearance to emerge from the fallout shelter, she was overwhelmed with requests for interviews and statements. She resisted the urge to appear before the cameras and announce that Texans were safe, because that was yet to be determined. She needed information and an honest assessment from her team before addressing her constituents.

During a time of crisis, the Texas Division of Emergency Management staffed and operated the State Operations Center in conjunction with Texas Homeland Security. In addition to monitoring threats twenty-four hours a day, the staff coordinated state emergency assistance to local governments.

Of course, a situation like this had never challenged the SOC before. Every state agency rushed high-level representatives to participate in the assessment. Noticeably absent, by design, were the Central Texas-based Federal liaison team, which included representatives from FEMA, the Federal Emergency Management Agency, and the director of the Department of Homeland Security, Texas Field Office, in McAllen. Governor Burnett wanted to meet with *her people* before the feds got involved.

In the hours before her arrival, the SOC was buzzing with activity. Certain outlying areas east of Beaumont on the Louisiana border and west of Lubbock, near New Mexico, were without power. Those areas had small independent utility districts that were not tied to the Eastern and Western Interconnection grids. However, through modifications to their infrastructure, they were capable of connecting to the ERCOT grid that controlled Texas.

Engineers were working to make the switchover, but in the meantime, local law enforcement was becoming overwhelmed with angry residents. Her first meeting, even before she learned of the details gathered by her team, was privately with Kregg Deur—adjutant general for the state of Texas and head of the Texas National Guard. She had total confidence and trust in Deur, not only because he had proven himself in times of natural disasters like hurricanes, but because he was a like-minded thinker when it came to the issue of secession.

"Kregg, before I meet with the rest of these folks, I have a question for you that we've never contemplated."

"Of course, Governor," said Deur. "I'll answer it the best I can."

"When we've discussed the prospects of secession in the past, it has always been under the assumption that a political struggle would occur in the State House here in Austin, and then later with the politicians in Washington who'd resist us."

"Right," he interrupted. "We both agreed that a power play like the Confederate states pulled a hundred fifty years ago would never work in this day and age."

She nodded. "Mainly because their army is bigger than our army, right?"

"No doubt, ma'am."

"Kregg," she hesitated briefly before continuing, "what if Washington and its powerful army was distracted as we made our move? What if we decided to circle the wagons around our borders first, and then give them the bad news that we're pulling out of the union? Have you ever given that any thought?"

Deur stood and walked across the room, slowly parting the curtains to observe the activity in the SOC. "I have not, but sometimes you can tell what a person is thinking by the questions they ask. If our information is correct, we've got power and they don't. By they, I mean the whole dang country, Canada, and much of Mexico."

"Why should a prepared Texas take on the burdens of an unprepared Washington?" she asked rhetorically.

"Arguably, other than being Good Samaritans, we shouldn't," Deur replied. "What are you suggesting?"

Governor Burnett hesitated because once the words came out of her mouth, there might be no turning back. "Close our borders."

"Marion, we're old friends," started Deur. "Don't get me wrong, I never considered our discussions surrounding the secessionist movement as pie in the sky. By the same token, I didn't consider leaving the Union as being likely. That said, this is the perfect opportunity to make that play."

"Think about it, Kregg. We've got the perfect opportunity to take advantage of an inexperienced president who is probably swimming in crisis-management decisions. She's got to worry about the safety and well-being of American citizens. Not to mention the fact that somebody, probably North Korea, has just started world war three."

Deur rubbed his hands together and looked at his palms. "I can't disagree with any of that, but it seems borderline treasonous to leave the nation under these circumstances."

"Even if it is in the best interests of all Texans?" she interrupted. "Listen, I'm not trying to kick America while she's down. But I've spent months on the campaign trail talking about Texas being strong and free. I firmly believe the majority of our fellow Texans would agree we should protect our own first."

"Okay, let's say you decide to secede, you've still got to convince the legislature, which is not in session."

The governor immediately responded, "I've already got my chief of staff arranging for an emergency session, regardless of whether the secession topic is to be raised. It'll send the message to our constituents that we're in control of the situation."

Deur ran his fingers through his thick hair and massaged his forehead before he continued. "You wanna know from me how we'd close our borders, don't you?"

"How do we secure them from masses of people entering like we did along the Rio Grande and the Mexican border?"

"I think it's twenty-eight hundred miles, give or take, if you take out the twelve hundred miles of common border with Mexico, which is secured already. We're a big state. This ain't Rhode Island."

Governor Burnett pressed him for an answer. She needed to meet with the rest of the team. "Can it be done?"

"I think so," he began. "Off the top of my head, we could reduce agents on the southern border with Mexico. The Gulf Coast could be protected by supplementing our existing resources with local law enforcement. From Beaumont around the Panhandle down to El Paso is the real challenge. We can create closings at the major interstate crossings first. There are seven of those. Follow that with creating roadblocks at the twenty or so state and federal highways. Yeah, it could be done."

"What about the gaps in between the roads?" asked the governor before adding, "Most of these refugees will be streaming in on foot, bicycle, horse, and lord knows what kind of transportation they'll use."

"We've got the benefit of the rivers along Louisiana and Oklahoma to help us. In the Panhandle and West Texas counties, we'll need a lot of help."

Governor Burnett smiled as she began to realize her lofty goals of the past might come to fruition. "I know where to get help for the rural counties. We'll call upon the ranchers."

"Marion, there are a lot of other considerations, but you've got the basics to make a decision."

The governor stood and made her way to the door of the conference room to allow the rest of her team to enter. "Keep this under your hat, Kregg. I haven't decided if this is the right thing to do, and I need to get the total picture. Agreed?"

"Of course, not a word."

CHAPTER 16

November 26
Raven Rock Mountain Complex
Liberty Township, Pennsylvania

"Thank you all for reconvening on short notice," started President Harman as her cabinet members and key military leaders took their seats. It was standing room only, as the president insisted upon all of her top advisors being present. "I have been in contact with key leaders in Europe, Russia, Israel, and Southeast Asia. There are some developments, which I'll relay to you in a moment. But first, any minute now, Kim Jong-un, in what is most likely a recorded address, will broadcast a statement from Pyongyang."

"Madam President," interrupted Acton, "the broadcast has started."

An image appeared on the screen with a caption generated by the State Department. Kim Jong-un was staring at the camera holding the text of his speech. As he read, his expression never changed. He displayed no outward emotion, but his words were full of anger and condemnation.

He began. "Just after the release of retribution upon the United States of America, I contacted the leaders of South Korea, Japan, China, and Russia through diplomatic channels. I advised them that the Democratic People's Republic of Korea and the Islamic Republic of Iran had detonated a superpowerful electromagnetic pulse over the skies of the United States.

"I told these leaders that many countries had been allowed to build, test, and maintain nuclear weapons while we have not. As other nations in the world were allowed—no, encouraged—to expand their nuclear arsenals, the nations of North Korea and Iran were told *no*.

"This was a decision I did not take lightly. After consultation with the government in Iran, we found this action necessary to protect the people of Iran and North Korea from the burdensome sanctions that cause famine and death in our countries. The actions of the United States were tantamount to a total economic blockade of our country. These sanctions imposed on our countries constituted an act of war!

"The electromagnetic pulse was used intentionally to avoid death to the American people. I do not hold them accountable for the actions of their leaders. However, the American people must learn to suffer as our people have suffered. The oppressive United States must learn a lesson from the decades of economic burdens placed upon Iran and North Korea. Nothing more.

"Let the American people learn to live without power and the unnecessary things that fill their homes and driveways. Let them understand what life is like to fish and forage for food. And let them know what it is like to live in fear as military powers threaten them daily, as our people have been threatened.

"My message to the American people is this. At one time, I promised to bring irrevocable disaster and disgrace upon your country. I have shown restraint. We mean no harm to you, which is why we didn't use our greatest weapons. But now, you can see how our two countries live. Now you can turn to your political leaders and say *you caused this!*

"Finally, here is a word to those in Washington, Tel Aviv, Seoul, and Tokyo who might consider retaliating against our countries. Do not continue your self-destructive ways. If you escalate this into a military conflict by attempting an attack upon our countries, we will turn you and your people into a pile of ash. The days are gone forever when our enemies can blackmail us with their nuclear bombs.

"It is true the military might of a country represents its national strength. It is only when it builds up its military might in every way can it develop into a thriving country. Today, we are on an equal playing field with the United States, both militarily and socioeconomically. What the future brings our nations will depend on America."

The monitor went black and then turned to gray. The sound of static continued to echo throughout the room after Acton turned off the television.

The president let out a sigh and motioned to Acton. "Charles, is there any way to get some air in this room? Or open the doors and post guards in the hallway to keep our conversations from leaking out."

"I'll look into it," said Acton as he left the room. The president held her hand up and paused while Acton made the arrangements.

The blood began to boil inside Secretary Gregg. In a way, he'd dodged a bullet, so to speak. Kim made no reference to the assassination attempt, which was probably the real catalyst for the EMP attack. That was something Gregg would have to live with for the rest of his life.

Now that Kim had fired off the first salvo, it was time to end this. Instead, he could feel he was destined for some kind of Kumbaya focus-group session where they all talked about how this made each other feel. He could feel the bile rising into his throat.

CHAPTER 17

November 26
Raven Rock Mountain Complex
Liberty Township, Pennsylvania

The president grew impatient waiting for Acton's return, so she started the discussion.

"There will be plenty of time to decode Kim's statement through State and the CIA. I'm interested in everyone's initial reaction. Carla, you first."

Pickering spoke on behalf of Homeland Security. "My initial reaction is that this is over unless we escalate matters. In Kim's mind, he has leveled the playing field between our countries. He's forced us to live as a third-world country just as the Iranians and North Koreans have lived for centuries."

"Madam Secretary?" The president turned to Jane Tompkins, the Secretary of State.

"The State Department's official position remains unchanged," Secretary Tompkins began. "An EMP attack, which most in this room consider an act of war, does not give rise to immediate loss of life other than through transportation accidents. We can recover and rebuild from this. A nuclear attack is significantly more lethal in both terms of human loss and environmental impact from the radiation fallout."

President Harman nodded and turned to Secretary Gregg. "Monty?"

He didn't hesitate or hold back. "We annihilate them! We leave no building standing and no bunker in place."

"But innocent lives—" Secretary Tompkins started to plead for restraint before Secretary Gregg shouted her down.

"You don't think people are gonna die in this country? Have you not read the numerous reports from the EMP Commission? Ninety percent! Ninety percent of the American people will likely die in the coming year. Innocent lives, as you call them. I don't give a tinker's damn about North Koreans. They have to pay for what they've done to our great nation!"

Acton came running into the room and closed the door behind him. "You've got to keep your voices down. This isn't the White House. Please."

"Yes, Monty, please," admonished the president. "This is an open discussion designed to help me reach a decision. We need to respect one another's observations and opinions just like we'd hope they'd respect yours."

Secretary Gregg simply nodded and stopped speaking. He was mad at himself for the outburst. He knew better than to let others know what he was thinking.

President Harman said, "Okay, let me tell you what I've gleaned from my conversations with world leaders today. Monty, let me say Prime Minister Netanyahu agrees with you. He's simply waiting for me to give him the word and he'll crush Iran. The new king of Saudi Arabia, Mohammad bin Salman, agrees, resulting in a rare accord between the Kingdom and Israel.

"That said, however, the key nations in Southeast Asia, China, South Korea, and Japan are firmly against a retaliatory strike."

"Madam President, with all due respect—" interrupted Secretary Gregg before she shut him down.

"Monty, there's no need to go on. I said the same thing you're about to say. Seoul and Tokyo seem pretty ungrateful. Trust me when I say, and Charles will confirm this, I told them this in not-so-diplomatic terms earlier."

Secretary Gregg nodded and stopped talking, again cursing himself for his outburst.

"There's an additional complication, as the Russians have inserted themselves into the situation," said the president. "After Putin learned of the attack, he immediately called leaders in London, Berlin, Brussels, and Paris. He told them, in no uncertain terms, to stand down and to encourage us to do so as well."

Or what? Secretary Gregg screamed in his head this time, allowing himself a slight smile for his restraint.

"Madam President," began Pickering, "perhaps we should take Kim at his word and focus on taking care of Americans at this time. If this is over, we can pull together, with the aid of the United Nations, and rebuild. Maybe this horrific act was what it took to bring the world together as one and put decades of hostilities behind us."

Secretary Gregg wondered if his face was turning blue from holding his breath. The president, Pickering, and Tompkins continued to talk in terms of recovery and strength through peace and loving one another. Secretary Gregg kept repeating one word over and over again in his head.

Texas.

CHAPTER 18

November 26
Deerfoot Inn & Casino
Calgary, Alberta, Canada

Not surprisingly, Palmer had slipped in and out of their hotel room several times over the course of the day and the guys were never awakened. Fortunately, the escalating emotions displayed by people hanging out in the lobby kept them occupied and drew them away from guest rooms with propped-open doors.

As she explored the upper floors of the Deerfoot Inn, she found the vending machines located in the hotel, which were full of typical snacks like chips and candies. However, the Canadian vendors had added trail mix, protein bars, and combination packaged items like tuna lunch kits.

Palmer didn't have an inner moral debate, nor did she hesitate, when she took the back end of her Buck Woodsman fixed-blade knife and gently cracked the glass on the second-floor vending machine. After a quick glance to determine if she'd been heard, Palmer quickly removed the Planters Sunflower Kernels, packs of Jack Link's Beef Jerky, Nature Valley and Quaker Oats bars, and Planters peanuts.

She shoved them into a trash bag she'd brought from the hotel room. Again, avoiding discovery, she had returned to the room for a total of six trips, procuring all of the healthy snacks from the upper floors and then returning to the lower floors to gather the unhealthy comfort foods as well. As the guys stirred awake after her last trip, a pile of vending machine products awaited them on the floor.

"Palmer, you're crazy!" said Cooper jokingly. "Kinda like the Grinch. Did you leave any morsels for the mice and the Who children?"

"Yeah, I left the raisin cookies. I hate raisins. They make me feel shriveled up."

"Hey, are those Cheetos?" asked Riley.

Palmer reached down and tossed the bag of Crunchy Cheetos on his bed. She sent a Kit Kat bar flying in the general direction of Cooper, who seemed dazed as he processed her haul.

The guys enjoyed their snack, and Palmer relayed what she'd learned. She opened the curtains to reveal the snowfall, which had tapered off. The bright reflective light drew moans from the guys, which Palmer ignored.

"Most everyone is gathered in the lobby, speculating as to what's happened," she began. "Most think it was a nuclear attack. Surprisingly few even knew what an EMP was. Somebody tried to explain how it worked, but they got it wrong. I just stayed out of it."

"I'm just curious, but did anybody mention cyber attack?" asked Cooper.

"One guy did, but he was immediately shot down because the mob said the lights could be restored right away after a cyber attack."

"Idiots," muttered Cooper.

Palmer nodded. "I agree. I stayed out of it. I was mainly eavesdropping to see what I could learn, but I was more focused on picking up anything of use."

"This is a lot of food, good work, sis," said Riley.

"Well, I hit the hotel kitchen, too," said Palmer. "I kinda flirted with a cute guy who was supposed to be watching over their food supply. I talked him into making me a sandwich. While he walked away, I loaded up my pockets."

Cooper started laughing as he admired his sister. "You're cracking me up! Whadya get?"

Palmer turned around to the desk under the wall-mounted television and began to reveal her loot. "Two butcher knives and a couple of knife sharpeners. Also, forks and spoons."

"Wow, this is great stuff," said Riley.

Palmer reached to the floor and set a cardboard box on Riley's bed. "No, there's more. He asked me to watch the kitchen while he went to the bathroom. I found an empty box and really went to work. Added some hard plastic plates and bowls. A manual can opener. An enamel coffee pot with coffee and a small aluminum pot for cooking."

"Coffee?" asked Cooper.

"You bet, and a stick lighter to build a campfire to brew it over."

Cooper got out of bed and used the restroom. Palmer had retrieved some snow in an empty plastic trash can. The melted snow worked to refill the toilet tank reservoir.

He took a dry bath towel and wiped the grime off his face. Normally clean shaven, he imagined his face with a full beard as he rubbed his whiskers. He had a razor, but he thought he might go to the old-time western look.

He returned to the room, and then Riley took his turn in the bathroom.

"Palmer, are they fallin' apart down there?" Cooper asked. "Other than arguing about who shot John, is anybody talking about how to get home, or where they're gonna get food, for that matter?"

"You know, I didn't stay that long 'cause those jerks from the Stockyards were right in the middle of it. Plus, I had work to do."

Riley emerged from the restroom and approached the window. The snow was letting up and the skies were clearing somewhat. "Coop, we better get going. We need to firm up our deal with Pacheco and Morales. With all of this food, we definitely need their help."

"You guys go on," said Palmer. "I'm gonna study the atlas from Daddy's truck and mark out a route. I looked at it some this morning."

"I know, seventeen hundred miles to the house," said Cooper. "Wasn't it about two hundred miles to the border?"

"One-seventy," replied Palmer.

Cooper sat at the end of the bed and pulled on his boots. "Well, it's like we talked about. One stretch at a time; otherwise it will be overwhelming."

"How far do you reckon we can travel in a day?" asked Riley.

"Pops used to say thirty miles on a good day," said Cooper as he watched the last remnants of the blowing snow. "Today is not a good day, for sure. But it's like Pops always said. Just keep movin'. You'll get there when you get there."

CHAPTER 19

November 26
The Armstrong Ranch
Borden County, Texas

By four o'clock that afternoon, the constant monitoring of the radio revealed nothing new except there were no new reports of nuclear bombs dropping from the sky. Major gave up on the HughesNet internet connection. The only explanation he had was that their low Earth orbit satellite had gotten caught up in one of the nuclear blasts. The odds were one in who-knew-how-many millions, but that was the way it went sometimes.

Over Lucy's objections, Major and Preacher decided to stick their heads out of the gopher hole. Armed with a portable radiation detector she'd purchased on Amazon, the guys powered up the device, cracked the hatch to the bunker and pushed it onto the straw-covered floor.

Fortunately, they'd forgotten about their plans to leave a pony in the stall. Most likely, their hands and the Geiger counter would have been trampled by the startled horse.

After several minutes, Major opened the hatch and grabbed the device. He and Preacher confirmed the findings, but they had to show Lucy before they were given clearance to leave the bunker.

Major recalled an old Bulgarian proverb he had learned. The man was the head of the family, but the woman was the neck. Where the neck turns, there will be the head watching!

While Miss Lucy allowed her husband the illusion that he was the lion, the proverbial king of the castle, it was she who ruled the roost.

After his wife gave him a kiss with a nod of approval, the two men readied their rifles and emerged into the cold, fresh air outside the bunker. They closed the hatch behind them and covered up their tracks with straw.

"Should we take the truck?" asked Preacher. "We can cover more territory and get back underground."

"Yeah," replied Major. "Let's feed the critters out at the barnyard first. Plus, we can gather some eggs. Before we go back down, we'll check the horses' water and feed."

"Let's ride," said Preacher as they headed toward the feed truck. "I hate to say this, boss, but your prized F-450 may be toast."

"Yup. It was a pickup, but it was loaded down with electronics."

"Listen, Major," started Preacher as the guys got settled into the front seat. Preacher turned over the engine and immediately adjusted the heat. "We haven't talked about the kids 'cause I don't wanna upset Miss Lucy. I've watched them three grow up. They're levelheaded and smart. Plus, they've got the survival instinct."

The older truck rattled up the gravel driveway toward the main gate. The heat began to warm the cab while Major stared silently out the window.

Preacher gripped the wheel but began to nervously wiggle his fingers. "Boss, I didn't mean to overstep."

"Nah, Preach, not at all. I have a hundred percent confidence in the kids. Trust me, I'm danged worried about them. Miss Lucy said a prayer and is certain God's guidance will get them home to us. I don't disagree. However, the obstacles of weather, food, and water don't concern me. It's who they run up against that worries me the most."

"Oh, yeah. Our fellow man. Aren't human beings wonderful?"

Major pulled his hat over his eyes and readjusted it. He let out a sigh. "I've seen people do horrific things to one another during my career in law enforcement. I mean, so god-awful that you couldn't make a movie about it."

Preacher approached the front gate, and the men stopped the truck for a moment. Nothing appeared out of sorts, so Preacher turned along the fence toward the barnyard.

Major continued. "Here's the thing, Preach. Prior to this EMP attack, people had laws and law enforcement to deter them from doing despicable things to one another. Now the rules don't apply. Law enforcement may try to keep the peace for a while, but I believe that will stop in favor of protecting their own. The kids will encounter desperate people looking for food or willing to take anything they may have by force. The scenarios running through my mind are making me nuts."

"I get it, Major. I wish we could go looking for them, but that's impossible. Heck, I wish they were armed. They had to cross the border into Canada, and those folks are very strict."

"Back in the day, I'd tell my new recruits that firearms and gunfights are not the best solution to a hostile situation. Now, if you don't have a gun to defend yourself, when it really gets bad, you'll probably die."

They approached the chicken coop first since the setting sun was taking away their natural light. Preacher positioned the truck so the headlights shone on the chicken yard and the coop. The men exited the truck, with their weapons.

"We've gotta carry these at all times, Preach. Sidearms too. Even though the power didn't go out in Texas, some of the same issues the rest of the country is experiencing will apply here."

"Like what?" asked Preacher as they approached the barnyard.

"America was a ticking time bomb ready to explode," started Major. "I think our nation was in decline. I always felt deep in my gut there would be a shock to the system. You know, some catastrophic event that would upset the apple cart."

They began to gather eggs in two baskets from Miss Lucy's prolific egg-laying hens. She considered her chickens to be one of her best food preps.

Major continued as they worked, taking a moment now and again to survey his surroundings. "Not all shocks are catastrophic, including something as brazen as what happened on 9/11. But when the right one comes along, like this one, well, it's kinda like explosives. We've worked with dynamite. We gotta handle it gently, and it's best not to light up a cigarette around the stuff. Semtex, the military-type stuff, is different. You can drop it, kick it around in the dirt, and even toss the brick on a bonfire. Nothing will happen. It requires the right detonator to cause an explosion.

"To me, America began to look like a tractor trailer rig loaded with Semtex. It kept getting filled up but was only as dangerous as a truckload of lettuce. However, add the right detonator and you're the push of a button away from totally devastating life as we know it."

"Armageddon," muttered Preacher as the men returned to the truck with nearly four dozen eggs. "Really, societal collapse."

"There ya go," said Major. "It's been comin' on for years. Our morals are in decline. Society has become undisciplined, unrealistic, and selfish. After the Depression years in the thirties, through World War II, Americans were taught that frugality and prudence were prized virtues. Communities were cohesive, and usually activities revolved around the church. People were brought up with a conception of proper morals and the ability to distinguish between right and wrong."

"Yeah, I get it," added Preacher. "Every month there's another mass murder and people slough it off. Yesterday, people stormed into a Walmart and pert near beat each other to death over a curved-screen television on sale."

The men pulled out the feed bags and walked around dispersing corn to the chickens and pigs.

Major continued. "Decades ago, events like these would create major news headlines and spark conversations. Now, despite the fact it's depressing, immoral, and sometimes vulgar, it isn't considered catastrophic. It's the new normal."

As they finished up, the stars were shining brightly, and the cold night air settled on Armstrong Ranch. Major pulled his coat closer, trying to ward off the chill caused by the weather and his concern for his kids.

"Major, do you think the kids understand this? Do they know what to expect when they hit the road?"

"God, I hope so."

CHAPTER 20

November 26
Texas Homeland Security Operations Center
Austin, Texas

Governor Burnett had spent the entire day in the SOC, watching reports come in from around the world concerning the situation in the rest of the country. She was also able to monitor in real time the law enforcement activities within Texas.

After she'd received the reports from Beaumont and Port Arthur about looting and streams of refugees entering the state at Interstate 10 over the Sabine River, she instructed the Department of Safety to close access to the bridge and to notify Louisiana Highway Patrol officers on the other side of the state line that the bridge was unsafe for pedestrian travel.

Despite the EMP destroying electronics on automobile systems, some cars along the Gulf Coast were not impacted, probably due to their distance from the point of detonation. Thousands of people were trying to cross over the Sabine River bridge while sparse vehicular traffic was moving as well. One person was injured when they inadvertently stepped off the sidewalk along the outside of the bridge into traffic, which resulted in two broken legs.

Governor Burnett saw the bridge closing as a test or experiment for a broader range of options dealing with the border. If it succeeded, she'd expand the closings to all the interstates tomorrow under the auspices of exercising safety precautions.

At six o'clock that evening, she planned on addressing Texans via radio, television and emergency band radio broadcasts. She had not ordered martial law because, for the most part, the citizens of Texas were behaving and helping one another. The only hot spots for Texas law enforcement agencies on this first day of the collapse of America was near the state line with Louisiana and in El Paso, where the city was having difficult controlling their overcrowded conditions.

The governor had just completed a meeting with the federal liaison from the Department of Homeland Security and three members of the FEMA operational team within the state. They briefed her on what they knew of the federal response in the rest of the country but were not able to provide her any information on the potential for a broader war. They were also tight-lipped on what, if anything, the president might ask of her during a phone call that was scheduled in five minutes.

Governor Burnett asked to be left alone in the conference room, not to prepare for her conversation with the president, but rather, to weigh the pros and cons of secession at this moment of crisis. The dilemma for her was a moral one. Politically, she despised Washington and its career politicians for what they'd done to America. It no longer resembled the freedoms envisioned by the Founders.

She, and her predecessors before her, had taken Texans through many economic sacrifices in order to protect the state from a catastrophic event like this one. On the one hand, she understood the perception of Texas turning its back on the nation would draw the ire of every citizen of the rest of the country. However, how could she justify to her constituents that she was going to open the state and its limited resources to millions of others? If folks were at the grocery stores cleaning out the shelves already, imagine what would happen when they were told to share with millions of people entering the state rather than their own families.

A gentle tap on the door of the conference room interrupted her thoughts. It was her chief of staff.

"Governor, we have the president on the line. You'll be on speakerphone with her and Charles Acton, her chief of staff."

"Thank you," replied the governor, looking down at the satellite phone she'd been provided earlier. "Do I press this button in the center?"

"Yes, ma'am. Also, please be mindful to let the other party finish their sentence. There can be a slight delay, which will result in you talking over one another."

The governor nodded and pressed the button. She paused for a moment and listened to background conversation coming from the White House.

"Good afternoon, Madam President."

"Governor, thank you for taking my call," started President Harman. "These are trying times, to say the least. There are many issues, both domestic and internationally, to attend to that have delayed my reaching out to you. My apologies for that."

Peaches and cream. She wants something.

"We understand completely, Madam President. It's our hope the country will not be subject to further attack, naturally."

"Same here, obviously. Our military stands ready to defend the United States, and our response to this heinous act will be dealt swiftly once we've received all the facts. That's not the reason for my call, however."

The governor shifted uneasily in her seat. The president still had command of the armed forces, including the hundred thousand plus based within the Texas borders. Now was not the time to appear confrontational.

"Of course, Madam President. How can I assist?"

"Well, frankly, Governor, we're not quite sure yet. I realize, of course, that you have your hands full with safety obligations to the citizens of Texas, but we all have to look at the big picture. Luckily, the power grid of Texas appears to be unaffected by the attack."

Not luck, Madam President. Planning and preparedness.

The president continued. "We will utilize one of our hardened aircraft as a shuttle flight between Andrews and Lackland in San Antonio. I'll be sending a team of advisors from Homeland Security, Health and Human Services, and Commerce to assess your situation and how we can use Texas's good fortune to help the rest of the nation during this catastrophic event."

Governor Burnett was silent, not because she was being *mindful*, as her aide had admonished regarding the use of a satellite phone, but she wanted to choose her next words wisely. She needed time to make a decision before Washington opened the floodgates and dumped their problems on Texas.

She finally spoke after an excruciating five seconds. "That's a wonderful idea, Madam President. We do have our hands full today, and tonight I need to address my fellow Texans. If you'd like to send your contingent tomorrow afternoon, we can have our ducks in a row and a much better idea of how we can help."

The president paused, but Governor Burnett could hear conversation in the background. She waited until the president finally addressed her.

"I suppose that's the best we can do, Governor. I will let our people at FEMA and DHS know that you'll be available tomorrow afternoon and they should plan accordingly. Thank you."

"It was a pleasure—" started the governor before she was interrupted by a rapid beeping sound emanating from the phone. She pressed the center button, totally disconnecting the call. "Well, I guess that conversation is over."

PART THREE

Sunday, November 27

Chapter 21

November 27
Deerfoot Inn & Casino
Calgary, Alberta, Canada

The snow had begun to taper off the night before, so the group of five took two-hour shifts with the horses to allow everyone ample sleep. Barring an unforeseen weather change, they planned on leaving at first light.

Thus far, the rodeo kids' ability to make quick, informed decisions had served them well. Immediately after the EMP hit, they were quick to reach a logical conclusion that North America was in big trouble. They'd gathered their things and headed for adequate shelter, for them and their most valuable assets, the horses.

Growing up, they'd learned that situational awareness helped protect them from untimely accidents and unforeseen events. *Awareness is ninety percent of preparedness.* Cooper had repeated this phrase repeatedly since the lights went out.

Once they'd arrived back at the hotel before everyone else, they'd established a regiment to rest and watch over the horses. Palmer quickly set about foraging for food and supplies while others in the hotel spent their time in the lobby complaining or bemoaning their condition.

They made a decision to return home because the prepper education they'd received from their parents taught them this was a catastrophic event, and waiting to see how things developed was a mistake.

It was a long trip back to Texas. The three Armstrong kids got their minds right and saddled up as the sun rose on the Great Plains to their east.

Cooper got settled into his saddle. The horses were in high spirits, anxious to move and get their body heat up. He surveyed each of his riding companions. The five of them looked like they'd just ridden off the set of a *Young Guns* movie.

"Let's do this," said Cooper as he encouraged his horse through the snow. Around the lean-to shed they'd used for shelter, four-foot drifts had accumulated because of the wind. Luckily for the riders, that same wind had helped clear the roads and keep the snow depths to under eight inches in most places. The temperatures were still below freezing, but there wasn't a cloud in the sky, enabling the warm sunshine to do its work.

They agreed to ride until around four o'clock that afternoon before looking for adequate shelter for the night. Pacheco had the only operating watch, an old kinetic timepiece made by Seiko. The lack of miniaturized electronics had saved it from the bombardment of electrons created by the EMP.

Everyone knew their horses and their capabilities. All of their rides were between the ages of six and ten, ideal for a long equestrian journey. All of their horses were calm and sensible, but none had ever been ridden in traffic. The group laughed when Riley suggested they keep an eye out for snowplows clearing the road.

This group of five had an advantage over novices who kept horses as possible bug-out transportation. They were comfortable in their saddles. Eighty percent of saddle sores came from improperly fitted saddles. Another benefit to a horseman's experience, they knew a wool saddle pad was the best investment you could make.

The first day, they headed due south along Canadian Route 2 toward the Montana border. Following the cavalry system, they stopped for five to ten minutes every hour to allow their horses to graze where grasses were available.

Within minutes of leaving the Calgary city limits, they were in the wide-open countryside. With the Rocky Mountains rising high to their west and the vast plains spreading out to their east, there was much to see and admire.

During the apocalypse, especially in a world without power, the human mind gets to admire nature in its natural beauty without noise, moving vehicles, or electronic devices to capture the attention. It was serene, peaceful, and in many respects, an improvement on the way of life people had grown accustomed to.

They made incredible time that first day. Traveling nearly forty miles, largely on the enthusiasm of the horses, so it was closer to 4:30 when they approached the first town along the highway—Nanton.

Suddenly, peace and serenity were replaced by police and security.

CHAPTER 22

November 27
Raven Rock Mountain Complex
Liberty Township, Pennsylvania

President Harman was in an untenable position. It was now the third day from the single greatest attack on America since its founding and she had not yet made a decision on whether to fight back against the enemy, the dual menaces that had been responsible for unrest in the world for decades.

Diplomatically, she quickly learned that America's allies were there in name only. Both South Korea and Japan feared an escalation into a war that would necessarily be fought on their soil. Both Russia and China had geopolitical interests in keeping the flawed North Korean regime in power; therefore they used rhetoric to back down the United States from retaliating. And finally, the Europeans, who had proven for twenty years that they were more than willing to fight a United Nations-sanctioned battle, with the U.S. leading the way, asked to opt out of this one. Short of a UN mandate, they were unwilling to put their nations' lives at risk for another.

Only Israel and America's newest ally in the region, Saudi Arabia, were willing to take on the Iranians. Iran, as the largest state sponsor of terrorism, had escalated its attacks on Saudi Arabia in recent years by arming Yemeni rebels with small arms and missiles. Iran had sponsored Hezbollah, Shia militias, and Hamas, all direct threats to Israel.

The president had been informed, via the State Department, that Israel and Saudi Arabia—unlikely allies, but two nations who agreed to come together to fight a common enemy, Iran—were waiting for her green light.

They would first unleash a barrage of missiles on Iran military interests and nuclear facilities followed by a precision air attack upon the Iranian Revolutionary Guard. An invading ground force wouldn't be necessary, as the two countries had no desire to occupy Iran but, rather, to destroy its military capabilities.

This morning following the presidential daily briefing, President Harman called her top military leaders into the conference room to provide her a full assessment of her military strike options that did not include a nuclear attack.

"Here's the way I see it," said President Harman after making a few introductory remarks to her top military advisors. "If the consensus of world opinion is that an EMP attack on another country does not give rise to a nuclear attack, then military strikes upon North Korea by us, and upon Iran by our regional allies, should not constitute the beginnings of a world war. If we've been warned against use of nuclear weapons, then we should be able to warn China and Russia against interfering with our punishment of Kim Jong-un."

Secretary Gregg smiled slightly and nodded his head. He wished the president had reached this conclusion earlier. If she had, then the debilitating EMP attack could have been avoided.

The president continued. "Today, I intend to make a decision on our course of action. Fish or cut bait, as they say. First, I'd like to get a total picture of each country's military assets in the region. Secretary Gregg, please proceed."

Secretary Gregg? She's being formal today. Tread lightly, Monty.

"Thank you, Madam President. I've prepared a graphic for us to use as a reference based upon our best information just prior to the attack. I suspect the troop movements of the Russians and Chinese have shifted considerably toward the border of North Korea."

"Why is that?" asked the president.

"Not for invasion purposes, Madam President," replied Secretary Gregg. "Their concern is millions of North Korean refugees fleeing the war zone and flooding their countries seeking refuge."

He powered on the monitors, and the screen revealed a detailed graphic depicting the Korean Peninsula, together with each country in the region, showing troop-strength levels and key military assets.

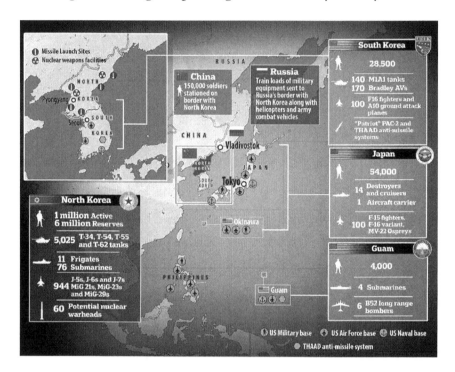

Secretary Gregg continued. "First, in the top left of the graphic, you'll see there are five clearly marked missile launch sites and two nuclear weapons manufacturing facilities. These are hard targets that would be a first priority in our attack."

"What about their mobile launch capabilities?" asked the president.

"Yes, those are an issue. The DPRK began to retrofit Chinese trucks originally sold to them for hauling timber. The trucks were modified into transporter-erector-launch vehicles, or TELs. These vehicles are naturally mobile and capable of moving an ICBM into position and launching it on the desired trajectory. We have tracked these in the past, but with our deployment of Constant Phoenix, as we discussed yesterday, we'll have instantaneous notice of a launch."

The president studied the graphic and pointed to the right side, which summarized the South Korean and Japanese military contribution. "If the decision is made to attack the North, we will assist South Korea in its defenses and a possible ground invasion. Japan will only assist to the extent of air support and patrolling the Sea of Japan for North Korean vessels."

"That's correct, Madam President," said Secretary Gregg. "South Korea will deploy their newly developed blackout bombs to paralyze the North's power grid. It's part of their three pillars of national defense. First, their Kill Chain program will detect, identify, and intercept incoming missiles. Secondly, the South will focus on Kim's command and control structure by launching attacks against government leadership targets. Lastly, they'll use the blackout bombs, an EMP weapon similar to the ones we used in the Gulf War in 1990 and as used by NATO in Serbia a decade later."

"Okay," interrupted President Harman. "North Korea's army is massive. Their air capabilities are more than double ours in the region. They have over five thousand tanks ready to move on South Korea. And their million-man army has grown with the addition of six million in reserves. That's a formidable force."

"It is, Madam President," said Secretary Gregg. "Over the years, as I've said before, prior administrations have been singularly focused on the nuclear weapons programs of both Iran and North Korea."

"Rightfully so," interjected the president.

"I agree; however, recent events have strengthened the traditional military capabilities of both nations. Iran's military spending in recent years has quadrupled. Naturally, in any conventional military conflict, Iran wouldn't stand a chance against the United States. They can hold their own in the Middle East. Further, they've expanded their naval assets considerably. They have placed a considerable amount of emphasis on building frigates and destroyers, some of which have sailed into the Gulf of Mexico in the past. They should not be underestimated."

The president sighed and referred to her notes. All eyes were upon her as she studied the graphic provided by Secretary Gregg.

"I'm not interested in getting mired down in another Vietnam or extended Gulf War. If I decide to move forward with military action, my goal is to retaliate, stand them down, and hopefully pave the way for the removal of the Kim dynasty from power."

"Madam President," interrupted Secretary Gregg, seeing this as his best opportunity to convince the president of the right tactic to follow, "we can accomplish your goals in around fifteen minutes after you give us the order. Operation Airborne Alert has been ready to deploy for years. If we deploy our full nuclear retaliatory capability, within minutes, there will be nothing left of Kim and his rogue state."

CHAPTER 23

November 27
The Armstrong Ranch
Borden County, Texas

While the wives assigned kitchen duty gathered dishes and utensils from the thirty-some underground dwellers of the Armstrong Ranch nuclear bunker, Major, Lucy, and Preacher moved into the small walk-in closet that stored weapons and doubled as their communications room. They had taken rotating shifts—alternating between sleep and monitoring news reports from the AM radio.

"After hearing that little dictator's speech, I feel better about moving out of the bunker," started Major. "It appears that he's made his point."

"Well, the WBAP news commentators seem to think most countries are in full support of the U.S. standing down," added Lucy.

Preacher nodded in agreement. "Why make a bad situation worse, right?"

Major let out a deep sigh. "All things being equal, we'd stay in here for another week or so just to be safe. But like so many things, the number of people this shelter can protect looked good on paper, but not in practice. We've got twice as many in here as we can support."

"We can't play God with their lives," added Lucy. "How could I possibly look in their faces and say *you can stay, but you must go?*"

"I agree," replied Major. "I think we can all leave this morning and return to our homes. Our daily focus has changed substantially."

Preacher ran his fingers through his hair and furrowed his brow. He pushed out his jaw and placed his well-worn cowboy hat on his head. "Well, if the news reports are correct, we could be overrun by millions of refugees from New Mexico to Colorado to California. We need to set up our security, Major."

"It's less than a hundred miles to Hobbs from here," said Lucy. "If they're walking, they could be here within days. In older cars, anytime."

Major pointed toward the door handle to indicate there wasn't anything else to discuss. "I think we're secluded enough as not to be the invading hordes' first stop, but we also have to be wary of others in our vicinity. Borden is a small county of less than seven hundred known residents. But as we all know, there are still a lot of illegals who work from ranch to ranch for their daily pay. Most ranchers aren't as generous as we are. There's a good chance those folks have been kicked out into the cold and will be looking for food. We're the largest and arguably most successful ranch in the four counties surrounding Lake Thomas, along with the Four Sixes and the DeWitts' place. My guess is we'll be high on the local refugee list, if you know what I mean."

Preacher grasped the handle and led them out as he added with a sense of urgency, "I think we need to get started."

Major waited for Preacher to grab Antonio and two other ranch hands. They were assigned rifles, and the four men emerged through the hatch into the empty stall. The sun was just beginning to rise, revealing a light fog hovering over the river in the distance.

The horses sensed the activity and began to get excited. Major couldn't decide if it was because they were agitated or simply glad to see their human companions.

The hands were instructed to walk around the barns and storage sheds while Major took Preacher around the ranch house. They carefully checked every room and potential hiding space for anyone who might have snuck onto the ranch overnight. After they were satisfied the area was clear, they began bringing the families out of the bunker.

The women brought their personal belongings and assisted their children into the fresh air. The rising sun and the cool, fresh air had an instant effect on everyone's demeanor. Both a sense of relief that their world was intact, coupled with the prospects of normalcy buoyed their outlook.

Major recognized their euphoria and immediately realized it was time for some blunt talk. Life might look normal, but it was far from it. He instructed Antonio to work with the ranch hands to retrieve the weapons cache and the many cans of ammunition out of the bunker.

One by one, green duffel bags of rifles, hard plastic cases of handguns, and dark green steel cans of ammo were handed through the hatch. After everything was topside, Major instructed Preacher to divide the weapons among the fourteen households.

Each of the families was assigned a twelve-gauge shotgun, a rifle chambered in .308, and a nine-millimeter handgun. Major had a minimum of a thousand rounds for every weapon he'd acquired, but he didn't distribute the full allocation to each family. One ammo can contained sixty double-ought buck shotgun shells. Another contained two hundred forty .308 Winchester Core-Lokt bullets. The third can contained six hundred one-hundred-fifteen-grain nine-millimeter rounds.

As the weapons were assigned, Major spoke to the group in English, with Antonio translating into Spanish. Over the years of employment at Armstrong Ranch, the Mexican families were encouraged to learn conversational English and use it daily. Most adults had become fluent, and their children all were. To prevent any misunderstandings, Major insisted Antonio provide a Spanish translation as well. This was about their survival and security. Conversations about life and death were not an appropriate time for English class.

"Good morning, everyone," he began. "It's cold this morning and I know you're anxious to return to your homes. I want you to understand something. The world has changed. As we told you the first night, America was attacked by another country. All of the electrical power across the country is not working except in Texas. We are the only state that can still turn the lights on, pump water from our wells, and listen to the radio.

"That's good for us, but it also comes with bad news. Soon, the grocery stores around the country will run out of food. This may even happen in Texas. People from other states will become desperate, and they will try to come into Texas to survive. We don't have enough to feed everybody, only our own. This means the new people will be hungry, scared, and eventually, angry.

"We will have a new job at the ranch, one that we took for granted before—security. Here's what that means. Every minute of the day and night, we have to stand watch over Armstrong Ranch and the families who live here. Right now, all I care about is all of you and the food resources we take care of every day. You must constantly be aware of your surroundings. Watch for intruders. If a fence is mysteriously knocked down, come to us immediately. Take nothing for granted. Always trust your instincts if you sense danger.

"You have all been assigned weapons. A rifle and handgun for the ranch hands. A shotgun for the adult who stays at home. Men, carry your handgun at all times, even when at home. Ladies, your children will no longer go to school. When you come to the barnyard or the garden to help Miss Lucy, bring your children. Even the young ones. We will set up school and activities for them. We will teach them to take a role in the garden, the barnyard and around the ranch as their age allows.

"At night, I need you to keep your lights dim. We live on flatland that can be seen for miles. Anyone driving along the highways and roads, even from a long distance, will see our lights on. This will bring them to our doorstep.

"Avoid outdoor fires, even in your chimeneas. From now on, we'll be burying our garbage down in the ravine. The smoke from fires can be seen for many miles. This will also bring us unwanted visitors.

"We need to be focused, aware, but not paranoid. Constantly look around and survey your surroundings. Later this morning, we will deliver a two-way radio to each home and show you how to listen to our frequency and how to contact us. These are simple radios, but a vital resource to our survival."

Major finished and then Lucy stepped in front of him. "We love you as we love our own children. Everyone here is a member of the family. Let's all protect one another, and we'll get through this just fine. I promise." Then Lucy paused, and with a tear in her eye she continued.

"*Dios te bendiga.*" God bless you.

CHAPTER 24

November 27
Nanton, Alberta, Canada

The group came to a stop as they rode over a slight rise in the road when Nanton came in to view. Palmer retrieved the binoculars, which were packed in her get-home bag. The Bushnell compact zoom binoculars had an incredible zoom capability and were easy to focus.

She studied the road and handed the binoculars to Cooper. He grunted and then muttered, "This didn't take long." He returned the binoculars to Palmer and then pulled his rifle out of his scabbard attached to the rear of his saddle.

"What've we got?" asked Riley.

Cooper responded as he stretched to deliver his rifle to Pacheco. "It looks like the town has closed off access with a roadblock. They've got a couple of old pickup trucks blocking the way, and I counted at least three men milling about."

"That's what I saw, too. Should we go around?" asked Palmer.

"Let me ride ahead and see what they have to say," replied Cooper. "It's time for us to rest for the night, and a hotel room would be better than a barn. While I'm gone, two of y'all ride down these side roads and see what might be available to hole up for the night. If need be, we'll go around the town."

"Dang, Coop," started Riley. "I hope every little podunk town ain't like this. If they're buildin' roadblocks, what are we gonna run into when we hit the U.S. border?"

Cooper nodded and contemplated Riley's statement. The main highways were the most direct route, but every town could present a dangerous challenge. The realities of travel in the apocalypse just set in. And they were only on day one.

Cooper approached the roadblock with caution as the three men instantly took up positions around the temporary barriers and the pickup trucks, which were parked sideways in the road, nose to nose.

He rode up nonchalantly and tipped his hat to the three men, who were clean shaven. One of the three wore a police uniform. Cooper decided to address the officer, assuming he was in charge.

"How are you fellas doin'? My name's Cooper Armstrong, and we're headed back to Texas. I'll get right to the point, Officer. We don't want any trouble. We're looking for a place to stay tonight and some hay for our horses."

"All right, Mr. Armstrong, straight shootin' is always the best approach," replied the officer. We don't have any power or water. The hotels aren't taking on any guests. This roadblock is to keep people from coming into town and not leaving through the other side."

"Well, y'all could escort us through," said Cooper. "Like I said, we don't want any trouble nor do we wanna be a burden."

The man to the officer's left lowered his weapon and approached Cooper. "I know this young man, Dave," he said to the officer. "You're the bull rider, right?"

"I am."

"My brother owns Cowboy Country Western Store down the road." The man pointed his thumb over his shoulder.

Cooper sat up in his saddle to look beyond the roadblock. Across the street from a small fighter jet mounted atop a steel pole was a brown metal building that resembled a large Tractor Supply operation.

"Dave, he's a well-respected young man. He won't cause any trouble. In fact, brother would put him up for the night if he didn't mind talkin' bull ridin' for a while."

"We've got rules to follow," started the officer. "You and brother are gonna have to be responsible for them until he leaves in the morning."

"Um, I've got some folks with me," said Cooper hesitantly. "My younger brother Riley and my sister, Palmer. Also, two of my fellow bull riders from San Antonio. All of us are in the rodeo."

"Five of you? I don't know," said the officer, his voice trailing off as the larger group started to concern him.

"Seriously, Dave. Brother and I will be responsible for them. Their horses can stay in the fenced utility yard behind the store. We've got hay, and there's probably water in the feed troughs from the melted snow."

"Okay, it's on you," said the officer. "I'll let the chief know what's goin' on. Mr. Armstrong, you and your group behave yourselves. I'm telling you this as a courtesy. We've adopted a zero-tolerance policy here for looting and other crimes. Our jail doesn't have the ability to house prisoners and feed them. We're also not going to let you go. Get out of line, and you're likely to get shot by one of our officers or one of our good Nanton residents. Are we clear?"

"Yes, sir. Like I said, we don't want any trouble," said Cooper, who then returned his attention to the man who'd been so helpful. "I'll be right back with the rest of the group. Thank you, sir." Cooper tipped his hat and started to turn.

"Sometimes you gotta take a chance and help your fellow man," he replied.

CHAPTER 25

November 27
Governor's Mansion
Austin, Texas

"Governor, I've received word that the president's advisory team has arrived at Lackland," announced Governor Burnett's chief of staff. The governor could feel the pressure, as time for making a decision was running out.

"Is everyone assembled in the conference room?" asked the governor as she swung around in her chair and looked out the window upon the mansion's grounds. If she didn't know better, it would have seemed like any other weekend morning in Austin. Relatively sparse traffic, only a few pedestrians, and a sense of normalcy except for the Texas National Guard troops surrounding the governor's mansion with their weapons held at low ready.

For security reasons, they'd relocated her office from the State Capitol to the Governor's Mansion to minimize her time outside the well-protected confines of her home.

"Adjutant General Deur just arrived, ma'am. He was carrying bundles of maps under both his arms. It was kind of comical, actually. You know, watching him trying to juggle all of that by himself."

"Trust me, I know the feeling," said the governor under her breath. She rose out of her chair and followed her chief of staff out of the office. "It's decision time."

After exchanging some pleasantries with her closest advisors within the Texas government, the governor began receiving their reports. She planned on saving Deur's for last, as it was, in her mind, the most important and most likely the determining factor as to whether she moved forward.

Commissioner Crawford of the Texas Department of Banking started the meeting by informing the attendees that both state and federally chartered banks would remain closed until further notice. Their automatic teller machines had been drained of their cash by Saturday morning. In addition, there was a genuine concern that armored car services moving from branch to branch might come under attack.

He further stated that all retailers had converted to a cash or barter system as a method of payment for goods or services. Credit card processing was obviously not functioning due to the nationwide collapse of the internet. With the banks remaining closed, stores were refusing to accept checks. Cash remained king except for certain commodities like weapons, precious metals, and prescription medications.

The word *inflation* was bantered about, as a concept rather than a quantifiable number. The price of perishable goods had tripled, and nonperishable foods had increased as much as tenfold. They all agreed it was impossible to police price gouging in light of the circumstances.

The Public Utility Commission of Texas announced power had been restored to the remote areas of Texas with their own independent grids now tied to ERCOT. Water and sewer treatment facilities were functioning properly. Any electric or water utilities that relied upon the internet for their operations quickly and efficiently converted to manual systems.

The commissioner expressed concern over retaining workers during the crisis. With grocery stores and gas stations going to an all-cash method of payment, employees in all public works sectors needed to be paid in cash as well.

The lieutenant governor reminded the attendees that Texas had a larger cash reserve than nearly the rest of the states combined. Through decades of fiscal responsibility, they had amassed over ten billion dollars in cash reserves, roughly equivalent to twenty percent of the state's gross domestic product.

This so-called rainy-day fund was about to be put to use. The reserves would be used to pay law enforcement, first responders, hospital personnel, and utility workers first. This was considered the critical infrastructure of the state and hence would receive priority.

Welfare payments to the poor would be paid in kind using the state's stockpile of emergency preparedness food and supplies. Families with young children and the elderly would move to the head of the line. Able-bodied Texans would be assigned jobs to meet the state's critical infrastructure needs.

Next, the Texas Railroad Commission, represented by Commissioner Ackerson, presented an assessment of the state's oil and gas industry. In addition to regulating public transportation and the railway system, their oil and gas division worked closely with refineries, liquid petroleum gas companies, and surface mining operators to produce what was most likely Texas's greatest natural resource—fuel.

Commissioner Ackerson stated the major fuel-producing companies from oil to gas to coal had all raised similar concerns as discussed by his fellow commissioners. They were prepared to work overtime to meet the state's energy needs, but they required cash to pay their employees and armed security to protect their investments.

Governor Burnett suggested an agreement be reached between the major banks and the fuel industry leaders. The banks needed to loan their cash back to the refineries and miners to keep them in full operation. They would be allowed to charge a nominal rate of interest. Otherwise, the refineries could come to the state for cash loans, but they would be far more limited in availability than what the large banks could provide.

Before the adjutant general provided his report, Governor Burnett realized that at some point, the Texas government would run out of cash. She was thankful for former Governor Greg Abbott's efforts to repatriate Texas gold reserves from HSBC bank vaults in New York and have them returned to Texas. In 2015, he established the nation's first ever state-level gold depository.

The action did more than save the million dollars a year charged for storage, it created a safe haven for the state's gold that could not be confiscated by the federal government, as it had done during the Great Depression under orders from President Roosevelt. Texas had several billion dollars in gold reserves at the end of the 2021 fiscal year.

The governor's mind wandered toward the establishment of an alternative currency to the U.S. dollar. The currency being traded between retailers and their consumers was probably worth pennies on the dollar. A gold standard needed to be established for Texas during the crisis, regardless of whether she pursued a secession option.

The Texas Bullion Depository could be the state's functional equivalent of the Federal Reserve. It would become a gold-backed bank. This crisis would enable Texas to establish an honest and sensible monetary system founded on real value, gold, rather than debt-based paper notes conjured into existence by the Federal Reserve. Over time, the good money, gold and silver, would drive out the bad money, the old U.S. dollars backed by the Federal Reserve.

"Governor? Shall I get started?" asked Deur.

Governor Burnett snapped her mind back to the present. *Juggling. Lots of juggling.*

"Yes, Kregg, please do."

"Governor, every hour we receive reports from around the state of people pouring across our borders with nothing but the shirts on their backs. We closed major bridges and established checkpoints at highways where the rivers don't act as a natural boundary, but refugees are streaming in by the thousands."

"How?" she asked.

"They're crossing the rivers in aluminum, flat-bottom boats using boards as paddles. Some are swimming. Others are riding mules and horses in remote locations of the Panhandle."

Governor Burnett raised her hand and Deur stopped speaking. "I get it. What do you propose?"

"Well, I can't fix how big we are, but I can deploy more assets to act as a deterrent to people crossing our borders from Louisiana, Arkansas, New Mexico, and Colorado."

"What kind of assets?" asked the governor.

"People. Unemployed people," responded Deur. "Until we can build a fence around the state's boundaries, we can hire responsible adults to help police our borders. We'd have to pay them out of the rainy-day fund, or with food, based upon budgetary constraints."

The governor nodded as she warmed to the idea. People without jobs needed a way to support their families. By employing them, they would be less desperate and therefore not likely to commit crimes to feed their families.

"How would you find these folks, and would they be armed?"

"Good question," replied Deur. "I would start with the Texas concealed-carry database and move on to our access of the National Firearms Registration and Transfer records provided to my department by the Bureau of Alcohol, Tobacco, Firearms, and Explosives. The former would provide a list of trained Texans who've shown a reliable propensity to carry a weapon and use it responsibly. The latter database from the ATF would give us a list of weapons owners who've passed background checks in the past. We'd simply update that information through our criminal databases."

"It would be like a small army," said the governor.

"Yes, ma'am. All Texans would be identified and vetted electronically first, and then approached by our seasoned law enforcement veterans for a face-to-face interview."

"Sounds like an arduous task," interrupted Governor Burnett. "How long would this take?"

"By focusing on communities nearest our weakest points along the border, we can minimize the influx right away. The recruitment of these deputies who already have firearms will fill gaps in our border security. Then if we can immediately install security fencing in the high-traffic areas that I've identified on all of these maps, we could have the state sealed off within a week."

The governor leaned forward in her chair and studied one of the maps Deur had rolled out on the conference table. "And who would build the fence?"

"Same concept, Governor. Able-bodied Texans looking for work who've shown a propensity for being responsible citizens. We'd start by advertising in communities near the state's borders, eliminate or accept them to the next level of the interview process through our database information, followed by a final hiring determination based upon the local contractor who will work with them directly in the counties where they reside."

Governor Burnett nodded her approval. "We provide the concept and funding, then delegate the work to the local county government that is best capable of overseeing the work. I like it."

Commissioner Ackerson raised his hand. "As you know, I was formerly in the Navy. Kregg, I have a question. What are our rules of engagement along the border? Especially as it relates to these new recruits. Are we giving Texans authority to fire upon fellow Americans?"

Deur glanced at the governor and leaned forward to respond. As he did, the satellite phone, which sat unnoticed in front of her chief of staff, began to buzz. The sudden vibration on the table startled everyone.

At first, the shock of the vibration on the table froze the governor, but then she motioned to her aide to answer it. The room remained silent while she took the call.

"Hello, you've reached the office of the governor of Texas."

After a pause, she said, "Yes, sir, she is here."

Another pause.

"Yes, of course. Please hold."

Her aide covered the mouthpiece with her hand, the nervous pressure causing her knuckles to turn white. She leaned over and whispered to the governor, "You'll want to take this call in private, ma'am. It's urgent."

CHAPTER 26

November 27
Black Friday
The Armstrong Ranch
Borden County, Texas

The ranch hands were split into groups. A group of four were responsible for bringing the cattle to the grazing fields closest to the ranch. Two sets of two were immediately assigned perimeter patrols. The rest worked with Major on specific ranch assets such as the barnyard, the barns, the garden and points of entry off the local roads.

The ranch house was located on the east side of their nine thousand plus acres, overlooking a bluff where the high plains turned into the Colorado River Basin below Lake Thomas. For perimeter security, two hands focused on the northern boundary along the river and over toward the western boundary just beyond FM 1205.

FM stood for farm-to-market road in Texas, a name that arose during the Great Depression. The Texas highway commission had authorized a pilot program for seven thousand miles of farm-to-market roadways connecting rural communities with population centers to buy and sell farm goods.

FM 1205 divided the Armstrong Ranch in half. A driveway built by Pops decades ago stretched east to west from the ranch house to the western border of the ranch. This enabled vehicles to quickly cross the entirety of the property on a paved asphalt road in all types of weather.

From above, the X created by the driveway and FM1205 created a perfect bull's-eye in the center of the ranch. From the ground, it was a perfect way to mobilize his hands in case they had to defend the ranch.

Major and Preacher stood in the middle of FM 1205 and looked for a mile in both directions toward their northern and southern boundaries.

"Do we blockade the road, Major?" asked Preacher. "This is the way most folks travel north and south across the county."

"There aren't a dozen cars that use this road on a normal day," said Major. "I'd like to close it, but we'd have to keep four men, two on each end, watching at all times."

"But if we don't, we're inviting folks right through the heart of the ranch. They could turn east and be on top of the house in minutes."

Major thought for a moment. He instantly wished he had more men. "We have to work with two-man teams, at least at night. During the day, we could post one man at each gate and assign rovers to patrol the perimeter but stay within a quick ride to each post."

"That would work," said Preacher. "A man each on the north gate and the south gate. We don't need to cover the center because we're closing off the country road. The boys assigned to the perimeter can be there to help in minutes. Plus, you and I will constantly monitor the radio."

Major saddled up and Preacher did as well. As they continued west along the driveway, the men discussed the ranch security in more detail.

"The biggest threat is the unexpected," started Major. "If the North Koreans wanna drop a nuke on Borden County, there's not much we can do about that. Odds are they'd hit more important targets like DC, New York, Chicago, and LA."

"And we're gonna stay on top of the radios, too. Information is very valuable under these circumstances."

"True. But make no mistake, Preach, Texas got lucky. I mean, the separate grid and all of that was brilliant in hindsight. But from what I know of these EMPs, depending on where they were detonated and at what height, electronics and components in Texas certainly could've been fried. Think about it, if they'd dropped an EMP over

Missouri, the heart of the country, we'd be out of luck."

"Well, frankly, if the state lost power, we'd be okay here at the ranch anyway, don't you think?" asked Preacher.

"Absolutely," Major replied with a slight smile. "When we decided to lead a preparedness lifestyle, we planned for a worst-case scenario—a downed power grid, whether by an EMP nuke or a solar storm. The only thing more devastating would be an all-out nuclear war."

"Would they strike Texas?" asked Preacher. "Like you said, they have better targets than us."

"It's hard to understand what that madman might be thinking," replied Major. "The nuclear silos at Valhalla outside Abilene have been decommissioned for years, but North Korea may not know that."

"That's too close for comfort," quipped Preacher.

"Dang straight. If North Korea is really on top of their game, they'd hit us at the Pantex Plant in Amarillo. It depends on how many nukes Kim Jong-un has. After he takes out our major cities and missile silos, he might go after the primary nuclear weapons assembly facility in the country—Pantex."

"Great," muttered Preacher as they continued to ride west.

"I might as well remind you about Walker AFB in Roswell," continued Major. "There are a dozen Atlas missile silos there. The heart of New Mexico might be a secondary target for North Korea."

"We're right in the middle of all three places," said Preacher as he pointed toward one of the ranch hands who was approaching them.

They arrived at the western end of the ranch and spoke briefly with the young man who was patrolling this side of the ranch. He'd just rode the fence toward the north and he was heading back southward. Preacher gave him instructions to work his way toward the house and meet them there shortly. They'd be constructing a fence and barricade at the south and north entrances to the farm in about an hour.

"I don't know what things are like in the big cities, but I can only imagine," continued Major. "Logic tells me that people will begin to flee the lack of resources and violence in the large population areas and head into the countryside seeking safety, shelter, and food."

"Major, Texas will be like a giant magnet drawing them here in droves. We have power; they don't. I can't see it any other way."

Major nodded his agreement. "I know, and we have to get ready. There will come a time when we may have to deal with large hostile groups. The best thing we can do is deter them from coming after our ranch. If we give them an appearance that we're prepared to fight, they'll move on to easier targets. And there will be easier targets, believe me."

They guided the horses down a dry creek bed past one of the homes on the ranch lived in by a single young man named Jose. The simple rectangular structure with a slightly rusted tin roof stood alone among some trees and tall grasses. As they approached the Colorado River, which created their northern boundary, the sparse grasses and rocky soil gave way to trees and plant life.

Major continued. "Natural boundaries, like the river, help us deny them access to our land. If they have operating vehicles, they'll have to go around, and all of our gates will be manned. If they're on horseback, they better be careful crossing the river. It's deeper than they might realize, and the silt bottom is like quicksand."

"Hopefully, with our constant patrols, we'll see them comin'," added Preacher.

"Detection is just as important as our deterrent and denial efforts. Even with knowing our land and having armed men at the ready, those extra seconds and minutes will give us the upper hand."

"Major, we've discussed this many times when you and I have been riding the ranch. I believe we're as ready as we're gonna be. Those people who wanna enter Armstrong Ranch and take what we have are gonna be in for an unexpected surprise. By the same token, we have to think like they do as well. What's our biggest weakness?"

"To put it bluntly, Armstrong Ranch is too big to defend. Our world needs to get a lot smaller."

CHAPTER 27

November 27
Raven Rock Mountain Complex
Liberty Township, Pennsylvania

President Harman met with Chief of Staff Acton, Secretary of State Tompkins, and DHS Secretary Pickering in the president's private quarters. It was a meeting intended to be away from the prying ears and eyes of the hundreds of military personnel performing their duties within Raven Rock. Other members of her cabinet, Secretary Gregg in particular, would question why they were excluded from the meeting. Especially since the meeting included the State Department, which dealt with international affairs, and Homeland Security, which focused on domestic matters—both of which necessarily involved a discussion of national defense. Not unexpectedly, internal politics within an administration didn't disappear with the advent of the apocalypse.

"I trust the three of you more than anyone else in our government," started President Harman. "Let me say first that I'm perfectly capable of handling our domestic crisis and waging a war in Southeast Asia at the same time. That said, under these extraordinary circumstances, I would be remiss to focus the entirety of this administration's efforts on retaliatory efforts against Kim Jong-un while the American people need my undivided attention."

"How can we help, Madam President?" asked Tompkins.

"Jane, we've heard Monty Gregg make the case for war, ad nauseum," replied the president. "Actually, let me clarify. He seems to be interested in annihilating the North Korean regime via a nuclear first strike."

"Madam President, let me start with a blunt assessment of North Korea and where they are headed as a nation," said Tompkins. "The EMP attack upon us does not change their standing among world leaders nor does it suddenly escalate the DPRK from an impoverished nation to an economically emerging one. Kim Jong-un presides over a dying society, nothing more than a prison camp of twenty-eight million miserable, starving souls masquerading as a country. In economic terms, North Korea lags somewhere behind Ethiopia while their sister country, South Korea, ranks thirty-first in the world, well ahead of Russia. North Korea ranks nowhere."

"Then what is the end game for Kim?" asked the president.

"He has to control his people through fear," replied Tompkins. "Fear of his iron fist and fear of an imminent American attack. Just like Hussein, Hitler, or Stalin, a dictator like Kim maintains power by spreading fear among the people and placing themselves as the nation's only salvation. By manufacturing an external threat like the Jews to Hitler's Germany, or the entire West to North Korea, he keeps the society on edge and paranoid as well."

"Jane, please, honest opinion. Do you believe Kim's statements from yesterday? Do you think he has designs to attack our allies, or us, with nuclear weapons or by conventional means?"

"No, I do not. While he has the capability, my belief is it would have happened already. One could argue that, at least in his mind and apparently in the mind of several world leaders, he was justified in taking the action against us and is showing the world his restraint by not taking it further. If we attack him, we could be portrayed as being the bad guys."

The president contemplated Tompkins's statement. "You would stand down?"

"Yes, I would. Perhaps we could build up our forces in the region for added protection in the event he did start a ground war against the South, but I think our position should remain the same as it was prior to the EMP attack—isolation, sanctions, diplomacy, and surround him with our military strength."

President Harman turned her attention to DHS Secretary

Pickering. "Carla, in all healthy organizations, dissent happens face-to-face. We gave Secretary Gregg his opportunity this morning, and now I'm looking to my trusted advisors to make their case. I'm leaning in the direction of Jane's way of thinking. When I took office, I intended to follow President Billings's lead by focusing on the health, welfare, and advancement of the American people. I wasn't interested in fighting wars abroad. First, give me your opinion on whether we should retaliate."

"Madam President, I look at this situation, oddly enough, like a domestic violence case involving a shooting. Our first goal is to treat the patient and prevent her from dying. Then we focus on arresting and prosecuting the perp. If North Korea escalates, we hit them with all we've got. Otherwise, we can deal with the situation later when we're back on our feet. For now, we need to focus our efforts on saving American lives and restoring order in the streets."

The president referred to her notes. "I have reports compiled by Charles that violence exploded last night within all major cities and most population centers over one hundred thousand residents. Is our society collapsing faster than you envisioned?"

"This is day three, and people are becoming increasingly desperate," replied Pickering. "Grocery shelves are bare. Fresh water is nonexistent because there isn't power to operate water treatment facilities. Garbage is piling up in the streets. The instances of gun violence are astonishing."

"What about law enforcement? Is their presence being ignored?" asked the president.

"Madam President, I'm being told that many officers are not appearing for duty. Some blame it on lack of adequate communications between the officers and their local governments. Others surmise that the police are staying home to protect their families in light of the rising levels of violence."

"I suppose I can't blame them for that," said the president. "Let me ask you this, I despise the concept of martial law and the violation of civil liberties it necessarily entails. However, it must be declared. I've been working with the attorney general on a draft declaration, which will be ready for review shortly. Do you think we've reached that point?"

"I do, Madam President. We have to restore order before we can safely deploy relief efforts into the cities. We can't put our relief workers and FEMA teams into danger. It's not fair to them or their families."

"Carla, if we declare martial law, it will need to be enforced by the military. The attorney general is working on the constitutional issues of such enforcement. Let us consider the practical aspects. If we can't get law enforcement officers to show up for their shifts, what incentive can we provide our military to risk their lives in these domestic war zones?"

"Two words—food and shelter," replied Pickering. "We can offer our military personnel and their families base housing. We will marshal our assets to feed them first, and use that promise of security as an inducement to work with FEMA to deliver relief supplies as well as maintain order in the streets."

"Might I add, Madam President," interjected Tompkins, "if you elect to increase our troop levels in the Southeast Asia theater, as a show of force, that will increase room within military bases to effectuate Carla's proposal. I think it's viable."

"Jane, how do you feel about martial law?" asked the president.

"Same as you. I don't like it, but it's absolutely necessary under the circumstances."

The president propped her elbows on the round kitchen table within her sleeping quarters and stared at the blank wall in front of her. There were no good options, only well-thought-out solutions.

"Charles, I need you to draft a memo to the cabinet and the Joint Chiefs of Staff for immediate dissemination. Let's keep it simple because I don't need to get into a lengthy explanation as to how I arrived at my decision. When we meet for tomorrow's daily briefing and subsequent cabinet meeting, we will have a new primary focus."

"Yes, Madam President," said Acton. "I'll keep it short and sweet. Bullet-point style."

President Harman continued. "Number one, we will not retaliate militarily against North Korea at this time. We will bolster our defenses with an increased military presence in the region.

"Number two, I will issue a declaration of martial law as early as tomorrow afternoon. This declaration will set forth specifics including direct military control of normal civilian functions of government with a focus on restoring law and order.

"Number three, I will expect all members of the cabinet to prepare a proposal to utilize the good fortunes bestowed on the state of Texas for the greater good of the citizens of the afflicted areas of the United States. I want all federal agencies to work in concert to develop a plan to use Texas resources for distribution to severely impacted regions of the country. Also, I want to establish a refugee program to transport displaced citizens to Texas. It's a big state. They've got plenty of room to help others."

CHAPTER 28

November 27
Raven Rock Mountain Complex
Liberty Township, Pennsylvania

Secretary Gregg was a man without words. He'd read the president's short memorandum and walked around the small living area in which he and his wife resided within Raven Rock. Using his closed-communications telephone system, he called for his aide-de-camp, Jackson Waller, to join him. His next call was to Colonel Baker, requesting that he shut off the call logs for his phone. Secretary Gregg had weighed his options and was ready to reach out to Governor Burnett. First, he had to lay the groundwork with Waller and then his wife.

"I asked Jackson to join us because I have an important decision to make," started Secretary Gregg. "The president has reached a determination wholly contrary to my recommendations, the person who's charged with the responsibility of protecting our nation. I firmly believe that she is exhibiting weakness by not retaliating, and worse, she's leaving us open for further attacks, both nuclear and conventional, by not taking the battle to Kim on North Korean soil. I will not allow my career to be tarnished by her reckless inaction. I believe it is time to resign."

"Monty, the timing is awful," plead his wife. "We are still in this bunker for a reason. We could be hit with nuclear bombs at any time."

"Dear, I understand your trepidation. There are other bunkers and locations in the country that are just as safe as this one. My decision is bigger than our immediate safety, which I will always provide for.

It has to do with my principles. I don't like the direction this country is headed. It's a sinking ship after decades of failed leadership. It's time to consider other options."

"Monty, I've stood by you as your career took us all over the world," said his wife. "I will continue to stand by you, but please, don't be cryptic. If you have plans for our future, tell me."

"Jackson has kept me informed on activities back home in Texas. The three of us have been friends and supporters of Governor Burnett for years. As you know, she is an advocate of the Texas secessionist movement. I don't know if she'll agree with my opinion, but I believe the time is ripe for Texas to be restored to the independence it enjoyed from 1836 to 1846."

Secretary Gregg's wife interrupted him. "Monty, that was a long time ago. Things have changed."

"But the Texas mindset has not. In 1846, Texas joined the United States only to secede again in 1861 with ten other states. The secessionist movement has remained a part of the political discourse in Austin for over one hundred fifty years. It's been ramped up in the last decade, and I believe they have the perfect opportunity to break away now."

"I wouldn't mind returning to Texas," said Mrs. Gregg. "What about you, Jackson?"

"My heart never left the hill country, ma'am."

"Billy and his wife feel the same way," added Mrs. Gregg. "Would they be included in this?"

"Yes," replied Secretary Gregg. "If you both agree, I plan on setting the wheels in motion with a phone call to Governor Burnett shortly."

Waller and Secretary Gregg's wife looked at one another and shrugged. The three of them had become close over the years, as Waller continued to be a trusted confidant of Secretary Gregg's. Following the death of Waller's wife, Mrs. Gregg was there to support him during those difficult times.

"I'm in," announced Mrs. Gregg.

"Me too," said Waller. "Although, I have a suggestion. Don't resign just yet. I have some thoughts on the matter as it relates to the president's reaction to the secession. We might want to speak to the commanders of Bliss and Hood beforehand. In other words, ask them to stand down."

Secretary Gregg sat a little taller in his chair and puffed out his chest.

"I'm gonna do more than ask them to stand down. I'm gonna ask them to stand with us!"

CHAPTER 29

November 27
The Governor's Mansion
Austin, Texas

Defense Secretary Montgomery Gregg's call caught the governor off guard. The first thing that went through her mind was the president had learned of her activities with regard to the border and was using Secretary Gregg to set the stage for her advisory team's arrival. She surmised that Secretary Gregg was supposed to warm the governor to federal control of her state. After her chief of staff left her office, she nervously picked up the phone.

"Hello, Monty," she said hesitantly to her old friend, whom she believed to be of the same political mindset.

"Marion, it has been a while, unfortunately. I'm going to dispense with the preliminaries and get right to the point."

Great, this is worse than I thought. She decided to exude confidence. "Well, Monty, there is more to discuss than the weather and whether the mackerel are runnin' along Matagorda."

Monty laughed, which helped ease the tension. "Marion, I'm coming to Texas in the morning, with my wife and top aide."

"Okay," she said, drawing out the word. "I take it this is not a social call."

"Marion, the president's advance team will be arriving at your doorstep at any time," he said before being interrupted.

"Monty, you said *advance team.* I thought these folks were advisors of some sort."

"No, Marion. Make no mistake. This is an advance team sent by President Harman for a single purpose—taking over your state."

"What?"

"You heard me correctly. The president and her precious advisors have every intention of stripping Texas of its assets and redistributing them throughout the country according to whom they deem needs help the most. In exchange, they plan on bussing in millions of people for you to watch over, feed, and coddle."

"Monty, we can't—"

"Nor will you, Marion. Now listen to me. There isn't much time. When her people arrive, put on that *welcome to Texas* charm that you're known for. Blow all the sunshine you have to. Give them countless hours of dog and pony shows. But you must give them as little information as possible."

"Okay, I can do that. Monty, what's the plan? I mean, you're coming here with your wife, and Waller, I presume. And you may not know this, but I had a handwritten note delivered to me by Billy Yancey this morning. He's back in Texas at his ranch outside Amarillo. This is not coincidental, is it?"

"I didn't know Billy was going to reach out to you, but he's good people, and I'll speak with him tomorrow as well. This is much bigger than a social gathering of old friends, Marion."

"You know where I stand on Texas and its sovereignty, Monty. I've been wrestling with a decision that has me torn between protecting fellow Texans and trying to help the rest of the country. I don't know what the president has in mind, but we can't do what you've just suggested."

"Marion, I'll just come out with it. It's time for Texas to become a republic again. However, you can't do it alone. You're going to need an army, and I'm the cavalry that will help make that happen."

"It's hard to argue with that," said the governor.

"Good. Upon my arrival, I'll get a message to you. Find a place where we can meet unnoticed from even your closest people. We can't trust anyone until everything is in place."

"Monty, I look forward to seeing you. Let's talk more tomorrow."

They hung up without saying another word. She set the phone down on her desk and paced around the room, digesting the conversation. Then she stopped and looked at the flags that flanked the left and right side of her desk. She held her palm flat and raised it to obscure her vision of the United States flag so only the Texas flag was visible. She began to smile.

I'm going to have an army.

CHAPTER 30

November 27
The Sabine River Bridge
Interstate 10
Near Orange, Texas

The Sabine River had a storied history. The river was created by the confluence of three tributary forks in northeast Texas at the Louisiana border. It meandered untamed, as locals say, through the bayou country until it reached the Neches River and ultimately the Gulf of Mexico.

Prior to forming the Texas-Louisiana border, it acted as the border between the Republic of Texas and the United States. The Sabine River had been the subject of controversy since the Louisiana Purchase in 1803, as map makers consistently drew it incorrectly. Finally, in a treaty between Washington and the Republic of Texas in 1836, the center point of the river was identified, and the Sabine River began to serve as the western boundary of America.

Just three days ago, as many as fifty-five thousand vehicles crossed this bridge that connected the two states. Interstate 10 stretched from Los Angeles to Jacksonville and was one of three transcontinental interstate highways stretching from coast to coast. Now, the bridge was devoid of vehicles except for the Texas Highway Patrol cars blocking both the east- and westbound lanes at the crown of the Sabine River bridge.

The bridge, which rose nearly one hundred feet above the river, was not empty, however. Foot traffic was sparse, as the Louisiana State Police issued advisories to pedestrians that the bridge was closed, as was Texas.

Individuals who could show proof of Texas residency were allowed to pass through the checkpoint on the Louisiana side of the bridge, but others were not. On the morning of the third day, Governor John Bel Edwards ordered the state police to perform other duties. He was upset when he learned Texas was denying access to Louisiana refugees for the foreseeable future. His written communiques to Governor Burnett went unanswered, at which point he vowed to let Texas deal with the mass of people gathering in Louisiana who were seeking the oasis known as Texas.

Throughout the day, hundreds and then thousands of people began to gather at the checkpoint entering Texas. The Texas state troopers called for backup and immediately halted the processing of Texas residents until the situation was under control.

Chief Armando Smith of the Houston Police Department's SWAT team was dispatched to the bridge. After making the two-hour trek, two dozen members of the tactical squad arrived in armored personnel carriers. In addition, two black armored water cannon trucks arrived to reinforce both the east- and westbound lanes.

The imposing vehicles were fully protected against ballistic, mine-blast and improvised explosive devices. Its fourteen-thousand-gallon water tank was capable of throwing a powerful, high-pressure water jet up to two hundred feet. They took up a position immediately behind the barriers, approximately forty feet from the growing crowd.

The Texas Army Guard leadership team in Austin was monitoring the events by radio, but delegated operational control to the state troopers and the Houston SWAT team commanders.

After the reinforcements arrived, the crowd was expected to disperse. However, their anger only grew in intensity. Those Texas residents attempting to get into the state shouted their frustration, hurling insults and profanities at the officers. The thousands of others from Louisiana and other nearby states demanded fairness. No single complaint could be discerned from another as the roar of hostilities rose to a crescendo.

Witnesses on the scene later recounted that a single gunshot was fired from somewhere at the back of the crowd, followed by another. The effect of the loud retort was to frighten the herd of people who were pressing against each other to cross into Texas. There were cries for help as women and children were forced to the concrete pavement and trampled.

The mass of people was about to overwhelm the HESCO barricades put in place by the Texas Guard. Made of collapsible wire mesh and filled with sand and dirt, these heavy defensive containers were used for flood control and military fortifications. The refugees were climbing on top of them to avoid the crush of the thousands of people pushing forward to avoid the gunfire.

When several young men scaled the barriers and began shouting with their arms raised in defiance, the commander of the Houston SWAT team gave the order. Inside the state-of-the-art command control system of the armored water cannons, two gunners opened fire, applying the full force of the water in the direction of the young men.

The first blast hit one young man in the chest, driving him twenty feet in the air and over the side of the bridge, over eighty feet to his death. The second powerful burst, which came from the other water cannon, struck its target high, causing the man's face to be crushed into a torn mass of bloody flesh before ripping his head from his torso.

Shrieks of fear filled the air. The crowd panicked and attempted to run from the devastating blasts of the water cannons. In only a matter of seconds, the relentless high-pressure stream of water knocked bodies over, broke the limbs of others, and caused several to seek relief by taking their chances in the river.

On both sides of the bridge, people were diving to their deaths—arms flailing, bodies contorting in a feeble attempt to land feet first, only to break their backs when they hit the murky waters below.

It was a gruesome scene, a horror that would be replayed in the minds of everyone present for the rest of their lives. It also marked the moment when a line in the sand was drawn at the Texas border. The line came with a warning notice to all—*Texas is closed*.

PART FOUR

Monday, November 28

CHAPTER 31

November 28
Sinmi-do, North Korea

The comatose state—a fate that's only comparable to death. Typically the result of a massive head injury, a coma created a profound state of unconsciousness from which a person cannot be awakened. The person was not brain dead, a condition where both conscious and cognitive functions have permanently ceased. Someone who was in a comatose state was completely unable to move or respond to their environment.

Duncan Armstrong couldn't move, but he could sense his surroundings. *I am alive!*

He heard creaking floors, feet shuffling, and muted voices coming from above him. Duncan's brain was temporarily confused as he struggled to regain full consciousness. His desire to rejoice in his survival was tamped down by his innate instinct to be careful.

He allowed his eyes to open ever so slightly in an attempt to survey his surroundings. A kerosene lantern flickered on a table in the corner of the room, drawing his attention. He dared not open his eyes further for fear that his awakened state might draw attention.

Sensing that he was covered by heavy blankets, Duncan took a risk and slowly, imperceptibly curled his toes. Everything was intact. He alternated flexing his quadricep muscles to confirm his legs were free from injury. *Good. I can run.*

The voices came into focus. *Korean.* His memory came back to him, slowly at first. He recalled falling and then floating. He'd been lifted upward, but not easily. It had been a struggle for the hands that hoisted him upward.

He barely moved his fingers, simulating typing on a keyboard. Then he flexed his biceps as he continued his self-diagnosis and inventory of his limbs. *All body parts accounted for, sir!*

Duncan couldn't suppress a slight smile. Not only was he alive, but he was unrestrained.

"*Abeoji! Ppalli wala! Budi!*" shouted a young woman's voice from behind him. *Father, come quickly, please!*

Her sudden outburst startled Duncan and his body shook slightly. There was no hiding his awakened state now. He had to make a decision. Play possum or try to escape. His mind raced as he struggled to regain full consciousness from the deep sleep he'd experienced. He analyzed what his mind could sense.

Dark basement. Single kerosene lamp on a table. No concrete, no steel, no block. A young woman standing vigil over him, alone.

He was not imprisoned. He was being treated, helped by unknown persons in a very foreign land.

"*Kkaeda?*" a voice asked as squeaky hinges revealed a door was being opened. *Awake?*

"*Ye. Ye.*"

More excited voices began to speak from the doorway. The man lumbered down the stairs and the door was closed behind him. Duncan couldn't make out the number of people moving about the floor above him. Three, maybe four. His focus was now turned to the two people in the room.

His muscles tensed, prepared to pounce on any aggressor. Yet he still resisted the urge to reveal his fully conscious state. He listened and observed through his senses. One hostile move toward him and he'd fight without hesitation.

The man spoke again. "*Yeong-eo.*" *English.*

The voice of an angel whispered in his ear, soft and delicate. "Mister, I am Sook. My father is Chae. We help you."

Decision time, Duncan thought. Everything he could discern from the last five minutes indicated she was telling the truth. Could he have been so lucky to have survived the fall and icy waters? Only to be rescued by locals at the fishing village on Sinmi-do by a family who, despite living in a nation where paranoia required reporting anything unusual to the authorities, nursed him back to health.

There is a God, but then, Duncan always knew that. He opened his eyes.

He opened his eyes and was shocked at what he saw.

CHAPTER 32

November 28
Joint Base San Antonio
802nd Mission Support Group
Lackland Air Force Base
Bexar County, Texas

Nearly one and a half million active-duty personnel for the five armed services were stationed within the borders of Texas. Of these service members, it was most likely to be a fellow Southerner in uniform than from any other state. For decades since the Vietnam War, recruiting efforts in the Northeast and most urban areas had been on the decline. Most enlistees came from Florida and Texas.

Not necessarily by design, but more as a result of fate, the lead commanders for the Army and Air Force in Texas were Texans. The commanders from Fort Bliss and Fort Hood were native Texans brought up through the ranks by then General Montgomery Gregg.

They'd pledged an oath to obey the Constitution, but they continued to follow the direction of Secretary of Defense Gregg. When they were summoned to Lackland Air Force Base to meet with Secretary Gregg, both commanders jumped at the opportunity. They were not told the nature of the meeting when contacted by Waller, only that it involved the most important decision of their career. They were also to use complete discretion regarding the confab.

Lackland Air Force Base in West San Antonio had been used following the EMP attack as the primary gateway for travelers from Washington to Texas. Part of Joint Base San Antonio, JBSA, commanded by another Gregg protégé, Lackland afforded the former general meeting facilities where he could gather his most trusted confidants to discuss his plans before he traveled to Austin to meet with Governor Burnett.

In addition to the commanders of Fort Bliss, Fort Hood, and JBSA, in attendance were his aide-de-camp, Waller, and Billy Yancey, who was unknown to the military leaders. Secretary Gregg considered omitting Yancey from the conversation, but as a specialist in regime change, which was arguably about to happen, he was adept at reading people. He was there to study the reactions of the military leaders and provide Secretary Gregg an honest assessment as they listened to his proposal.

"Gentlemen, this is going to be a very difficult conversation," started Secretary Gregg. "I am going to lay out a proposal, a life-changing option for all of us, but one that I haven't considered in haste."

The military men looked at one another, and General Mickey Brooks, commander at Fort Hood, spoke on their behalf. "General, um, Mr. Secretary, excuse me. I—"

"No formalities today, my friends," said Secretary Gregg. "We've been comrades-in-arms, red-blooded Texans, and friends for many years. In this room, right now, we are six old buddies trying to make a decision that's best for our families, our fellow Texans, and possibly the nation, although some may not see it that way."

"Okay, Monty," said General Brooks, looking to his fellow generals for acquiescence. They smiled and nodded. "In that light, let me speak for all of us in saying over the years, we've all hitched our wagons to the same horse. You, sir. No matter which direction this conversation goes, we'll consider all options without judgment."

"Good, that's all I ask," said Secretary Gregg. "Let me get right to the point. Our nation has been dealt a bad set of cards, to be true. By the same token, our president, and many before her, recklessly gambled with the lives and future of the American people. As a result, that dictator in North Korea, with the help of Iran, has stricken us down with a blow more devastating than most politicians were willing to acknowledge. America is on her knees, my friends, waiting for the final strike to take her down, if she doesn't collapse on her own in the meantime."

"Monty, we're aware of the difficulties around the country," said General Brooks. "Our limited contact with other base commanders reveal disjointed and conflicting orders from the administration. As the president turned over domestic deployment matters to Homeland Security, a move we deemed in contravention of your authority as Secretary of Defense, morale has suffered. Are we fighting to defend our country and attack those who brought this down upon us, or are we to become a police state?"

"I understand your frustration," interjected Monty. "You can imagine mine. Gentlemen, I've left Washington for good. Although I haven't formally resigned as Secretary of Defense, it is apparent that I've been cut out of the decision-making process, and most likely, I'm being set up as the scapegoat for the attack."

"Sir, that's ridiculous," protested the Lackland base commander. "The Air Force has led the charge in warning the other branches of the military about the EMP threat, especially from Earth-orbiting satellites. I know you've advocated for stepping up our defense of this particular threat. It's unfair to claim you haven't done what's necessary to protect the country."

"It's politics, my friends. I could've declined the opportunity to be Secretary of Defense, which would've kept me out of this precarious position. I honestly thought I could advance our military from within the administration while protecting the country at the same time. The president believes I've failed."

"Not true," said General Brooks.

Secretary Gregg continued after glancing at Yancey, who provided him an imperceptible nod. His approach was working.

"After this meeting, as you know, I'll be traveling to Austin for a private meeting with the governor. You know Marion Burnett as well as I do. There is no greater advocate for our military and Texas than she."

"First class," added General Brooks.

"Yes, she is, although a little rough around the edges." Secretary Gregg laughed. "But not quite as rough as Ma Richards." This drew an uproar of laughter from everyone in the room as Secretary Gregg reached behind him and retrieved a spoon from near the coffee maker and tapped it on the bottom of his shoe.

Ann Richards, nicknamed *Ma* by her political opponents, had been governor of Texas in the early nineties and was famous for making a speech at the Democratic National Convention deriding presidential candidate George Herbert Walker Bush. Mocking his wealthy upbringing in the Northeastern United States, she famously said in an exaggerated Texas drawl, "I'm delighted to be here with you this evening. I figgered after listening to George Bush all these years, you needed to know what a real Texas accent sounds like. Poor George, he can't he'p it. He was born with a silver foot in his mouth!"

After the hilarity died down, Yancey was smiling, and that was his cue to Secretary Gregg to make his pitch.

"Gentlemen, unless I've read the political tea leaves incorrectly, two things are about to happen. Tonight, the president is going to declare martial law, imposing direct military control over all aspects of our government, law enforcement, and business. She will put her cronies from California in charge of this effort, which would effectively force me out in many respects."

"Honestly, Monty, I can't say I'm surprised," said General Brooks. "We haven't felt the impact here because we have power. But the rest of the country is in chaos. What else is going to happen?"

Secretary Gregg took a deep breath. "Marion has called the legislature into special session tomorrow. I believe she is going to secede from the union, restoring the Republic of Texas in the process."

"I thought that was all bluster on the campaign trail," said the commander from Fort Bliss. "Do you think she can pull it off?"

"She has already closed the borders," added General Brooks. "The next step is to have a vote to make it official."

"What about us?" asked the commander from Fort Bliss. "We swore an oath to uphold the Constitution."

"Yes, you did," said Secretary Gregg. "But all of us are avowed oathkeepers, and there are certain orders we refuse to obey. For example, her martial law declaration might order the military to disarm American citizens. It's likely she'll order the confiscation of excess supplies and food from households deemed *hoarders*, simply because they were prudent and preparedness minded. After the secession is announced, it's likely she'll order you to overtake the Texas government with the ultimate intention of disbanding the state's government and seizing its assets."

"Texas is a sovereign state now," said General Brooks. "Washington has no right to invade from within its borders using the soldiers under our commands, nor should it send troops from other nearby bases."

Secretary Gregg leaned back in his chair and studied the faces of the men sitting around the table. "You have choices in the matter, but here's what I'm asking of you. First, stand down when the president issues orders to you in violation of your oath. Governor Burnett is trying to protect our fellow Texans from a crush of outsiders entering the state who are putting our families at risk. Next, consider this. I will meet with the governor this afternoon to propose something radical. Some might call it treasonous; others, especially those within our charge, will see it as a step toward survival and self-preservation."

"What's that, Monty?" asked General Brooks.

"I want to provide the Republic of Texas its own armed forces. Texas, through its planning, sacrifice, and dedication to its political roots, has managed to avoid the calamities besetting the rest of the nation. As Texans, we have the opportunity to jump off a dying ship and restore the republic to its former greatness."

The generals talked among themselves while Secretary Gregg drank half a bottle of water. He was parched from his flight and the lengthy conversation. He waited for a response.

"This is only slightly different from the Civil War," started the commander of Fort Bliss. "The Union forces garrisoned in the South were primarily Northerners. The few native Southerners abandoned their posts and joined the Confederacy. The vast majority of troops within our command are Southerners and likely to be pro-Texas."

"We're going to have to convince our subordinates and all of those who fall within our command," said General Brooks. "As for us, we're in. We'd be honored to help Texas remain strong and free."

Secretary Gregg offered his advice. "Thank you all. Now, go back to your bases and tell them this. They can remain on post in the relative comfort of a new nation, the Republic of Texas, with power, energy, food sources, and a stable government. Or they can immediately be reassigned to a base of their choosing, out there, in the darkness. Wish them luck."

CHAPTER 33

November 28
The Armstrong Ranch
Borden County, Texas

"Miss Lucy!" shouted Major from the barn. "May we borrow you a minute?"

Lucy had just finished baking egg bread with some of her helpers. The recipe was a unique way to make Texas toast, which would later have a variety of ingredients added to make delicacies like cinnamon swirl bread, raisin bread or old-fashioned garlic butter toast.

Using ingredients stored in her pantry like flour, yeast, salt, and sugar, together with sustainable ingredients available from the barnyard critters such as milk, butter, and eggs, Lucy and her charges would knead the ingredients and bake it in her oven daily. Their system enabled the three women to create more than a dozen loaves of bread, one for each family per day.

Lucy approached the barn and found Preacher topping off her truck with gas. Two of the hands were standing next to the truck with their rifles.

"Y'all goin' somewhere?" she asked.

Major walked over to her and gave her a kiss on the cheek.

She smiled and touched his face. "What was that for?"

"Because I can," he said with a chuckle. "Preacher and the boys are going into Lubbock to talk with the folks at the slaughterhouse. We'd planned on selling off at least a hundred head of cattle before winter set in, and that's not gonna happen. I wanna see if we can slaughter ten and use the beef for stored food."

"What's the flatbed trailer for?" she asked.

"When I was over there a couple of weeks ago, Plain Meats had a large restaurant-style freezer for sale. With most of the horses kept out on the ranch all day, we have extra room in the barn. We figured we'd slaughter ten steers and divide them up between all our freezers or turn the meat into jerky."

Lucy thought for a minute. "After that, we could butcher them here at the ranch, one at a time, as needed."

"Exactly. Can you think of anything else they could pick up while in town?"

Lucy thought for a moment then laughed. "I reckon Albertson's has been wiped clean."

"As a whistle," replied Preacher, who'd joined the conversation.

"Preacher, stop by HF&C," continued Lucy. "If they're open, pick up some starter feed for the laying chicks this spring. We're gonna produce a whole flock of egg-layers. We've got plenty of cattle to eat, there's no sense in eating our egg-producing chickens."

"Got it," Preacher said as he took off his jacket. The day was warming up quickly.

"Two more things," Lucy said. "See if the slaughterhouse will sell you a roll of jumbo vacuum rolls for the food saver. If we're gonna slaughter our own cattle, we could use some backup vacuum bags. Also, while you're at HF&C, buy up all the Agri-cillin and Baytril they've got. We've still got a lot of calves out there. Let's not let them get sick."

Preacher headed for the truck after exchanging a few words with Major. Then Major spoke with Antonio and the other young man. They nodded and tipped their hats to her husband.

Lucy wandered away from the group and nervously wiped her hands on her apron as she faced the north. A single tear rolled down her face as a sudden sense of foreboding overcame her.

The truck pulled away and Major joined her. She quickly wiped off her face and forced a smile. She'd never been able to hide her emotions from her husband, and this morning was no exception.

"What's worryin' ya, Miss Lucy?"

"You know, little things like where are my children," she said with a chuckle, which only served to bring more waterworks.

Major put his arm around her and held her tight. "They're resilient and levelheaded. I know they'll make good choices."

She shook her head and wiped her tears once again. "Cooper can be a risk taker, and Riley is compulsive. I hope Palmer can keep them both grounded."

"Miss Lucy, they all have our best attributes, and they work well together as a team. Could you ever imagine a more close-knit group of kids, despite their differences?"

"It is amazing," she replied. "It was almost like we had two sets of kids. Duncan and Dallas were the adventuresome, see-the-world brothers. The rodeo kids were stay at home and traveled only to pursue their passion—rodeo."

"It does make me wonder if maybe while I was in Lubbock running Company C, the postman came sniffin' around the ranch a little too often," Major said with a laugh, which was short lived as Miss Lucy landed a well-earned slug to his arm. "Ouch!"

"You're lucky that new gun you bought me is sittin' on the kitchen table," she snarled playfully.

"Yeah, yeah. Let's continue to pray for all of our kids. You raised them well, Miss Lucy. Have comfort in knowing they're all survivors."

The conversation halted as one of the hands came racing toward them on his horse. As he pulled on the reins, causing the horse to snort and rear up slightly, he shouted to Major, "Two police cars want to enter. The governor sent them for you."

"They're here to get me?" asked Major.

"*Si.*"

Lucy's mind raced. *Why would they want to take my husband?*

"Major, what should we do?"

"I suspect it's fine," he replied, slightly unsure of his answer. "Maybe the purpose of their visit got lost in translation."

"Maybe," said Lucy.

"Go back and fetch them," ordered Major before turning to his wife. "Let's see what they have to say. Marion must have a good reason to send these fellows all the way from Austin at this early hour. It's at least a four-hour drive."

The two Texas Highway Patrol cars came down the long driveway to the house at a respectful, slow speed. It was in contrast to the sense of urgency of their message.

Major was being summoned to the State House to meet with the governor, the Secretary of Defense, and four dozen other key ranchers and business leaders from around the state. It would be a long, eventful day in the history of Texas.

CHAPTER 34

November 28
The Governor's Mansion
Austin, Texas

Governor Burnett made no effort to hide the presence of the Defense Secretary or his entourage, which included Waller and Yancey. If this meeting went well, it would lend additional credibility to her leadership skills as she navigated the state toward secession. If the meeting was a bust, she could spin it to her advantage—*she'd agreed to meet with the president's representative in a last-ditch effort to see eye-to-eye, to no avail.*

"Gentlemen, this is our adjutant general, Kregg Deur," said the governor as she started the introductions. "I've asked him to sit in, as he is in charge of the Texas Guard and is spearheading our border-control efforts. Please, everyone, take a seat."

The governor motioned for her chief of staff to leave and close the door. After everyone was settled, Secretary Gregg spoke first.

"Marion, if I may, I'd like to dispense with the formalities."

"Fine by me," said the governor. "For days, I've felt like I've been on the campaign trail again. That door has been revolving with one legislator after another offering advice and hearing what I have in mind."

"I understand," said Secretary Gregg. "Let's lay our cards on the table, Marion. I believe you are positioning Texas to secede from the union, and we're here to help."

Governor Burnett laughed. "Clearly, this is an unofficial visit. Unsanctioned by the president, correct?"

Secretary Gregg laughed. "She would consider this treasonous, and perhaps it is. Time will judge us for our actions."

"It's no secret that I've been an advocate of secession for years," started the governor. "I believe half of Texas agreed with me before this attack by the North Koreans. If polling were available to us, I'd wager that number is more like eighty percent right now. If I opened the floodgates on both ends of I-10, that number would rise to ninety percent or more."

"That's a fair assessment, as secession is, in a way, regime change," said Yancey. "While your government will continue to operate under your leadership, creating a new nation-state is the necessary result of replacing one form of government with another—state becomes nation."

"I suppose that's true," said the governor.

Yancey continued. "Regime change can be effectuated through several methods. Sometimes an outside, hostile enemy forces the overthrow of a government. Other times, a revolution or coup d'état takes place to replace a failed state. In your case, this is a friendly takeover of sorts, assuming you have the will of the people on your side."

"I believe we do," interjected Deur. "Texans have seen their food supplies dwindle. Gasoline is beginning to run out. The media within the state have warned that unless something is done, despite having electricity, Texas will fall the way of the rest of the nation."

"Not to mention the hundreds of thousands of people who are now threatening to enter the state," added the governor. "In those early days, we made a point to spread the news about refugees breaking into homes. One family was brutally killed outside Texarkana on Saturday. The news spread across the state like wildfire, thanks to the efforts of our public relations office."

"That single event helped me recruit thousands of new deputies to help close and secure our borders around the perimeter of the state," added Deur. "One important detail that was left out of the story, however, was the fact the killer lived in Wake Village on the Texas side of town."

"You created a false flag, well done," said Yancey.

Deur nodded. "Sometimes a situation presents itself to lay the blame on somebody else in order to advance the goals of government. Personally, I don't like it, but I have a job to do—protect our borders."

"Monty, we go way back and I know you well," said the governor. "What are you proposing?"

"Marion, the president is going to declare martial law. I believe it's her first step in exerting control over the country, including Texas. There is already talk behind the closed doors at Raven Rock of commandeering your assets, flooding your state with refugees, and taking control of the valuable energy industry here."

"I thought as much," muttered the governor. "Would she be so bold as to send troops into our state to force our hand? Or worse, use the million-plus already within our borders?"

"I don't know what's in her head, as she has kept me out of the loop," replied Secretary Gregg. "I don't think she'll invade per se. Rather, she'll call upon Bliss and Hood to do the dirty work."

"We can't fight that, Monty," said a concerned Governor Burnett. "Kregg and I have our hands full recruiting, feeding, and paying thousands of new deputies to protect our borders."

Secretary Gregg managed a sly grin and raised his hand to calm her concerns. "Marion, I've already laid the groundwork. All I need you to do is garner public support, have a successful vote in favor of secession, and remain steadfast as the political pressure is heaped upon you from Washington."

"I can do that," said the governor. "And if the president decides to abandon, or even skip over, the political pressure you mention?"

"You mean go straight to military force?" replied Secretary Gregg with a hypothetical question of his own. "Then I'll use my considerable influence over the U.S. commanders and ask them to stand down. Or we'll defend ourselves like any autonomous country would do."

CHAPTER 35

November 28
Woodhouse, Alberta, Canada

Luck was often beyond a person's control. But decisions were always in a person's hands. Good decision-making, coupled with preparation, could create both luck and opportunity. This was evidenced by the stroke of luck, and generosity, afforded Cooper and the gang when they'd arrived in Nanton the night before.

Cooper read the situation properly, took a chance, and as a result, a very generous family took them in for the night and provided them comfort. Not only did they have a warm place to sleep by a roaring fire, but they were fed two hot meals. More importantly, their hosts provided them hundreds of rounds of ammunition for their weapons, a critical element of their chance to survive.

After voicing their appreciation and issuing promises to come back *when things settle down*, the group of five hit the trail and continued their trek toward the U.S. border. Both horses and riders were rejuvenated as they made good time with full bellies and hearts filled with hope.

They were provided two tents large enough to sleep in, additional water bottles, and several cigarette lighters. The group was now relatively set for shelter and water, and with ammunition for their rifles, they could hunt for food. Now, their biggest challenge was to stay out of harm's way.

The folks in Nanton had provided the group some advice on the upcoming towns along Route 2, which led due south to the border town of Carway. Their most likely point of trouble would be the bridge crossing at Oldman River just north of Fort Macleod.

Rumors had spread that some of Fort Macleod's less savory characters had commandeered the bridge and were exacting a hefty toll from those attempting to cross. The town's motto of *small town, big heart* had been replaced with *give me what you got, no arguments.*

This was only the group's third day of travel, and they weren't ready to duke it out with a bunch of local thugs. After some discussion, it was agreed the group would stop early for the night just south of Woodhouse. They'd made good time that day, and it was a good idea to rest their horses. The group planned on breaking camp before dawn in order to arrive at Fort Macleod near daybreak.

Palmer studied the map with Pacheco while Cooper and Riley got the fire going. Morales volunteered for horse-feeding duty.

The fire was roaring now, as the group made no effort to hide their location from prying eyes. They hadn't seen a house nor human for miles. They camped near a shallow lake, which had thawed thanks to warming temperatures. Morales was pleased that the watering was easy as he allowed the horses to drink thirstily without concern of bacteria. Nothing could live in this cold water, he surmised.

Everyone settled around the campfire, where they enjoyed peanut butter and jelly sandwiches made by the folks in Nanton. Palmer laid out her proposed route, having taken on the unofficial title of navigator.

"If we veer off Route 2 at Mud Lake, we can take this back road due south to a railroad bridge crossing a half mile west of the bridge where the thugs are hanging out. I'm thinkin' we walk the horses across one at a time so it doesn't attract any attention. They'll just think it's a local crossing into town using a shortcut."

"Sounds like a plan," said Cooper. "We'll turn in soon, and I'll wake everyone up around two in the morning."

Riley, the notorious late sleeper, groaned. "Maybe we don't need to do that. I mean, they don't care about some old railroad bridge."

"You never know, Riley," said Palmer, who was best suited to control her brother. She'd always followed her momma's lead in that respect. "You can handle one early morning. After that, we should have a good clean ride to the border."

"All right," he acquiesced. "Hey, are you gonna finish that sandwich?"

Palmer laughed and volunteered the last quarter of the PB and J.

"Let me see the map," directed Cooper. "Sure enough, it's called Old Man River."

"Crazy, right?" said Palmer. "Just like the song."

Cooper studied the map closely for a moment in the dim light, realized the name of the river was *Oldman*, not *Old Man*, but shrugged off the misnomer. He reached behind him to retrieve his backpack. He pulled out a harmonica given to him by Pops when he was ten years old.

"Yup, just like the song," muttered Cooper, who was about to play before another groan was emitted by Riley.

"You ain't gonna go all *Brokeback Mountain* on us, are you, Coop? Seriously, are you gonna play that thing?"

"I am, and you're gonna like it," said Cooper with a laugh.

With near perfect melody and scale, Cooper played the instrument as darkness fell upon them. The smooth sounds flowed across the snowy fields for miles. For those few minutes, the group forgot about the long trip that lay before them and the dangers they'd face.

CHAPTER 36

November 28
Sinmi-do, North Korea

Her face was beautiful with soft features, and her smile forced him to let down his guard. Sook, as she called herself, tucked her hair behind her ears and reached for his forehead. Initially, Duncan flinched, and she stopped. Then her smile grew wider and he relaxed. She placed her hand on his forehead, feeling his temperature, and then lovingly pushed his hair to the side.

She whispered to him, "Much better. Welcome back."

Duncan opened his mouth and tried to speak, but he broke into a coughing fit.

Sook patted him on the chest. "Shhhh. I'll get you some water."

She reached behind her and retrieved a small plastic water bottle with a straw protruding from the lid. Duncan saw that it was marked with lines indicating the volume of fluids contained in the bottle. It appeared to be from a medical facility.

She allowed him to take a sip. "Slowly. Not too much."

His mouth was dry, and the water provided welcome relief. Duncan began to move his arms under the covers. If he had been unconscious, how had he been receiving nourishment? He shifted his eyes away from this angelic caretaker and looked to his left. An intravenous fluids line was draped from a bag hanging from the ceiling. A steady drip of fluids poured through the lines.

He turned back to Sook and whispered, "Thank you. Where am I?"

"Safe," she replied. "You are in our home. In Sinmi-do village."

"What happened?" Duncan managed to ask the question before

experiencing another coughing fit. Sook was quick to provide him water, which he took in too quickly, causing him to cough again.

"Slowly. You have many questions. Do not speak. I will answer."

Duncan smiled and looked to the man standing. He nodded, but Chae's wrinkled, worn face returned his gaze without emotion.

Sook began to recount the events to Duncan. "Four days past, Father and I were fishing in the river. As we paddled upstream, we saw your body wedged against a fallen tree. You were unconscious and very, very cold. Almost dead."

Duncan interrupted. "Your English is excellent."

"Yes, thank you. When I was a young girl, I traveled our country with United Nations. I learned English. With you, I can practice and make it more better."

Duncan managed a laugh. "It is very good, Sook. My name is Duncan."

Sook frowned as she studied his face. Something was wrong.

She spun around in her chair and reached for his phony German passport. She showed it to him. "Are you not Hans?" she asked skeptically.

He'd forgotten all about his cover to get into the country. Duncan had to make another decision. This family had cared for him, and now he could destroy the rapport they'd established. He opted to tell the truth.

"No, my name is Duncan. I am an American."

Sook studied the passport and compared the photo to Duncan's face. "You are a spy."

"No, um, yes," he said. "I was here with the United Nations, but I could not come into the country as an American."

Still unsure of his response, Sook nodded and set the passport back on the table. "The soldiers have been looking for you. My father, mother, and sisters helped hide you. I am a nurse. I have access to medicine and supplies. You've been in a coma."

Duncan was relieved that the conversation continued. He needed to regain his strength, and that required the family's continued help.

"What about my friend?" he asked.

161

"The man from the South? The soldiers told us he is dead. I am sorry."

Duncan closed his eyes and grimaced. He'd known the answer to that question before he asked it, but if the miracle of this family could save him, perhaps there was a glimmer of hope for Park.

He regained his composure and asked, "Are they still looking for me?"

"No," she replied. "But we must be careful. Something is happening."

"What?"

"The soldiers are preparing for war."

CHAPTER 37

November 28
The Governor's Mansion
Austin, Texas

After an hour-long reception in the large dining room, everyone was encouraged to settle down as Governor Burnett began her address. Her plan was twofold. Make a Texas-centric patriotic speech followed by one-on-one conversations with the most important Texans on the invitation list. She was also pleased that Secretary Gregg asked to be present. He was very well respected in the state and would provide comfort to those who might raise concerns about Washington retaliating.

"Ladies and gentlemen, first let me thank you for accepting my invitation to come this afternoon."

"It's not like we had a choice," quipped one of her largest donors. "You sent the cops to my front door and scared the bejesus out of my missus!"

The room burst into laughter, including Major, who knew the feeling.

"Well, I do apologize for that," the governor continued. "Important decisions are about to be made, and you all are my most trusted friends and confidants from around the state. I trust the people in this room with my life."

The group shouted words of encouragement and provided the governor a thumbs-up. The atmosphere in the mansion was beginning to feel like a campaign rally. A charismatic leader like Governor Burnett had that effect on people.

She continued. "Nearly two hundred years ago, winds of change swept across Texas. Our first settlers made camp near the San Marcos and Guadalupe Rivers with plans to make a life for themselves and their families. With the aid of a small cannon provided to these first Texans by the Mexican government, they fought off furious Comanche attacks.

"However, the relationship between the settlers and the Mexican government soured, an order to disarm these Texas settlers was given, and they demanded the return of the cannon. At this point, the cannon was worthless as a piece of artillery, mostly making a loud noise and a puff of smoke when it was fired. But it had become an important symbol of the settlers' resolve to protect their land from anyone who threatened it.

"Matters escalated and the Mexican forces dispatched a hundred men to take back the cannon. When they arrived, they sought a peaceful resolution, but the Texans remained strong. After a day, both sides were at a standoff as a thick fog blanketed the area. When the fog lifted, the Mexican commander was shocked at what he saw."

"Fashioned out of a white wedding dress donated by the daughter of the small colony's founder, the outline of a star was created above a crude drawing of the cannon in question. The handwritten words were written as bold as the challenge that it made—*Come And Take It.*

"The first Texans immediately took the fight to the much larger Mexican forces. Following their commander's orders, the Mexicans quickly retreated from the battle, which later became known as the Lexington of Texas, referring, of course, to the first shots fought in America's fight for independence.

"Ladies and gentlemen, today, Texas finds itself at a crossroads, just as it has six times during its storied history. God has provided us an incredible gift that has insulated Texans from the demise afflicting the rest of the United States. However, God's good graces can only be accepted and used for the good of all Texans because we have prepared for this eventuality.

"One unheeding administration after another has failed to protect the American people from this type of attack. Texas, on the other hand, foresaw the possibilities, took steps to protect our people, and now we stand alone as other states experience despair.

"My fellow Texans, just like the Mexican army was coming for our first settlers' cannon, Washington is coming for our resources. They have designs on our oil and gas. They want to redistribute our food and supplies. They want to inundate our state with outsiders who have no home, no resources, and most likely, very little to offer.

"As your governor and someone who dearly loves Texas, I cannot stand idly by and watch our resources decimated by a swarm of locusts. For that reason, I'm calling a special session of the legislature tomorrow to formally introduce, vote and pass a declaration of secession. It is time to restore the Republic of Texas."

Before she'd finished the last statement, Governor Marion Burnett received her answer. Everyone cheered, some more wildly than others, such as Major, who showed the appropriate respect by applauding but instantly considered the ramifications of secession.

Prior to Governor Burnett's speech, Major had learned the details of the border closings and understood the need. He didn't want thousands of people roaming around his ranch trying to kill his cattle or steal his chickens, or worse.

What he didn't hear from the governor was any attempt to

negotiate or compromise with the president. His first reaction was that the governor was using this as an opportunity to advance her dream—secession and formation of the Republic of Texas.

The governor continued. "Now, I know y'all have a lot of questions, and I didn't drag all of you up here just to hear me talk. As Texans whose roots run deep into our history, I need you to help our state through this transition by being advocates to your families, friends, and neighbors. Tell them to be patient with us as we form a new government. And, above all, let them know that we are taking measures to protect them from the hordes who are gathering at our border, or any form of retaliation ordered by Washington.

"Please, take some time to discuss this among yourselves. I will be available to speak with you, as are key members of my team. Also, as our special guest, all of you will recognize Secretary of Defense Montgomery Gregg. Monty, unlike most of our friends in Washington, is actually here to help.

"Thank you, everyone, and God bless the Republic of Texas!"

The cheering began again, and Major made small talk with several of the ranchers he recognized from other parts of the state. As they conversed and uniformly sang the praises of Governor Burnett's actions, Major drifted away and thought of Duncan. He wondered to himself whether the Secretary of Defense might be able to learn of his whereabouts.

Major moseyed through the crowd to the group that surrounded Secretary Gregg and his associate, a man who introduced himself as Billy Yancey. Soon, it was his turn to speak privately with the former general and his friend.

"Mr. Secretary, it's a pleasure to meet you," started Major. "My name is Duncan Armstrong, but folks call me Major due to my service as commander of Company C of the Texas Rangers in Lubbock. I was wondering if you could help me."

Secretary Gregg's face turned ashen. His eyes darted to Yancey and then back to Major's again. Thus far, he hadn't said a word in response to Major.

Feeling somewhat uncomfortable, Major continued. "Anyway, sir,

I wondered if you could help calm the fears of two loving parents. Our son Duncan is out there somewhere. We have no way to get in contact with him, much less find him. Is there any way you could locate him? You know, to make sure he's okay. Again, his name is Duncan Armstrong and he works for the CIA."

CHAPTER 38

November 28
The Armstrong Ranch
Borden County, Texas

It was approaching nine in the evening when Major returned to the ranch. He'd fallen asleep in the back of the cruiser after exchanging stories with one of the troopers. His father had been a field lieutenant at Company C during Major's tenure in Lubbock. The young man's father had been instrumental in manning a felony fugitive team made up of Texas Rangers and tactical support personnel. Like Major's ancestor John Armstrong, who made a name for himself as Leander McNelly's Bulldog, Company C had an excellent track record of tracking and capturing fugitives.

He offered to find the men a place to sleep for the night in the ranch house, but they insisted upon getting home to their own families. Lucy brewed a pot of strong, black coffee and sent them on their way with the hot brew to stimulate them. A bag of cinnamon swirl toast for the road made their day.

As they waved goodbye from the front porch, the two paused to stare at the night sky. More than half of the moon was visible, and the stars seemed to shine exceptionally brightly.

"There's nothing like a Texas sky at night," said Lucy in a whisper. "In a way, it's sad to think about what's happening in the rest of the country. I doubt they can enjoy this. We were very fortunate, Major."

Major hesitated before speaking. While the men were waiting for their coffee, he and Lucy hadn't had a chance to discuss the meeting. He was anxious to tell her, although he was uncertain of her reaction.

Truth be told, he wasn't a hundred percent certain he was okay with the decisions made this afternoon concerning the fate of Texas.

"Let's go inside," he began. "A lot happened in Austin that will change the course of Texas and our nation."

While Major got comfortable, Lucy fixed them a mug of coffee and a piece of cinnamon swirl bread. She spread some softened butter across the top for extra flavor. When she returned, Major had settled on the hearth in front of the fire. The warmth helped his aching back, which was sore from the six hundred miles of travel.

He dipped his bread in the hot brew and took a bite. *Nothing like it*, he thought to himself before he began.

"Lucy, Marion has done several things that we were unaware of. She has dispatched law enforcement to every major road leading into Texas and sealed our borders. With the help of Kregg Deur, she's recruited deputies along the border towns to assist in the effort. Essentially, Texas has closed itself off from the rest of the country."

"Wow, can she do that? I mean—"

Major cut her off. "Wait, there's more. After a lot of discussion, or should I say *convincin'*, today in Austin, Marion announced her intentions to gather the legislature tomorrow to formally secede from the union."

"Wait. You mean officially? All that talk over all these years is going to happen?"

"Yes. She claims to have the overwhelming support of the legislature, and the vote will be fast-tracked tomorrow. By the end of the day, Texas will be a republic once again."

Lucy set down her coffee and handed the rest of her bread to Major to finish. She rested her elbows on her knees and dropped her chin to her clasped hands. Major elected to let this information soak in for a moment. Finally, she spoke. "Why did she call you there?"

"Personally, I think Marion had already made up her mind about this. I think she was including ranchers and other community leaders from around the state to make us feel included. If there is any pushback from Texans, she'll look to us to help sell the benefits of secession."

"First, are you totally on board with this? And does it really matter?"

Major chuckled as he finished off her cinnamon bread. "It doesn't really matter. The decision is made. Now, I'm not sure who I'm supposed to sell it to. I don't plan on leaving the ranch very often unless it's absolutely necessary. And I'm sure as heck not gonna invite folks into our home to talk about it."

Lucy continued. "When would this take effect?"

"For all intents and purposes, it already took effect when she closed the border. Officially, as soon as the vote passes, she'll notify the president."

Lucy stood and walked slowly toward the window. She parted the curtains to look out into the darkness. Major anticipated her next question.

"Any Texan who found themselves out of state when this hit will be allowed through the checkpoints by showing their identification."

"What if they don't have any for some reason, like Duncan, who always has to travel in secret?" asked Lucy as she turned and studied the news broadcast from the BBC on DirecTV. The screen read *President to Issue Address*.

"It may take longer to get through the processing stations, but with social security and some basic identifying information, they'll be allowed in."

While Lucy's primary concern was for her children, she also considered the ramifications of secession. She pointed toward the screen, which caused Major to stand so he could see.

"The president will never stand for this, although I'm not sure what she's gonna do about it. My guess is she's preoccupied at the moment."

"It looks like we're about to find out," said Major.

CHAPTER 39

November 28
Raven Rock Mountain Complex
Liberty Township, Pennsylvania

The few members of the international media allowed into the Raven Rock Complex were growing restless. Over the last two days, outlets like the BBC, *Der Spiegel,* and CNN International from London had chartered planes capable of carrying their satellite news trucks to the United States. Each media team also included a maintenance truck to keep the vehicles fueled as they traveled from point to point, beaming up to their satellites the biggest news event since 9/11.

The media was told to prepare for a major address from the president followed by a brief opportunity to ask questions. The live feeds were rolling, and the reporters were struggling to fill up airtime as they awaited the president, who was fifteen minutes late.

The small media room resembled the White House press briefing room when in use by the president. The *blue goose,* the nickname for the large blue podium adorned with the seal of the President of the United States, was flanked on each side by the United States flag and the flag of the President of the United States, which consisted of the presidential coat of arms on a dark blue background.

To the casual viewer, the upcoming address did not seem out of the ordinary. However, President Harman was about to make history.

The president, followed by her chief of staff and Director of Homeland Security Pickering, finally appeared at the podium, wearing a classic MA-1 bomber-style flight jacket bearing the presidential seal. She nodded to the members of the media and wished them good afternoon.

"My fellow Americans and those watching from around the world, America is the victim of a brutal, unconscionable attack. Last Friday, two electromagnetic pulse weapons were detonated in the Earth's atmosphere near Portland, Oregon, on our west coast and in the vicinity of Trenton, New Jersey, on our east coast. At the moment of detonation of these nuclear warheads, a massive pulse of energy was spread across our magnetic field, overwhelming our electronics from computers to communications equipment to most vehicles.

"The attacks of Pearl Harbor and 9/11 pale in comparison to the severity of these nuclear detonations. At this time, forty-eight states are without power, with only Hawaii and Texas spared. Hawaii, which obtains the majority of its electricity from oil-fired plants, relies upon imported oil to maintain its power grid. Those imports have stopped because our West Coast ports are closed.

"Texas, through judicious planning in partnership with the federal government, continues to maintain its separate and independent power grid. As a result, the state of Texas will remain a valuable resource during our rebuilding effort.

"My highest priority as Commander-in-Chief is the security of the American people. Our military has kept us safe from terrorist threats by ISIL and al-Qaeda. They have effectively monitored and contained North Korea and Iran, until now.

"Although my focus tonight will be on the immediate issue of rebuilding our great nation, the perpetrators of this unprovoked attack, North Korea and Iran, will be held to account. The United Nations has already scheduled an emergency meeting in Brussels to address this issue. At this time diplomats are being evacuated from Washington and New York to Europe. Justice will be served in due course.

"We must first focus our attention on helping our fellow Americans through these difficult times. Americans are concerned about their health and safety. Many have already run out of food for their families. With winter approaching, proper shelter will become an issue. Without fully operational medical facilities, our citizens could die from common colds or simple cuts.

"At this time, my administration is working diligently to restore power with the assistance of our allies. Assessments of the damage to our grid are under way and the parts to repair the systems are being acquired from abroad. In the meantime, the Federal Emergency Management Agency, FEMA, working in conjunction with the Department of Homeland Security, led by Director Carla Pickering standing to my right, will begin disbursing food and fresh water to the largest population centers, where our efforts can impact the most people.

"I have signed a series of emergency executive orders regarding continuity of government, establishment of regional FEMA headquarters, and to insure the protection of our citizens, I've taken the extraordinary step of preparing a Declaration of Martial Law.

"This is virtually unprecedented within the United States, but these are extraordinary times. Throughout American history, martial law has been used under limited circumstances such as the aforementioned attack on Pearl Harbor and after major natural disasters. In order to restore order and protect the American people during this recovery process, there is simply no other way to gain control of the societal collapse our nation is experiencing.

"At this time, I'd like to allow Secretary Pickering the opportunity to read the executive summary of the declaration for the benefit of viewers. Complete copies of the Declaration of Martial Law will be distributed to the media present and later posted at public buildings across the country. Thank you."

The president stepped aside, and Pickering settled in behind the podium. She immediately began reading the summary.

"Thank you, Madam President. Let me expand on one of the president's statements regarding dissemination of this declaration. It will be delivered to the United States Postal Service for posting in a conspicuous place. It will also be made available through the offices of the governors of each state.

"Part one, purpose of this declaration. It is the policy of the United States to maintain a comprehensive and effective continuity capability composed of continuity-of-operations and continuity-of-government programs in order to ensure the preservation of our form of government under the Constitution and the continuing performance of national essential functions under all conditions. In addition, it is the duty of the United States to protect and serve our citizens. Therefore, the president through executive orders has declared the United States to be in a state of *catastrophic emergency*.

"A catastrophic emergency means any incident, regardless of location, that results in extraordinary levels of mass casualties, damage, or disruption severely affecting the United States population, infrastructure, environment, economy, or government functions. The authority granted to FEMA in this executive order shall be used to strengthen our national defense preparedness, and to assist federal, state, and local law enforcement during this catastrophic emergency.

"FEMA is hereby granted broad and sweeping powers to effectuate the purposes of this declaration. Each regional FEMA headquarters will continue to operate under the direction of the Department of Homeland Security.

"In order to maintain security and order and provide essential services to the citizens of America, curfews will be established, and until further notice, there will be a suspension of certain provisions of the United States Constitution, including, but not limited to, civil law, civil rights, habeas corpus, and such other and general provisions as may be determined in the national interest by the Office of the President.

"As a result, certain freedoms enjoyed by our citizens must be temporarily suspended as the recovery and rebuilding process takes place. This necessarily involves a suspension of certain rights afforded by the Bill of Rights.

"The First Amendment right of free speech and the press are hereby restricted to the extent such speech or written word is deemed intended to incite a riot or hostilities against the United States.

"The Second Amendment right to bear arms is suspended. All weapons, magazines, ammunition, and related accessories are hereby declared unlawful and shall be voluntarily, or forcibly, surrendered to law enforcement.

"The Fourth Amendment right against unreasonable searches and seizures is hereby suspended. No citizen shall hinder or prevent any action or process in furtherance of the duties of those appointed by the Office of the President.

"The Fifth Amendment right to due process is suspended. All persons subject to appearance before the state and federal courts of the United States will now fall under the purview of the military tribunals of the United States. In conjunction with this portion of the declaration, the right to a speedy trial and to civil trials by jury are also suspended."

Pickering paused and removed her glasses as she addressed the cameras. "The remainder of the declaration deals with implementation and enforcement of the president's directives. The penalties for noncompliance are strict and will be administered swiftly. My advice to the American people is this.

"Please comply with law enforcement directives. It is our hope that the nation pulls together to help their fellow man. Share your homes. Share your food and water. Lend a hand to those in need.

"Do not make an already bad situation worse for yourselves by attempting to circumvent the law or the Declaration of Martial Law. There will be a zero-tolerance order put into effect. Again, please heed my warning. Let's work together toward rebuilding. You can do your part by complying with our directives."

Pickering nodded to the president and stepped aside. President Harman made a few additional points.

"Thank you, Secretary Pickering. Let me add one thing. It goes without saying that these actions are deemed necessary because of the position we have been placed in by this unprovoked attack. The provisions of the declaration may appear onerous to some. They are not considered permanent. As soon as order is restored to my satisfaction, I will begin to rescind all or part of the declaration as appropriate.

"Furthermore, although these provisions have gone into effect this evening at 10:00 p.m. Eastern Time, I recognize it may take several days for the content of the declaration to be disseminated around the country. I will allow a seventy-hour grace period for the nation to be made aware of these provisions before full enforcement is authorized.

"I'll take a few questions before I get back to work."

CHAPTER 40

November 28
Raven Rock Mountain Complex
Liberty Township, Pennsylvania

Nicholas Grenfell-Martin of CNN International stood and asked, "Madam President, could you provide any details on the damage sustained to the power grid, and are you prepared to give the American people a time frame for its repair?"

"We are working with Homeland Security and local utilities to assess the extent of the damage. Because of the massive impact of the electromagnetic pulse, both computer technology and electrical transformers have been destroyed. Some of these transformers are unique to the particular location in which they were used. This may require the construction of new replacements. It will take days and possibly weeks to provide a final assessment. In addition to protecting the American people, these repairs are our utmost priority."

The president pointed to the reporter from the BBC.

"Thank you, Madam President. Jason Boswell, BBC News. We are receiving reports that Governor Marion Burnett has closed the Texas borders to any nonresidents. First, has the governor committed an act of treason by closing the state's borders? Second, is the state of Texas prepared to open its vast supply of oil and gas reserves for use in your rebuilding effort?"

"Governor Abbott has no legal basis for closing access to the state of Texas to any individual lawfully present in this country. Now, whether the actions of Governor Burnett give rise to an act of treason in the eyes of the attorney general is not for me to decide. I have contacted the governor, and we had a very frank conversation. An advance team has been sent to Austin to meet with the governor, and she has welcomed them with open arms. She should also be welcoming her fellow Americans into Texas so that Texans can do their part in the recovery effort."

"Follow-up question, Madam President. If Governor Burnett continues to block access to her state, what are your options?"

"It's too early to address the specifics, Mr. Boswell. I'm sure the governor will do the right thing. Just know that all options are on the table."

The president pointed to the next reporter. "Friedrich Marsh, *Der Spiegel*."

Marsh stood to address the president.

"Madam President, regarding the martial law declaration, does it apply to Texas as well?"

"Yes, it does. Our number one priority is providing assistance to our citizens in every state, including Texas. This attack was perpetrated on America, and despite Texas being spared, they are also indirectly impacted by the collapse of the power grid. They need the federal government's protection as well."

"Madam President, is it true that you've reassigned U.S. Customs and Border patrol agents to assist local law enforcement in San Diego, Los Angeles, and Tucson in their efforts to quell rioting and looting?"

"Large parts of northern Mexico were affected by the collapse of the Western Interconnection power grid, which generates electricity in the United States for their use. That is not their fault. If allowing our borders to remain open helps those folks affected by our problems, then so be it. And let me say this as well. I have been in contact with Mexican President Raul Dominguez, who is willing to consider a limited number of our refugees to come to Mexico in exchange for our removing the draconian and onerous barriers we have placed between our nations. I agree with him, and the recall of the Border Patrol agents is in furtherance of this policy."

The president pointed to the next reporter in line. "Next up, Luis

Ramirez, Voice of America Radio."

"Madam President, you mentioned the United Nations in your opening remarks. Has the UN offered any support in the recovery effort?"

"Yes, thank you, Luis. I should have expanded on that earlier. Whenever there is a disaster or a humanitarian catastrophe, the United Nations is on the ground providing relief, support, and assistance. Our situation is no different. Through the coordinated efforts of our Department of Homeland Security and Secretary-General Ban Ki-moon, the United Nations will be providing aid throughout the nation in primarily heavily populated urban centers. Also, while our forces help maintain stability across the nation, the UN has offered a sizable peacekeeping force, who will work with FEMA in more rural parts of the country. We are fortunate to have this asset to help implement the Declaration of Martial Law."

"Last question." The president pointed to a man seated behind the first row of reporters.

"Madam President, do you consider this attack an act of war? If so, when will you make a decision on engaging your enemies?"

Despite the buildup to the EMP attack and the reports of the suffering of the American people, President Harman was still unable to make a decision. It was a question that was gnawing on her every minute of the day.

Do we lick our wounds and rebuild? Or do we strike back with a vengeance, which could trigger a nuclear-dominated World War III? There wasn't a cut-and-dried answer.

PART FIVE

Tuesday, November 29

CHAPTER 41

November 29
Sinmi-do, North Korea

Recovering from a deep coma was not just a matter of waking up and, therefore, life returned back to normal. It took days of rehabilitation and oftentimes included learning basic functions like sitting upright on the edge of a bed or learning to hold your weight in a standing position with the assistance of a walker. One of the biggest issues a comatose patient faced was abnormal muscle stiffness that could occur due to inactivity when the brain was injured.

As Duncan tossed and turned through the night, managing brief stretches of restless sleep, all he could think about were his new friend's words. *The soldiers are preparing for war. Dear Leader is calling on all men and women to fight.*

His brain wanted to deny their statements. I killed Dear Leader. *You have an imposter leading your country.* Then he began to consider the possibility that he'd shot the wrong man. He was having difficulty recalling the events. His gut told him something was off, especially because the troops were able to surround them so quickly.

Had little sister duped everyone? Was this a setup to kill a body double to provoke a war? Or was this some kind of recorded message to the people of North Korea to mask their Dear Leader's death?

After hours of running the possibilities through his head, it began to ache, and Duncan finally drifted off to sleep. He awoke to the shuffling of feet above him. He had no concept of time or even whether it was day or night. He was well hidden for a reason. The DPRK soldiers would kill him. Then they'd place everyone in this house, and their extended families, into work camps for the rest of their lives.

Nobody in North Korea really knew what was happening outside their borders. However, if they were preparing for war and calling up all conscripts of their so-called million-man army, he needed to get moving and find a way out of the country. There was no time for rest.

Duncan slowly sat up against the wall that acted as a headboard. Today, the dizziness was gone, as was the headache from the night before. The herbal medicines used by Sook worked wonders. He racked his brain to think about the location of his rifle. He remembered hiding it near a fallen tree, just uphill from a creek bed that he followed before plunging into the small river.

His rifle was his security and the only way to defend himself. If he could locate it, then the next order of business would be a boat to take him into international waters and the Yellow Sea.

Duncan swung his legs around to the side of the bed and sat upright. He fumbled in the dark to locate the kerosene lamp, which had been placed on a table by his side. A box of matches sat on the base and he struck one, providing light in the room. After the lamp was lit, he surveyed his surroundings from a new perspective.

His clothes were neatly folded on a chair next to his boots. It appeared the blood had been washed out by Sook or her family. His chest rig was slung over the back of the chair. Ammunition magazines were still inserted in the Velcro pockets, but his sidearm was nowhere in sight. He presumed it was upstairs for safekeeping, or he'd lost it during his tumble into the river.

He wiggled his toes and found the smallish wool socks to be tight on his feet. The tingling sensation was no longer present, and he attempted to stand.

Duncan's legs failed him. His knees buckled, and he began to topple forward. His attempt to grab an empty chair for support did not help matters, as his unsure footing caused it to tip over as well. Duncan spun around and crashed into the wall with his back with a thud, knocking over the chair in the process. The commotion grabbed the attention of Sook and her father, who came running down the stairs.

Sook reached him first and bent down on her knees to inspect his head. "No. No. No. Too early! You must rest more."

Duncan dismissed the pain in his upper back and began to laugh as he thought of the old commercial in which the elderly woman lay on the kitchen floor needing help. Her words caused him to chuckle as he repeated them in his mind, *I've fallen and I can't get up.*

His laughter eased the tension in the room and instantly became contagious. Both Sook and Chae laughed along with him as they helped him off the floor and back to the side of the bed.

"Thank you," he said to each of them. He took a deep breath and regained his composure. "Sook, I have to leave."

"Too early. You need recovery. Much too early." She gently pushed against his chest and shoulders, attempting to force him to lie down.

He touched her soft hands and smiled. "No, Sook. I have to leave for your safety and mine."

Her father asked her a question in Korean and she quickly responded. He looked at Duncan and waved his index finger back and forth.

"*Ani. Ani. Neomu ppalli.*"

Duncan grinned and shook his head. He didn't need an interpreter. Chae was giving him the same admonishment.

He took Sook by the hands and spoke. "Sook, listen to me. I know I need rest. There is not time for rest. The soldiers will close the ports and waters. I must go very soon."

"Rest," was her response.

"No, I must go by boat to the South. Into the Yellow Sea."

Her father asked for an interpretation, and the two spoke back and forth for several minutes. The conversation appeared to be heated for a moment and was completed with the older man sitting defiantly in the corner with his arms crossed and his chin stuck out.

Tears began to fall down Sook's face, causing Duncan concern.

"What's wrong?" he asked.

Sook wiped the tears from her face and answered, "Father will help you escape to the South. He insists you take me with you—for a better life."

Duncan looked to Chae, who continued to maintain his defiant posture. He nodded his head once before sticking his chin up in the air a little higher.

"Sook, this will be dangerous. I may die. I cannot be responsible for you."

"I told this to Father, and he said I am strong young woman. I can help you. Duncan, I do not want to leave my family."

She then turned to her father and began to plead her case. The body language of father and daughter said it all. He was adamant.

"He will not change his mind. He is old and stubborn. But he loves me."

Duncan considered his options. Having an interpreter like Sook could be helpful if they encountered a South Korean fishing vessel or even as a stalling tactic when they were boarded by any North Korean patrols. Plus, if they were successful in reaching South Korea, he would need help communicating with the locals to find his way to a military installation.

"Sook, can you help me find my way to the creek where I fell into the river? I need to find my rifle."

She hesitated for a moment before answering, "We have your small gun upstairs. You can have it back."

"Thank you, but that is not enough. I need my long gun. My battle rifle."

She turned to her father and spoke to him in Korean once again. After a few minutes of arm waving and drawing a crude map on the dusty floor, she addressed Duncan.

"My father believes he knows the creek. This has been his home since he was born. He knows the woods and rivers very well. Tomorrow, we will take you there."

Duncan smiled and patted her on the hands again. "Today, Sook. We will go look today."

CHAPTER 42

November 29
DPRK Commando Headquarters
St. Louis, Missouri

St. Louis, Missouri—the gateway to the American heartland. Its iconic Gateway Arch rose high above the Mississippi River, paying homage to America's expansion to the west. It also served as a symbol of purpose to Kyoung-Joo Lee, a commander in North Korea's Lightning Death Squad who had spent years in Canada training operatives and then sneaking them into the United States with expertly prepared forged identification documents. He'd devoted nearly a decade to providing a gateway for his operatives to enter the United States. His efforts were coming to fruition.

The plan designed by Dear Leader many years ago was fully operational now. The first step was to recruit and train an elite fighting force specializing in *soldier power skills*, as Kim referred to them. North Korea had the largest special-forces organization in the world, numbering nearly two hundred thousand men and women. They were trained in unconventional warfare and, for the purposes of this mission, insurgency operations.

Lee was just one of several dozen commanders of the Lightning Death Squads spread around America. Initially trained to attack South Korea, Kim saw an opening, an alternative to conventional thinking. When a new president was elected in South Korea, one who seemed to turn his back on the West, Kim considered a different tack.

Rather than invade South Korea for purposes of reunifying the

Korean Peninsula, he would take down his real nemesis, the mightiest empire in the history of mankind—America. And, he surmised, it would be remarkably easy. As he'd learned while studying abroad, in the words of their revered President Abraham Lincoln, *America will never be destroyed from the outside. If we falter and lose our freedoms, it will be because we destroyed ourselves from within.*

Kim had seen economic and societal collapse in his lifetime in South America. Sometimes these things evolved slowly. However, collapse could be *encouraged*. The result of his analysis was the plan to take America down to her knees.

Lee was assigned to Canada, along with two other leaders of the Lightning Death Squads. They had three counterparts in Mexico, whose primary function was to smuggle arms and commandos using drug cartels in Mexico in exchange for laundering their money through North Korea.

The money-laundering arrangement was a win-win for Kim. The Mexican cartels had just begun to invest their ill-gotten gains in the unregulated bitcoin crypto-currency. The North Koreans had used Bureau 121, their highly feared cyber operation, to steal bitcoins from crypto-currency depositories around the globe and effectively manipulate the crypto-currency trading market.

The cartels provided access to the United States. The North Koreans assisted them in their money-laundering schemes. Both sides benefitted financially from the cyber capabilities of Bureau 121.

Over the years, the number of commandos in the United States grew to an astonishing force. Through advance planning, they remained hidden from scrutiny as America's immigration battles focused on the influx from South and Central America. Illegal aliens from Asian nations weren't on anybody's radar.

The numbers of commandos grew, and with the help of the Mexican drug cartels, they were well armed with weapons and high-tech communications gear. While most of America was unable to communicate with one another, the disciplined commandos had stored their electronics in simple Faraday cages consisting of a small galvanized steel trash can, a cardboard or foam lined interior, and heavy-duty aluminum foil to wrap each component.

When the EMP attack occurred, the commandos retrieved their weapons and electronic gear. They immediately accumulated in forty-seven large cities across the United States to receive their orders.

St. Louis was one of the regional DPRK headquarters because of its centralized location. This was not Lee's primary assignment. He was considered a *rover*, one of the higher ranked officers who'd be called upon to perform special tasks. Over the years, these chosen commandos were allowed to handpick their six-man squads.

They were assigned advanced weaponry and military gear. Lee was also provided two older vehicles, a 1970 Chevrolet Suburban and a 1969 Chevrolet Blazer, which were immune to the effects of an EMP blast.

The high-ranking officers of the Lightning Death Squads met in Cheltenham, a neighborhood in the Central West End area of St. Louis. This part of the city was known for its relatively large Asian population, so many of the commandos had settled there.

The leaders discussed the objectives originally assigned to them by Dear Leader. Disrupt the Americans' command and control structure, destroy transportation routes, including the bridges along the Mississippi River, and sow seeds of chaos in the inner cities to force the American military to devote their resources to controlling their own people.

However, a wrinkle had emerged in their plan—Texas. Several hundred DPRK operatives were located in the five major metropolitan areas of the state, including El Paso, Houston, Dallas-Fort Worth, San Antonio, and Austin.

Dear Leader had learned of this two days prior and immediately issued orders via their satellite communications linkup to destroy the Texas power grid also. This task must be completed from within, he ordered, as they could not risk firing another nuclear EMP at the United States.

Lee volunteered to spearhead the operation. With his men, he'd travel the seven hundred miles to the *Lone Star State*, he said sarcastically, and show them whose star shines brightest on this planet. He vowed to raise the flag of North Korea over the Texas capitol in honor of Dear Leader.

CHAPTER 43

November 29
Oldman River
Fort Macleod, Alberta, Canada

Fort Macleod was a small town of three thousand Canadians who were proud of their history as being the first Mounted Police settlement in western Canada. Built on the Oldman River, which stretched east-to-west from the Rockies to Hudson Bay, the town boasted that it was a *small town with a big heart*. Unfortunately, the apocalypse changed a person's outlook on life.

Every small town had a persona, so to speak. Woodstock, Vermont, had been labeled the *prettiest small town in America*. Destin, Florida, was known as the *Redneck Riviera*. Pacific Grove, California, was known as *Butterfly Town, USA*. All of those labels were thrown out the window when the panic hit the populations of these villages and hamlets.

An us-versus-them mentality took hold. At first, Fort Macleod residents rallied together to lend support. But as is typical in modern society, fingers of blame began to be pointed. News trickled into the town that the power grid had collapsed because an EMP attack had been initiated against the United States.

Anger and hostility grew towards the US as a result. Canadians in Fort Macleod became upset their happy lives were disrupted because of *American drama*, as they called it. Their first actions were to close access to the town to all travelers, a practice adopted by most small Canadian towns in the region.

Their second official act was to purge the town of American expats, including famous actress and comedian Amy Schumer, who'd denounced their citizenship and moved to Fort Macleod seeking a better life.

This action by the Fort Macleod municipal government was met with some resistance by longtime residents who opposed the purge. After some debate, a compromise was achieved. Following the purge, the properties and belongings of the Americans were seized for distribution to the Canadian-born residents. In compromise, and compassion, the Americans were given a ride to the U.S.-Canada border in horse-drawn carriages so they didn't have to walk.

The civic leaders of Fort Macleod were largely part of the Nationalist Party of Canada, an unregistered political group that advocated a strong national identity based upon the promotion of Canada's European heritage and culture. As a result, the town took on an independent streak that revealed itself after the power grid collapsed.

Located at the intersection of major highways traveling east-west and north-south, town leaders decided to exact a toll from any travelers who crossed through their town. The tolls varied according to the traveler's capabilities. Resistance to payment was greeted with denied access and, if argument was involved, with swift punishment.

Once again, some local residents objected to the practice as being inhumane. They said *we should be helping people rather than stripping them of their belongings and dignity.* But after reality was explained to them that soon the town would run out of food, even those in dissent acquiesced in order to share in the spoils.

It took Cooper and the rest of the riders longer than anticipated to reach the railroad bridge, and at ten in the morning, the town of Fort Macleod was in full swing. The group took a position atop a slightly elevated hill and shared time with the binoculars. They studied the town and placed most of their attention on Route 2 where it crossed the river.

"It appears they sucker people onto the bridge," started Cooper as he relinquished his turn with the glasses. "They have four guys manning the barricades on the town side of the river, two for each lane."

"Yeah," said Pacheco. "But I also see a group hiding behind those metal buildings. When travelers come onto the bridge, this group closes them in and traps them. Then they have to give in to the town's demands."

"Pretty low-down," mumbled Riley.

Palmer stood and looked back up the highway over Cooper's head. "Guys, there's a group coming from the north. It's a wagon pulled by two horses. Looks like a family."

She handed the binoculars to Cooper, who confirmed what she'd seen. He turned the binoculars back to the metal building and the men seen by Pacheco. They were scrambling around and taking up positions behind stalled vehicles.

"It's gonna be an ambush," said Cooper.

"Should we warn 'em, Coop?" asked Palmer.

Cooper grimaced and thought about it for a moment. "Nah. Sadly, by the time we get over there to warn them off, the people from town will see us and screw up our plan. Instead, let's use their problem as a distraction to help us cross the old railroad bridge."

"Do we stick to the plan of going over one at a time like we discussed?" asked Morales.

"Yes, when the wagon approaches the bridge, I'll go across first at an easy, nonthreatening pace. Pacheco, you come next. Then Palmer, Morales, and Riley."

"Okay," said Riley. "What if we run into trouble?"

"Good question," replied Cooper. He pulled the map out of his pocket. "Once you're across, immediately follow the old rail bed to Crowsnest Highway, which runs west to east into Fort Macleod. Cross the highway and we'll meet in this open area. I can barely see it through the binoculars, but it looks like a big field. Once we're together, we'll make our way south."

"And if there's trouble?" Riley asked again.

"The main thing is to stay separated until we meet up at the rendezvous point," began Cooper as he traced his fingers along the map to illustrate his response. "It'll be out of sight from the guys on the bridge. If things go really bad, then ride south along this small road, looks like it's called eight-ten. There's a lake on the west side of the road called McBride Lake. We'll meet up there."

"Coop," interrupted Morales, "it's time."

"Okay, everybody, here we go." Cooper looked into everyone's faces as he encouraged them. "We've got this, but just in case, have your rifles ready. We don't know what those folks are capable of. Got it?"

"Yeah, let's do it," said Riley.

"You first, big brother," said Palmer as she slapped Cooper on the back.

Cooper mounted his horse and began the thousand-yard ride in clear view of the men on the bridge. They would only be able to see him through binoculars, and he hoped the distraction of the travelers would keep the town guards focused on them rather than his group.

He reached the massive railway bridge without a problem and then dismounted. The bridge, formerly part of the Canadian Pacific Railway system, had been abandoned years ago. There were several tree limbs piled up in front to discourage pedestrians, but Cooper's horse easily stepped over the debris. The four-foot-tall steel rails along the bridge helped obscure him from the highway bridge that could be seen in a distance.

As Cooper walked toward the other side, he quietly patted himself on the back for avoiding the pitfalls that awaited the family on the horse-drawn wagon. However, he became keenly aware of the extra time it took to make this crossing. Suddenly, Texas seemed like a long way from where he was.

CHAPTER 44

November 29
Oldman River
Fort Macleod, Alberta, Canada

Cooper found a low spot behind a stand of trees and waited as Pacheco crossed without difficulty. Once Palmer started her ride, Cooper left and headed for the highway to cross into the field. As he rode, he constantly surveilled the fields to his left and right, looking for any signs of activity. There was a white block house to their west, but it appeared to be abandoned. There were no vehicles parked near it, and one of the windows had been broken out.

He reached the highway and crossed into the field, where he settled in to observe his surroundings. There was no pedestrian traffic or riders on horseback. It was deserted and appeared to be a perfect way to avoid town. The melting snow even provided him a pretty good view to the south along the small county road.

Within minutes, Pacheco joined him, which meant Palmer was standing watch on the other side. He sent Pacheco ahead toward their meeting place at McBride Lake. When Palmer arrived, Cooper sent her south as well, and he ventured onto the highway after retrieving the binoculars. Standing in the middle of a major highway without fear of oncoming vehicles was odd to Cooper. It was serene in a way, even enjoyable. But best of all, there was no indication that they'd drawn the attention of the men guarding the highway bridge or any other residents of Fort Macleod.

Then the sound of a gunshot pierced the quiet surroundings. Followed by another and another. A final shot rang out and he could hear the sound of men shouting at the railroad bridge.

Cooper pulled his rifle from his scabbard and raced toward the gunshots. Horses were galloping in his direction, with one of the riders slumped over the front of his horse and the other rider waving his arms as they got closer. Cooper encouraged his horse to go faster as it trotted along the old rail bed. Within a minute, he met up with Riley and Morales.

Riley was shouting. "He drew on us, Coop! The guy shot Morales in the back!"

The three horses almost collided as the adrenaline of both rider and horse pumped through their bodies. Cooper regained control of his horse and swung him back around. He pulled alongside Morales, who had blood pouring from the back of his shirt.

Clang! Clang! Clang!

A bell was being rung in Fort Macleod.

"They're sounding an alarm in town!" shouted Cooper. He leaned over to Morales. "Can you ride?"

"Yeah, Coop. Go!" he said with a groan.

The warning bell was ringing again, and the sounds of vehicles could be heard in the distance. Cooper assumed the town had a few operating vehicles that were too old to feel the effects of the EMP.

"We can't outrun their trucks," he shouted as he took off toward the highway. "We need to go a little farther west and then head down through the fields to the lake. The trucks will get bogged down. Plus, we can use that tree line at the foothills over there for cover."

Riley and Morales kept pace with Cooper. With Morales focusing on staying upright, Riley and Cooper continued to look behind them to see if they'd been discovered.

"They wouldn't know where to start," Cooper shouted to Riley. "Our tracks go in both directions. I hope they go to the railway bridge first. That'll buy us some time."

Minutes later they traveled up an incline and found themselves in the middle of a wind farm. Dozens of two-hundred-foot-tall wind turbines dotted the landscape. The large three-blade structures slowly turned with a swooshing sound. As they crested the top of the hill where the farm had the most turbines in operation, they were able to see McBride Lake in the distance.

"Whoa," Cooper instructed his horse to stop. He was still holding the binoculars in his left hand. While he had the high ground, he elected to see if they were being pursued. If not, he'd slow the pace after looking into Morales's wounds.

"What about it, Coop?" asked Riley.

"Nothing. I think we're good." Cooper dismounted and grabbed the reins of his horse and walked over to Morales. "How're you doin', buddy?"

Morales opened his coat with his right hand and revealed his left shoulder. "Caught me in the shoulder. I think it went all the way through."

"He shot you in the back?" asked Cooper.

"Yeah," replied Riley. "The guy came out of nowhere waving a pistol. He shot Morales and then drew on me. I shot him, Coop. Twice. I mean, I knocked him down with the first round, and then, like, well, I finished him off."

Cooper looked around again and mounted his horse. "Morales, listen. It looks like the bullet came through your shoulder and out the other side. I think that's a good thing, but honestly, I don't know. Are you sure you can keep riding? We've got a couple of miles to go."

"I'm good, Coop, but I'm gettin' cold. I know the sun's warmer than yesterday, but it seems to be gettin' colder, you know?"

Coop knew what that meant—shock. He turned to Riley. "Riley, I need you to ride ahead and find the others. Immediately find a place to camp for the night where we can keep our fire hidden from this road. Look on the west side of the lake, got it?"

"Yeah, what about you guys?" asked Riley.

"We're gonna take it easy so Morales doesn't get banged around too much. He's losing blood. Tell them to get a tent ready, fire, boiling water, and the medical supplies. We'll be along shortly."

"Got it!" said Riley as he turned to ride.

"Riley, make sure the camp is hidden from the road. These guys will come looking for us."

"I'm on it!" he replied as he took off.

"Coop, your brother saved my life," Morales said in a whisper as he mustered his strength to talk. "I never saw the guy comin'. He would've put another bullet in my back if Riley hadn't shot him first."

Cooper looked to the sky and rolled his neck on his shoulders. He recalled the conversations he'd had with Duncan and Dallas after they'd killed someone in battle. *A lot of guys never get over it*, Duncan had said. *It really messes them up.*

Cooper thought of those words as he considered the mental anguish his brother might be going through. Then he wondered to himself how many others they would have to kill before they arrived at the Armstrong Ranch.

CHAPTER 45

November 29
Main Post, Fort Hood
Killeen, Texas

The state of Texas had implemented an extravagant closed-circuit television system for the primary purpose of monitoring traffic conditions across the state. In addition, as a cost-savings measure, the governor's office instructed state workers in outlying counties to communicate with their various department heads in Austin via the closed-circuit system rather than waste time and taxpayer dollars on lengthy travel.

After her reaching an agreement with Secretary Gregg yesterday, and based upon her optimism regarding today's secession vote, Governor Burnett instructed her chief security officer to equip the Main Post at Fort Hood with closed-circuit TV access.

Today's special session of the Texas legislature regarding the secession vote had been closed to all media and the public. It would not be broadcast to any outlets except those connected to the CCTV communications network.

Secretary Gregg was joined at Fort Hood by Adjutant General Deur to discuss bolstering the state's border defenses. The debacle at the I-10 bridge near Beaumont had created a perception problem for the governor and her efforts. Several legislators began to question whether secession was feasible. Secretary Gregg and Deur were charged with finding ways to avoid the mass buildup of refugees at their border and to consider involving the military in the effort.

They paused from their deliberations to watch as the CCTV cameras went live, broadcasting the vote across the state. They caught the tail end of the governor's speech.

"Texas is more than a place on a map. It's our home and the place where we raise our families. Unlike other states, Texas has not been co-opted by the political points of view of outsiders. We have resisted the federal government's offers of grants and appropriations in order to force morals and values upon us that Texans don't agree with.

"Now we face a dilemma. All of our efforts, all of our planning, everything we've sacrificed has come down to this moment. Washington intends to strip us of our resources, including energy, food, and quite possibly, monetary reserves. They've made it clear that Texas belongs to Washington and the federal government. I disagree.

"Texans have taken measures to prepare for this type of catastrophic event while other states have spent their money like drunken sailors in a brothel. It would not be fair to Texans, nor would it solve America's problems, to allow the federal government into our borders for the purpose of leading us down the same path of ruin that they face.

"My fellow Texans, the bottom line is this. We have a duty to protect our citizens, first and foremost. The only way to accomplish that task is to remain strong, free, and independent. Secession is the only way, and today we can take the steps to recreate the Republic of Texas once and for all.

"Join me in this historic vote as we declare Texas to be free and independent. Vote a resounding yes for secession from the United States!"

The camera panned the joint session of the Texas legislature as nearly all of the one hundred fifty members of the legislature and thirty-one senators stood to applaud.

Secretary Gregg laughed and shook his head. "She can fire them up, can't she?"

"Oh, yes," said Deur. "I've watched her so many times. She has a knack for reading the crowd and telling them exactly what they need to hear to follow her lead. Don't tell her I said this, but she's a lot like a fortune-teller in that respect. She watches for reactions and expressions that give her insight into her audience. If something is working, she continues to emphasize that point. I've never seen anything like it."

"It's an incredible talent, to be sure," said Secretary Gregg. "Between us, will she be able to withstand the enormous pressure that President Harman will put on her? This news will hit Raven Rock like an H-bomb, pardon the pun."

"She's tough as nails and has nerves of steel. When she's standing on her convictions, nothing will back her down."

"That's good," started Secretary Gregg. "What you and I are planning for the protection of the new Republic of Texas will certainly not be deemed acceptable to President Harman and may cause Texans to shudder as well."

"Are you talking about the rules of engagement for the folks manning the border blockades?"

"Yes," said Secretary Gregg. "I experienced a period of time in the Middle East when the ROEs caused our troops more deaths than the enemy. Soldiers and law enforcement personnel can't be restrained in doing their duty by political concerns."

"I don't disagree, but it may be difficult to convince our people to fire upon their fellow Americans when the time comes."

Secretary Gregg took a deep breath and exhaled before he spoke. "That's just the thing, Deur. Those people on the other side of the border are no longer fellow Americans. They're from another country, and they're trying to enter ours."

CHAPTER 46

November 29
Sinmi-do, North Korea

For the rest of the morning, Duncan performed a variety of stretching exercises to bring his stiff body back to life. By lunchtime, he was able to climb the stairs to allow filtered sunlight to wash his body. He no longer felt like he was being held captive in a dungeon even though he voluntarily stayed in the basement for the safety of the family.

After a light lunch, he resumed his exercise, stepping up the pace in the cramped basement to the point he could jog in place for several minutes at a time. He was not ready to run a marathon, but he would certainly rely upon his drive and desire to hike up the mountain in search of his rifle.

Sook returned shortly after lunch. "Father and I took the small skiff up the river near the point where you fell in. He recognized the creek pouring over the bluff. He is certain the creek is the place to begin looking."

"How far upriver can we take the boat, and is it possible to climb the mountain?" asked Duncan.

"Walking up the road might draw attention, and we do not have a car. Father will take us by boat to a trail. That trail will lead up to the bluff. Then we can approach the road through the woods. It will be much safer."

"When can we leave?" he asked.

Sook reached into her left pocket and pulled out Duncan's knife and sheath, which he strapped around his leg. Then she removed his sidearm from her other pocket and set it on the bed next to him.

He hesitated, and before he picked it up, he considered the fact this was a huge leap of faith for Sook's family. They were now placing their trust in this unknown American. Duncan stood and reached out his hands to Sook.

She took them and looked down to the floor. Duncan was more than a foot taller than she was. He leaned down to look into her eyes.

"Sook, thank you. I have prayed and thanked God for you since the moment I woke up. I will do my best to protect you and your family. Okay?"

Sook smiled and then surprised Duncan with what she said. "We, too, have prayed to God for your health, recovery, and safety."

Duncan was surprised. "Wait. You have? You've prayed for me?"

"Yes, Duncan, we have. We are Christians, but it is a well-hidden secret, just as we hide you. There are many of us in North Korea. We cannot practice our faith, as religions are forbidden and severely punished."

"I had no idea," mumbled Duncan.

"The Great Leader, Kim Il-sung, only allowed the state philosophy of *Juche*, which means self-reliance. Dear Leader has said individuals are the masters of their own destiny, and as a collective, all North Koreans are masters of the revolution to achieve true socialism."

"Do you have a Bible?"

"Yes. My grandfather gave it to Father before he died. The pages are worn, but the words are alive within us."

Duncan smiled and spontaneously hugged Sook, which surprised her. Yet she didn't pull away. He finally leaned back and they broke their embrace.

"Sook, you and I, with God's help, will leave here safely. I believe we've been brought together for this reason. You are an angel and I am one of God's soldiers. Together, we'll survive."

She wiped a tear from her face and smiled. "Yes. Time to go." As she led Duncan to the stairs, she provided him a tattered jacket and a fisherman's cap. Duncan found them to be a perfect fit, and he pulled the cap over his face.

As he emerged at the top of the stairs, nine women and children awaited him. They all looked at him in wonder as he towered over the group. Slowly and cautiously, the children approached him and hugged his legs. Soon, he was surrounded by half a dozen young kids under the age of eight. He reached down and picked up the youngest, a little girl barely out of diapers. She grinned from ear-to-ear and playfully grabbed at his cap.

Duncan suddenly wished he had a camera to show the world what life in North Korea was really like. It wasn't just made up of wealthy dictators and unscrupulous soldiers. There were families trying to survive with few or no possessions. Eating was just part of the challenge. Avoiding suppression from Kim Jong-un's tyrannical rule was the other. This Christian family, in the most unexpected part of the world, had taken him in, an American, and nursed him back to health despite the risk of being separated and thrown into work camps.

All they asked in return was he help the family's oldest child find a better life away from this madness. Duncan promised God he'd deliver on that commitment.

CHAPTER 47

November 29
McBride Lake
Alberta, Canada

Palmer readied the tent and gave instructions to Riley and Pacheco. She had studied how to deal with gunshot wounds with her mother. The two women of the Armstrong family had taken it upon themselves to learn about first aid techniques and dealing with certain types of trauma. They agreed there was no substitute for a real medical professional, but after TEOTWAWKI, they would have to act as the family medical team.

"Coop, carefully help him off his horse," she began to bark the instructions. "Even though the bullet went through, he may have broken bones or arteries we can't see. He has a lot of blood loss, probably forced out of his body from the ride."

Cooper and Pacheco helped Morales dismount. They assisted him inside the tent, where Palmer had laid out a sleeping bag and several towels. She also had a stack of blankets at the ready.

"Help me lay him flat on the sleeping bag," she continued. "All of this blood loss can cause his blood pressure to plummet. If he's been complaining about being cold, it's possible he could be going into shock."

Morales lowered his body and then he smiled. "Hey, Doc. I'm right here, you know. All that *he* and *him* makes me think I'm missin' something."

Palmer laughed and then placed a towel under his shoulder. "Okay, mister patient. You lie flat so the blood can circulate to your brain. Here's a small pillow to keep you comfortable."

"Much better, thanks," said Morales.

"Pacheco, keep pressure on the front and rear wounds for me. You'll need to apply pressure with both hands to keep him from squirming."

Then Palmer turned her attention to Morales. "I need to get you bandaged up and then wrapped in these horse blankets. Then I'm gonna zip you up in the sleeping bag. I've got to move quickly, so I apologize for jostling you about."

Cooper stuck his head out of the tent and looked outside. "Palmer, if you don't need us, we need to establish perimeter security. The town may come looking for us, and I'm pretty sure none of us wanna be lyin' there next to Morales gettin' fixed up."

"Good idea," she said. "If I need anything, I'll holler. Before you go, will you fetch that warm water in the campfire coffee pot for me? I need to clean his wounds."

"I'm on it," replied Cooper. "Send Pacheco when you're done with him."

Palmer looked in the small medicine kit included in their get-home bags. There were two large sterile gauze pads, which would be used to cover the wounds after she cleaned them. The smaller gauze pads worked to wipe blood away from the openings.

Then she retrieved two tampons from her backpack. She opened the first one and began taking it apart.

"Hold up!" said Morales, suddenly finding the strength to raise his voice. "What's that thing for?"

"I gotta plug the holes, mister patient. Deal with it."

Palmer smiled as she wiped the wound clean one last time and irrigated it with bottled water. After a pat down with a towel, she gently inserted the tampon into his shoulder. Morales groaned in pain.

Palmer moved quickly to apply Neosporin antibiotic ointment around the wound. Then she set into place the large gauze pad before she ripped first aid tape into strips and gently placed them across his shoulder.

"Now I'm gonna do the other side. I'll need you to roll over."

She and Pacheco worked together to put Morales on his side. The bleeding had slowed, allowing for a quicker cleanup. Following the same procedure as the front, she plugged the wound, sealed the area with gauze, and then wrapped his entire shoulder by stretching self-adhering bandage tape over the wounds, under his armpit, and back over again until the injured area was immobilized. As she finished the wrapping, she let Pacheco join the others to watch over the camp.

"Thank you, Palmer," said Morales.

She zipped up the sleeping bag and covered him with the blankets. "Are you feeling warmer now?"

"Yes, much better. The pain is not too bad. It just throbs, and my shoulder feels really hot."

Palmer rolled off her knees and sat with her legs crossed under her. She took a cloth and wiped the sweat off his forehead. She didn't like the fever.

"I'm gonna give you some Tylenol. It may or may not help with your pain, but it might bring this fever down. Morales, I'm not gonna lie. You need a real doctor and some antibiotics as soon as possible. All I've done is stop the bleeding. That's the immediate life-threatening problem."

Morales reached for the water bottle with his good arm, and Palmer gently raised his head to help him drink.

She continued with her honest assessment. "If I thought help was only an hour or two away, I wouldn't be concerned. We can't go back to Fort Macleod, and the next decent-sized town is in Montana."

"I get it, Palmer. I'm gonna die." His smile told her that Morales was kidding.

"Joke like that again, and I'll punch you where it hurts!"

"Just kidding! Gee, Palmer. So serious. You've fixed me up great. A good night's sleep and I'll be ready to ride. It'll feel better when I'm back in the States."

The two continued their chat when Cooper reentered the tent. "I've got good news. It doesn't appear that they're gonna chase us down here. We'll stay on guard, but as far as I'm concerned, we can hunker down here for the night."

"Great news," said Palmer.

"We'll try to wake up again before sunrise," Cooper continued. "Will he be able to ride?"

"I'll be ready, no matter what. Another day or so and we'll be in Montana. I'm not gonna hold us up. I swear."

CHAPTER 48

November 29
Undisclosed Bunker
Pyongyang, North Korea

While military strategists around the globe debated Kim Jong-un's next move, endlessly exploring ICBM trajectories, payload weights, and re-entry shields, Kim and his top advisors continued with their preparations for the ground invasion of the United States.

As a defensive precaution and a show of strength, the DRPK military positioned a dozen Hwasong-15 missiles throughout the country on their mobile launchers equipped with Kim's super-large heavy warhead—a hydrogen bomb.

The Hwasong-15 ICBM weaponry system was placed on hair-trigger alert by the military. If fired upon by the U.S. or its allies, Kim vowed not to hesitate. He intended to fulfill his promise to other Southeastern Asian countries to avoid an all-out war. However, if provoked, he warned the total annihilation of South Korea, Japan, and the United States would be achieved.

He'd gathered his top leaders, and his sister, Kim Yo-jong, to be present during the back-channel discussions with the Iranian leaders. The Iranians had been promised the opportunity to attack Israel with its newly procured nuclear weapons and rid the planet of the infidels once and for all. Kim asked them to stand down in order to determine whether a larger nuclear conflict could be avoided.

Kim was walking a fine line between keeping his Iranian partners happy and foolishly entering into a nuclear Armageddon with the Americans. After a briefing from the vice chairman of the Worker's Party Central Committee, who assured Dear Leader that the entirety of their nuclear forces was ready, Kim instructed his aides to bring the Iranian leadership onto their large-panel monitors in the room.

The conversation occurred through an interpreter.

The head of Iran's Revolutionary Guard confirmed they had achieved a range of sixteen hundred miles with their missile technology—enough to strike all of Europe. He continued. "We have kept the range of missiles at twenty-four hundred kilometers, but not due to a lack of technology. You have provided us the ability to reach farther points, perhaps even the United States' southeast coast. However, we are following a strategic doctrine, just as you. So far, we have not seen Europe as a threat to us, so we did not increase, or test, a longer-range missile. However, if Europe wants to provoke us in order to protect the infidels in Israel, or if America participates in any form of retaliatory strike, we will certainly adjust accordingly."

Kim spoke next. "Your missiles can reach most American forces and interests in the region. They more than cover your enemies, Israel and Saudi Arabia, if they intervene."

The Iranians were silent for a moment. Suddenly, they all stood as the country's Supreme Leader, Ayatollah Ali Khamenei, made his first appearance before Kim Jong-un. Surprised by his appearance, Kim stood out of respect. The rest of his leadership team did as well.

Ayatollah Khamenei took a seat in the center of his contingent, flanked by the president of Iran and the heads of the Revolutionary Guard. Without introduction, he spoke directly to Kim.

"Our people have been waiting for this moment for centuries. Our two mighty nations have worked together to share technology, innovation, and military strategies. Our promise to you was to distract the American forces who could attack you from the west. At the same time, we stand ready to unleash the wrath of Allah upon Israel. All of our ballistic missiles are ready to launch strikes on the U.S. forces who surround us. However, each day of delay in launching our attack allows the enemy to prepare.

"Further, we have, as promised, committed our new naval vessels to carry your ground forces to North America. These ships will make port in Mexico by tomorrow. The flag of our Islamic Republic flies proud as we escort your elite forces to do battle.

"Chairman Kim, all of our obligations to you are fulfilled. It is now time for action."

The Ayatollah had laid down their position in less than two minutes. Kim had expected this ultimatum, just not so soon.

"I appreciate your kind words, Ayatollah Khamenei. Do not mistake the Democratic People's Republic of Korea's delay as a sign of us losing our resolve. Our forces require forty-eight hours to position themselves for the next phase of the attack on the United States. I understand your frustration, but I ask for your patience as we properly position ourselves militarily and politically with our mutual allies."

"Chairman Kim, forty-eight hours. Then we unleash our fury on Israel."

The Ayatollah stood and bowed slightly. Kim jumped out of his chair and bowed in return. The much younger man, who had been in power in North Korea for eleven years, rarely got the opportunity to speak directly with the leaders of other countries. For decades, the rogue state was treated as a geopolitical outcast, tolerated by the likes of Iran, Russia, and China for strategic purposes, but ostracized by the rest.

He was ready to take his place in history, but he needed two more things to fall into place—his commandos must be in place in America, and he needed an excuse to unleash the hounds.

CHAPTER 49

November 29
Sinmi-do, North Korea

Chae owned two fishing vessels. One was a twenty-eight-foot trawler, which enabled him to go to the far reaches of Korea Bay and, at times, when conditions were right, into the Yellow Sea and international waters. His second boat, a small flat-bottom boat, resembled a Boston Whaler fishing vessel with no canopy. The center console had no dials or gadgets, only a steering wheel, a throttle, and an old dash-mounted compass.

He used the flat-bottom boat for fishing the rivers and inland coastline. The trawler was used for deep-sea excursions. At times, he'd take both toward the Yellow Sea, one to catch black-faced spoonbill or grouper, the other to catch the occasional shortfin mako shark. It was considered a delicacy in North Korea, and a catch was often traded to the DPRK's port authority for a larger portion of his regular haul.

Chae had a good reputation with the local government officials and was rarely questioned about his activities. He'd learned early on that absolute power corrupts absolutely. By occasionally offering a trophy fish as a gift, he could feed his family better than others and would be given a pass if his haul that day was shy of his expected quota. Chae's goodwill could play an important role in assisting Sook and Duncan as they attempted their escape.

Chae fired the Evinrude E200 outboard engine with ease. Manufactured in the United Kingdom many years ago, the E200 provided him lots of power for offshore fishing excursions and excellent fuel mileage. The four five-gallon gas containers at the rear of the boat provided him long-range capability when deep-sea fishing.

He took the boat upriver at a steady pace, not wanting to attract the attention of any onlooking soldiers or curious residents who might feel compelled to notify the authorities of Chae's perceived suspicious behavior. He slowed and pointed toward a sandy bank that was tucked into the bluff.

As he pulled in, Sook commented to Duncan, "I know this trail. It is a steady climb to the top. We can begin your search easily."

Duncan looked upriver toward the bluffs as they rose above the river. None of it looked familiar to him. Only his body could sense the fall he'd experienced into the fairly shallow river.

Sook hugged her father and smiled at Duncan. Chae encouraged them both with his best English. "Go. Go."

While Chae fished from the bow of his boat below, Sook and Duncan climbed to the top of the bluff. Understandably winded, Duncan stopped periodically to catch his breath and stretch his limbs. In about thirty minutes, they reached the top of the trail, and Sook led the way toward the road. Their plan was to walk higher up the terrain about fifteen feet from the road bed to avoid detection. Then they could begin their search for Duncan's Barrett.

Duncan was impressed with Sook's movements through the forest. The melting snow made their footing precarious, but it did prevent the threat of snapping branches. Fortunately, the sun's warmth had prevented the wet snow from forming into a crunchy ice, which would have taken away their opportunity to remain hidden.

Sook slowed and raised her hand, indicating that Duncan should stop. She pointed to her ear and cupped her hand to listen carefully. Duncan did the same, and he picked up the sound of trickling water up ahead. She turned to look at him, and he shrugged, mouthing the word *maybe*.

They pressed forward, side by side now, as the babbling brook grew louder. Sook picked up the pace as they reached the small trickle of water. Duncan tapped her on the arm and pointed.

"There. Do you see the fallen tree by the road? Also, do you see the bark shredded off that pine tree? The rifle should be there."

"You first. I will hide by the road and watch for soldiers."

Duncan moved swiftly toward the tree. The memories were returning. Park had been shot, and Duncan had hoisted him on his shoulder. It was impossible to use his rifle for defense, so he'd kicked the weapon under the fallen tree and pushed pine needles up against it.

After crawling up a slight incline, he reached the tree and fell to his knees. He was frantically digging out the wet snow and debris when he heard voices. A man was speaking authoritatively from down the road. He could see two figures jogging up the gravel shoulder in his direction. Then he heard Sook's voice.

She'd stepped onto the road and was speaking to the two soldiers. Their weapons were raised as they ordered her to raise her hands above her head. As she did so, she unbuttoned her jacket and allowed it to open. Then her tone of voice changed.

Naturally, Duncan couldn't understand what she was saying, but there was no mistaking her tone. She was using God's greatest gift to the female gender. The ability to disarm the male of the species with her sexuality.

Duncan kept his eyes on the three of them as Sook worked her magic. The soldiers shouldered their weapons and offered her a cigarette. They lit it for her and the game commenced. Sook playfully swatted at the soldiers, even running her hand down one of the men's faces. She playfully spun around and wandered toward the other side of the road, causing the young men to turn their backs to Duncan as they followed their prey.

It was the opening he needed. Resisting the urge to use his sidearm for fear of drawing unwanted attention, Duncan gently removed his knife from its sheath and grabbed the steel blade with his fingers. Catlike, he climbed the slight embankment and steadied his nerves. He could disable one of the soldiers, but he'd have to move quickly to overtake the other to keep Sook from being in danger.

As she continued the playful conversation, Duncan gripped the blade, ready to throw it at his target. Lightning fast, he found his narrow throwing line and focused on the base of the man's skull. Unconsciously, from a lifetime of practice, he aimed, pulled his arm back, and released the knife like he was throwing a baseball.

The blade stuck deep into the back of the soldier's neck, whose now dead body stood in limbo for a moment before collapsing. Duncan tried to close the gap and tackle the other soldier, but his right foot slipped out from under him, causing him to drop to his knees.

The soldier deftly pivoted and unshouldered his rifle to fire upon Duncan when he heard the loud sound of a crack like a tree limb had been broken over someone's knee.

The soldier screamed in pain and fell toward the pavement. As he dropped, Sook swung her right leg around and kicked the soldier in the temple, causing blood to fly through the air on the snowy ground in front of Duncan.

Silence.

Neither soldier moved. Duncan found his footing and pulled his sidearm as he approached the two men who lay dead on the road. With his weapon pointed at their heads, he checked for a pulse to make sure. He shrugged as he pulled the serrated blade out of the upper spine of his kill, leaving a hole for blood and spinal fluid to ooze onto the snow. He crouched over the dead bodies, staring at the results as he wiped off the blood on the man's uniform and returned the knife to its sheath. Then Duncan turned his attention to Sook.

She stared at the bodies for a moment and casually walked to retrieve her jacket. Duncan helped her put it on and then studied her face. Her eyes were steely cold. With two well-placed kicks, she'd killed one of the DPRK's menacing soldiers.

"Are you okay?" he asked her as she buttoned her coat.

"Yes. My grandfather taught me taekwondo."

Taekwondo was a Korean form of martial arts that emphasized head-height kicks, spinning kicks, and fast, reactionary kick techniques.

Duncan wasn't sure what to say, so he expressed his feelings. "Wow, Sook. That was amazing."

"Please do not tell Father. He would not approve of killing this man."

Duncan nodded as he looked up and down the road. Nobody was in sight.

He picked up the men and dragged them over the embankment. First, he stripped them of their weapons and ammunition. Then, while Sook brushed snow over the bloodstained road with her feet, Duncan pulled the bodies down the hill along the same creek bed he'd carried his partner, Park, several days before.

He looked over the bluff and found an area where rain had eroded away the soil. A tree had toppled over and exposed the roots near the bottom of the bluff. Duncan positioned the bodies carefully and dropped them on top of the tree, where they remained suspended fifteen feet in the air.

He hustled back up the hill and found Sook with two North Korean Type 58 rifles slung over her shoulders and his Barrett rifle in her hands.

Duncan couldn't suppress his smile. With her short hair and smudged face, she looked like one of Kim's million-man army. The difference was this girl was able to kill without hesitation. As they quietly retraced their steps back to Chae's boat, Duncan wondered if she'd killed before.

PART SIX

Wednesday, November 30

CHAPTER 50

November 30
Raven Rock Mountain Complex
Liberty Township, Pennsylvania

"What?" President Harman was shouting at her chief of staff. It was just after midnight when she'd received word from the president's advance team that Texas had passed legislation to secede from the United States. "Are they out of their minds? They can't do that!"

Acton handed the president a manila envelope, which contained a letter from Governor, now acting-President, Marion Burnett of the Republic of Texas. Included was the resolution and legislation passed with eighty-two percent of the votes in the Texas State House.

Her hands shook as she read the letter. "Republic of Texas? That's absurd. Right, Charles? Seriously, is this some kind of joke?"

"No, Madam President, I believe all of this has occurred in the last twelve hours."

"Where were our people?" she asked. The president was incredulous. "Did she lock them up or something?"

"No, Madam President. The governor had them escorted away from Austin under the guise of displaying the state's vast food storage resources to share with the rest of the nation. After what was reported to me as a wasted day traveling to El Paso, the governor ordered your team expelled."

"What?!" she shouted. "Expelled? As in kicked out of the state?"

"No, ma'am. As they relayed it to our communications team, they were kicked out of the country—the Republic of Texas."

President Harman wandered around the room and rubbed her

temples. She found her way to a chair in the corner and plopped into it. She rolled her eyes and shook her head in disbelief.

"How could we miss this, Charles? The woman has spouted off about seceding for years. Of course she's taking advantage of the crisis to further her goals."

"Madam President, there was no way to anticipate her actions," replied Acton. "You want to give every American, especially a political leader, the benefit of the doubt when it comes to a catastrophic event. It's one thing to be under attack and then kicked while we're down by our enemies. It's another thing to be stabbed in the back by our fellow Americans."

The president leaned back in the chair and rhythmically thumped the back of her head against the wall, symbolically trying to knock some sense into herself.

"Charles, I'm gonna need the AG and Carla Pickering in here. This can't wait until morning."

"I've already requested their presence, ma'am. Although, I instructed them to be here at half past the hour. I expected you'd need a moment alone."

She chuckled and rolled her head on her neck. After standing, she found a window into a corridor, where she could see her reflection. Her eyes were sunken, and dark rings had formed. She hadn't enjoyed a restful sleep since Thanksgiving night.

"Thank you, Charles. Please, before they arrive, what's your honest assessment?"

Acton was philosophical in his response. "Lincoln faced a similar crisis situation. The country was being ripped apart over the issue of states' rights, although slavery was principal among them. Foreign nations had continued to circle the relatively new nation and were considering support of the South, both economically and militarily. However, you have an additional challenge. Madam President, we've experienced five days without power in this country, and the results are horrifying. It is impossible to control and assist three hundred million people. I am beginning to believe the predictions of the EMP Commission to be true. Under these circumstances, without a herculean effort by the government, nearly ninety percent of Americans will die in the coming year."

"Thanks for the vote of confidence. Just bottom line it for me, Charles," interrupted the president. "What are you suggesting?"

"Madam President, if you throw our military resources toward retaliating against North Korea, you are depriving the American people of much-needed protection and support. There are no courts in operation to challenge Governor Burnett and the Texas legislature's actions. Even if you won, they might ignore the rulings."

"Then what?" she asked.

"You would have to rectify the situation by force using our military. Once again, the other three hundred million Americans would suffer because of the distraction. So, to sum it up, while we fight Kim Jong-un, and perhaps the Russians and Chinese too, Americans will be dying. While we use our military strength to fight our own in Texas, Americans in the rest of the nation will be dying. You could win both of those fights only to learn that the American people died during the process."

"Well, aren't you full of great options," said the president sarcastically. "All of this boils down to the proper use of our military resources. I guess we'll need to take that up with Monty this evening. Have you notified him to meet with us also?"

"Madam President, he's not available. I believe he's still in Texas."

"Wait. I understand he was going to deliver his wife home and then return immediately. Did something go wrong?"

"No, ma'am. He never came back."

CHAPTER 51

November 30
Port of Piegan
United States Border Crossing
Carway, Alberta, Canada

Morales declared himself good to go although Cooper had his doubts. The Brazilian was tough, and the pain would never bother him. After speaking with Palmer early that morning as they broke camp, Cooper's biggest concern was infection. Despite the near zero temperatures when they continued their ride south in the early morning hours, Morales continued to sweat.

He broached the subject with Pacheco, who was Morales's closest friend. Pacheco was also aware of the potential complications of the gunshot wound, as he'd lost a cousin to a gunshot when he was a child. The two oldest guys agreed the best course of action was to get Morales to Great Falls, Montana, which was due south from their present location.

A bigger city would be more welcoming to refugees, they thought, and would be able to provide some sort of medical attention. Great Falls was at least a three-day ride without an injured rider. If Morales deteriorated, then it would take longer. It was, however, their only option.

It was early afternoon and the warm sun created a beautiful day to ride. Although the temperature never approached freezing, the sunshine melted the snow and provided their horses better footing. The combination lifted their spirits until they came across a group of riders who'd stopped to feed and water their horses.

Cooper dug his heels into his horse's sides and rode ahead of the group while Pacheco and Riley readied their rifles. As Cooper approached, he saw that the riders were unarmed and appeared to be tired. He doubted that they'd seen a meal in a couple of days.

"How are y'all doin'?" he asked as he approached the group of three men and two women, all of whom appeared to be in their forties.

"We've seen better days," one of the men responded. "Where you headed?"

Cooper told a white lie, although he wasn't sure why. "South. My family has a place on the Colorado River."

"Well, we were too," said one of the women. "They were kicking people out of their homes in Fort Macleod, and we figured they'd be after us next. So we gathered up these horses and headed south."

"Why'd they kick folks out?"

The first gentleman responded, "They were Americans. The good people of Fort Macleod decided to blame all Americans for their troubles. We left before they took our horses from us."

Cooper shrugged and decided not to pursue the matter further. He was glad to put Fort Macleod in the proverbial rearview mirror.

"All right then, y'all have a nice ride. I reckon we'll see you on the other side of the border."

Cooper pulled on his horse's reins and started to return to his group when the man spoke up again.

"Maybe. Maybe not. There's a three- or four-day wait to get into the country. You have to have two forms of identification and be processed by Customs and Border Patrol agents. They've set up a tent city outside the border-crossing facilities."

Cooper gave them a puzzled look. "Three or four days to get across? That's crazy."

The man continued. "Yeah, everybody agrees, but they've got soldiers manning the post with automatic weapons. There was a rumor of a guy getting shot trying to push past the gates."

"Well, thanks for the heads-up," said Cooper, who once again attempted to leave.

"Oh, one more thing," the man shouted after him. "Be prepared to turn over your weapons. They're confiscating guns from everybody whether they're granted admission into the country or not."

Cooper waved his left arm in thanks and broke into a gallop back to his group. It didn't matter what was happening at the border checkpoint. They were gonna find another way into the good old U S of A.

CHAPTER 52

November 30
Korea Bay
Fifty miles south of Dandong, North Korea

Big risks bring big rewards. In Duncan Armstrong's case, failing to take the risk of traveling into the unknown likely meant death for himself and all of Sook's family. As he rested the few hours in advance of their escape to South Korea, Duncan considered other options, all of which were horrible. His best chance of decent treatment was to escape into Russia, although like a fisherman who throws his catch back into the lake, it was likely the Russians would return him to the North Koreans. An escape into China would most likely result in his being used as a propaganda tool, only to be disowned by his own government.

He decided to take his chances, albeit with another life placed in his charge—Sook. Duncan made one last effort while they sailed south into the darkness of Korea Bay to convince Sook to remain home with her family. He laid out the risks. He tried to make her feel guilty. He encouraged her to remain in order to help her family and neighbors.

All of his arguments fell on deaf ears. Chae continued to sail his trawler south for a day of fishing, towing the whaler behind him. Sook interpreted Duncan's words for her father, but his chin remained firm and his resolve steely. Chae's daughter was escaping the prison known as North Korea for a better life. Duncan was her ticket to freedom.

"Father will tow us as far as he can with his available fuel. He must fish today, or he will face trouble tonight when he returns."

"I understand," said Duncan. "Sook, we don't have a map, and our only means of navigation will be the shoreline. If we get too close, we'll draw the scrutiny of patrol boats."

"Father knows this. He has calculated the travel. His methods are crude, but they should be accurate."

Chae pressed down on the throttle, causing the bow to rise slightly before planing over the surface of the water. Duncan turned to Sook as the faint lights of Sinmi-do began to disappear in the distance. A few tears began to stream down her face as she quietly murmured *annyeong*, goodbye.

Duncan gave her a hug and she sniffled. Duncan was a straight shooter, not a manipulator. He refused to use the emotional moment as a last-ditch opportunity to convince her that this trip was too dangerous. Instead, he comforted the girl who saved his life.

"Are you okay?" he asked finally.

"Yes, thank you. It is time to say goodbye. A new adventure awaits."

"Sook, um, you know—" started Duncan before being interrupted.

"No, Duncan, my mind is made up and Father insists. I suspect he has planned this for me for many years. You are, as they say, my white knight in armor."

Duncan laughed, drawing the attention of Chae. The older man took his eyes off the sea for a moment to smile and start laughing himself, completely unaware of the conversation.

"Okay, I'll be your white knight. Now, tell me about your father's calculations."

"We have to get within the Northern Limit Line. This will place us out of the grasp of the patrol boats, I hope. The army is on high alert. They may stretch their tentacles into international waters and the Yellow Sea."

The 1953 Armistice Agreement, which established a cessation of hostilities between North Korea and the United Nations Command following the Korean War, provided for a line of demarcation along the 38th parallel, effectively dividing the peninsula in two. However, an issue immediately arose regarding the territorial waters of the two nations.

North Korea insisted on a demarcation line from their shore of twelve nautical miles, beyond which the Yellow Sea would be considered international waters. The UN Command insisted upon three nautical miles.

Over time, the issue festered but not over ownership and the right to defend the disputed waters militarily, but rather over economic matters, especially the rights of fishermen. Presently, Pyongyang did not recognize the UN-dictated boundary and routinely sent their fishing boats, escorted by North Korean naval vessels, to the twelve-mile line and beyond. While the South did not attempt to challenge the fishing rights around Hwanghaenam-do, their patrol boats were very active in the area.

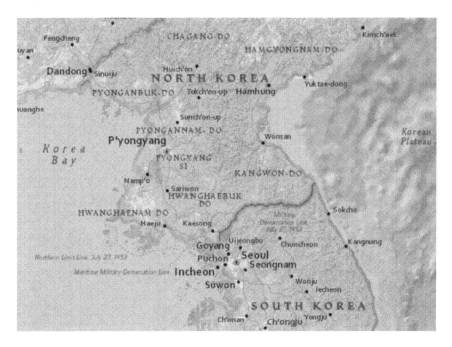

By heading in a south-southwesterly direction from Sinmi-do, Chae was skirting the twelve-mile boundary off the western shore of the Korean Peninsula. Sook explained to Duncan what would happen next.

"We do not have sufficient fuel to make it from Sinmi-do to the South without help. Very shortly, Father will stop the boat and we will be on our own. He has calculated the miles to clear the Hwanghaen peninsula, which places us beyond the Northern Limit Line and into international waters. This travel distance will require three fuel cans. When those cans are empty, we will switch to the remaining three fuel cans and change our direction to the east toward Incheon in the South."

Duncan shook his head. In a world full of global-positioning satellites, talking watches, and maps that could be viewed in a multidimensional hologram, he was trusting his fate to the calculations of an old North Korean fisherman and the accuracy of plastic cans of gasoline.

You can't make this stuff up.

CHAPTER 53

November 30
The Armstrong Ranch
Borden County, Texas

It was three in the morning when Major was awakened by pounding on the front door. He and Lucy simultaneously turned on their nightstand lamps and looked at one another to confirm what they'd heard. The pounding commenced once again followed by shouting. The Armstrongs never locked their front door, even after the apocalypse.

"Mr. Major! Miss Lucy! Come quick! There is a fire. Jose's house is on fire!"

Major jumped out of bed and ran through the bedroom door to the railing overlooking the large family room and the foyer. "I'll be down in a minute. Is he okay?"

"Yes," replied one of his ranch hands. "He was on patrol. He saw the flames coming out of his window and rode to his house. Two men broke through the front door and ran away."

"Which way did they go?" asked Major.

"Along the river toward the barnyard."

"Major, we can't let them get there," Lucy pleaded as she got dressed. "If they're vandals, they could destroy everything with a fire."

Major heard his wife but issued directives to his hand. "Bring a truck around. Where's Preacher?"

"He's hunting down the men now."

"Okay, go. I'll be right down."

Major quickly dressed and strapped on his holster. After kissing his wife, he bounded down the stairs and pulled a shotgun and a flashlight off the foyer coat rack.

"Lucy, I'm gonna have this man stay with you. I want you protected until we can catch these guys. Please lock all the doors and have your gun ready. There could be more than two."

"I will. Please be careful!"

Major bolted outside and slammed the door behind him. The feed truck was ready for him, and Major quickly gave the young man instructions to make regular patrols around the perimeter of the house and around the barns. His instructions concerning engaging these men were simple.

If they're unarmed, fire a warning shot until they comply with your orders. If they're armed, shoot to kill without hesitation. We don't risk our lives for trespassers.

It took less than five minutes to reach the barnyard. As he arrived, the buildings were all dark, which was not unusual for this time of night; however, agitated chickens were out of the norm.

The headlights on the old feed truck were weak, but they illuminated the hog pen and the adjacent small enclosed field where the chicken tractors were used. A chicken tractor was essentially a chicken coop on wheels, which allowed the chickens to forage freely across a certain area while protecting them from predators.

The hands would move the two chicken tractors across sections of pasture every day, which gave portions of the flock fresh vegetation to forage on. As the tractor was moved, the chickens left nitrogen- and phosphorus-filled manure behind them. The penned-in area was ideal for foals to graze.

The chickens in this area were raising a ruckus. Major reached into his pocket to retrieve his two-way radio when he realized he'd left it in the charger back at the house. He had a regular morning routine that included retrieving his radio, but in his haste to address the emergency, he'd run out the door without it. He had no way to reach Preacher, which meant he was on his own.

Using the light from the truck's headlamps to aid his vision, Major readied his shotgun and grabbed his Maglite flashlight. He tried not to overreact to the chickens. It didn't take much to scare the hens. A small field mouse or a snake slithering past could send a whole coop into a frenzy.

He slowly worked his way around the hog pen and carefully approached a small shed used to store fertilizer. Major continued to work in the dark, feeling his way along the perimeter of the barnyard, using his knowledge of the layout to his advantage.

As a Texas Ranger, he'd stalked fugitives in close quarters before. He'd learned to rely on instincts and experience. He'd learned that certain methods of movement, firing stances, weapon positioning, and reflexive shooting were useful in any confined-area encounter.

It was that experience that led him to choose his shotgun over a rifle when he left the ranch house. Shotguns were useful for mid-range and close-quarters combat. Major used to describe close-quarter pursuits as *eye-gouging distance*. At twelve to twenty feet, the powerful impact of a twelve-gauge shotgun could not be denied.

He caught movement out of the corner of his eye. A shadow seemed to dash from one of the chicken tractors to another. Once again, the chickens voiced their fear and concern. His mind raced to assess the size of the predator that had dashed across his periphery.

In the distance, he heard the sound of dogs barking. Preacher and his men must've employed the Texas gun dogs. Most hunters on the high plains of Texas had a variety of German shorthairs, English setters, and Labrador retrievers that were specially trained to ignore the loud sounds made by hunting rifles and be patient until the hunter gave instructions.

The dogs around Armstrong Ranch had been trained to hunt hogs and coons. None of the Armstrongs had ever showed an interest in hunting birds duck or quail. They were a beef-eating family.

Major trusted Preacher's ability to flush out the intruders. If they were still on the ranch, he'd chase them in this direction. Major would have somethin' for 'em when they arrived at the barnyard.

As the chickens calmed down again, Major decided to move forward alone. The battery on the truck was running down, causing his lights to dim. If it became totally dark, he'd lose his advantage.

He lowered himself and moved along the fencing that held the hogs. Then he heard a loud thud. It was the kind of sound when somebody ran headfirst into a low header in a barn. He knew this because he'd done it before.

He had to move fast. While there were no guns hidden in the barn, there were plenty of weapons, from long knives to machetes. If the guys were correct, he was dealing with two or more men. He had the upper hand by being armed, but they could get the jump on him if he wasn't careful.

Major slipped the flashlight in his pocket and darted across the field to the first chicken tractor, careful not to get too close. If he bumped the cage, he'd give his position away. He crouched and walked behind the egg-laying boxes, the barrel of his shotgun leading the way.

He stepped into the open and dashed to the next chicken tractor. The barnyard was deathly silent. Major began to question whether he'd seen or heard anything at all.

Creak!

One of the barn doors was opening. It wasn't the double front door, which hung on tracks. This sounded like the side doors on their rusty hinges. *If I don't move in, they'll escape toward the lake. We can't chase them down the ridge.*

The barking dogs were getting closer. Major wanted to fire a warning shot into the air to notify Preacher to come to the barn, but what if he was wrong? His mind could be playing tricks on him. Sometimes the mind looks and listens for things that go bump in the night, and creates them subconsciously. If he distracted Preacher and his men from systematically clearing the thickets along the river, the men could get away or, worse, harm one of his men.

Patience. Think smart. They're more afraid than you are.

Another creak of the barn door. Major swiveled his head back and forth as he sought any signs of wind. There was none. They were exiting the back side of the barn, the farthest point from his position. Whoever these men were, they were careful and fairly quiet. Somehow, they sensed Major was alone, and they were taking advantage of the time they had before the dogs arrived.

He started toward the barn and then he caught a break. The two men dashed for the pickup. They must've assumed the keys were still in it and planned on making their escape in the feed truck.

Wrongo! Major thought to himself with a grin as he thought about the keys in his pocket.

He revealed himself from behind the chicken tractor and yelled, "Stop!"

When the men continued running, he racked a round into the chamber of his shotgun and fired a round of birdshot into the air.

The booming sound of the Remington echoed across the ranch at this early hour. Hogs, chickens, ducks, and every other barnyard critter erupted in a panic. The explosive sound did not, however, deter the two arsonists. They continued to streak across the graveled area in front of the barn toward Major's truck.

Although Major was at least fifty yards away, he racked another shell into the chamber. This one was double-ought buck. He always staggered his shells in the eight-round, extended-tube magazine. One bird, two buck. One bird, two buck. And so on. This enabled him to fire his warning shot and most likely shoot to maim rather than kill. The twelve-gauge double-ought was intended to be a *game ender.*

He fired again, this time directly at the fleeing men. At fifty yards, well beyond the maximum effective range for buckshot, he was not likely to kill them unless the unfortunate arsonists took some of the shot to the head.

The lead runner groaned, spun around and fell into the grill of the truck. The other man continued to run, tripping over his partner's legs, and then quickly scrambled to the side of the truck. He crawled around the open door and pulled himself into the front seat behind the steering wheel.

Major now assumed the men were unarmed. He took off around the hog pen, with his shotgun pointed directly at the truck. Inside the cab, the uninjured man was frantically searching for the keys, rummaging through the glove box, under the floor mats, and above the visor.

"Get out of the truck with your arms up! Now!"

The man continued looking for the keys, and when he couldn't find them, he tried to scoot across the cab and out the passenger-side door. It was too late.

Major ran past the front of the pickup and the rapidly dimming headlights. He glanced down at the other man, who was alive, but writhing in pain, blood streaming down his arm and jeans.

Clumsily, the man emerged from the passenger side only to be thrown to the ground by Major.

"Please don't kill me! Please!" the man begged as he lay crying facedown on the gravel drive.

"Spread 'em! Spread your arms and legs out like a snow angel, which you aren't. Do it now or I'll put you down, I swear it!"

The man quickly complied, and after kicking the truck door closed, Major slowly walked backwards to check on the other man while keeping a close eye on his crying partner. Much to Major's delight and appreciation, the wounded man had complied with Major's orders too.

"We're comin'! Major, is that you?"

"Yeah, come on in, boys! I've got these two."

Major allowed himself to relax, exhaling a long puff of foggy condensation from his lungs into the cold air. He hadn't chased down any fugitives in a dozen years. Somehow, he didn't think this would be the last time.

CHAPTER 54

November 30
The Armstrong Ranch
Borden County, Texas

Preacher quickly dismounted, and one of the hands tied off his horse. With his pistol drawn, he reached Major first and immediately slid to his knees next to the injured man.

"Where's the woman?" he shouted as he pressed the barrel of his sidearm into the back of the man's head. "Answer me!"

"I dunno. We got split up," the man said with a moan.

Preacher pulled on his jacket until he found where the man's wounds were. Switching the gun to his right hand, he pressed the barrel against the base of his skull and began to squeeze the blood-soaked sleeve of the arsonist.

"Tell me! Don't mess with me, boy! Where is she?"

The man screamed in agony as Preacher pressed his fingers into the wound. "The river. She tried to cross the river. We told her not to. I swear, mister. Please, I swear!"

Preacher gave the man's arm another squeeze and then mashed his shoulder into the gravel.

He stood and turned to Major. "We've got this, right? I need to send the men back to the river to find the girl."

"Yeah, send 'em."

Preacher shouted orders to his men, and Antonio led the way back toward the riverbank where they'd just abandoned their search. The sun was beginning to rise, which would make their task easier.

Preacher stomped back to the pickup and growled at both of the men. He was angry.

"Don't either of you move or I'll shoot you. Hear me? I've killed before and I will kill you, God help my soul. Got it?"

"My arm, it's burnin'," moaned the man in front of the truck. "Can you please help me?"

Preacher pulled his leg back and kicked him in the ribs as hard as he could, causing the man to writhe in pain. "There! That'll make you forget about your arm."

Major watched Preacher, slightly alarmed at his longtime friend's hostility. Then again, he supposed what Preacher was doing was less painful than the buckshot that peppered the man.

Keeping an eye on the two men, Preacher and Major backed away several paces so they could catch their breath and decompress from the chase.

Preacher wiped the sweat off his forehead and adjusted his hat. "I don't think the girl is armed, but we don't know for sure. We need to find her before she causes any more trouble."

"The boys will find her. What happened out there?"

"You know, we've got those three homes on the far western edge of the ranch," started Preacher. "They're the only homes on that side of FM 1205. Anyway, Jose was on patrol and he saw the fire from a distance. He called for backup on the two-way, but by then, flames were coming out of the windows, and he saw these two bailing out of the house and running this way along the river."

"It seems you all were on top of them pretty quick," interrupted Major.

Preacher nodded as he wandered over to his horse. He reached into his saddlebag and pulled out two bottles of water. He gave one to Major.

"Jose raised me on the radio, and I was out the door," said Preacher. "Listen, I ain't made a big deal about it, but I haven't been sleepin' much. This whole thing kinda has me spooked, I guess. Anyway, I've been sleepin' in my clothes, and it took me all of thirty seconds to mount up to ride toward the fire."

"What about the house?" asked Major.

"I don't know, but the way it was burnin', probably nothin' but block and ashes now."

This seemed to build up the rage in Preacher again and he stomped over to the arsonists, who were still spread out on the gravel.

"Why did you burn the house down?" He shouted the question.

Neither man responded.

"Tell me!" Preacher demanded as he kicked the injured man again.

"We were cold and hungry. We'd been walking since Clovis, tryin' to get to my friend's place in Abilene. We're just tired, dude. You know. Lookin' for food and a place to stay warm."

"I ain't your dude!" Preacher yelled at the man and then stomped his boot on the man's hand, forcing it into the half-inch limestone gravel.

"Please stop hurting him!" the other man shouted.

"Okay, I'll hurt you instead," responded Preacher as he stomped around the truck toward the man, who immediately curled up in a ball.

Major stepped in to stop the impending beat-down. In Preacher's state of mind, he might just beat the man to death for interrupting the interrogation. It was a side he'd never seen in Preacher and something he intended to discuss with him when his temper simmered down. For now, Major attributed it to sleep-deprived stress.

"Preach, hold up. Come back over here, and let's talk about what to do with these two."

Preacher stopped, exhaled and shook his head side to side. He holstered his pistol and slowly walked back to Major. Through gritted teeth, he asked, "Can we hang 'em?"

Major laughed. "Even in the old days, they didn't hang a man for stealin' or burnin' down a house."

"What did they do to them?"

"Well, they didn't hang them all," replied Major. "Most times, they held them in jail and then stuck 'em on the next train out of town. Eventually, territorial prisons sprang up around the West, where the prisoners were locked up in their cell all day until somebody decided to push them out and make room for another. Every once in a while, thieves would be flogged in the town square as a deterrent."

"That'll work," said Preacher with a devious chuckle. "Let me flog 'em with a horse whip."

Major laughed and shook his head. "No, Preach. I think it would be best if we chained them in the back of the pickup and deliver them to Sheriff Allison up in Gail. We'll let Benny deal with them."

"Do we still have courts?" asked Preacher.

"I think we do. The president declared martial law, but the state seceded from the union first. As far as I know, we're officially a country, and Borden County is, well, like a state now."

"The state of Borden. Has a nice ring to it."

"I don't know if that's the case, Preach. That would mean Texas has two hundred fifty-four counties, um, states. I don't think its gonna work like that, but either way, we're taking these two to Gail and dropping them off on Benny's doorstep."

The sound of horses grabbed their attention, and they swung around to see who was approaching. It was Jose and Antonio followed by two hands riding on a horse together and a fourth horse carrying the body of a woman slumped over the saddle.

The two prisoners turned their heads toward the riders and began to shout.

"Mary! Mary!" yelled one.

"What's wrong with her?" asked the other.

Preacher made them stay on the ground while Major went to investigate.

He slowly approached the body and saw the woman's blood-soaked hair. He felt for a pulse and didn't feel one.

"Where'd you find her?" he asked Antonio.

"She was tangled up in the beaver dam. She must've hit her head and drowned. The current carried her downriver until she got stuck."

"Wonderful," Major mumbled to himself sarcastically. Then he gave instructions to the ranch hands. "Boys, grab some chains out of the barn and a couple of padlocks. Meet me over at the pickup."

He grabbed the reins of the horse carrying the girl's dead body.

Slowly, he returned to the prisoners.

"Well, boys, hope you're proud of yourselves. Your friend here, Mary, hit her head on a rock and drowned."

"Oh no," the injured man wailed. "She was my girl. How could this happen?"

"It happened 'cause you tried to steal something that wasn't yours and burned a house down in the process. Mary paid the ultimate price for your stupidity!"

The man was delirious as he cried. The emotional outburst touched Major's heart, who handed the reins to Preacher and helped the injured man off the ground.

"Say goodbye to your friend," Major whispered into the man's ear. "Then get your mind right. You're goin' to jail."

CHAPTER 55

November 30
Korea Bay
South of Sinmi-do, North Korea

Duncan fought back tears as Sook and her father broke their embrace. Even the stoic, proud North Korean man managed to frown and well up with tears. Duncan didn't have to understand Korean to know that he was giving his daughter his blessing and final words of encouragement.

Duncan had pulled the whaler alongside Chae's trawler and tied it off to the cleats after placing the dilapidated bumpers in between the two boats. Chae grabbed Duncan by both arms and looked him in the face. He mustered a few words of broken English. *Sook good girl. You help.*

"I will, Chae. I'll get her to safety. Thank you."

The two men hugged and Chae smiled. "Go. Go. Sun. See."

Duncan looked to the east, and the sun was peeking over the Korean Peninsula. The two boats needed to hurry in separate directions before they were noticed by others. As Duncan scrambled to untie the lines, Sook fired up the powerful Evinrude engine. Duncan climbed aboard, and she began to slowly pull away from her father's trawler. The old man gave a final wave, and Sook returned the gesture with a smile.

The scene was surreal for Duncan. He witnessed father and daughter saying goodbye to one another knowing full well they'd never see each other again. It made him think of his parents and family. When he left them to report to duty, it was always presumed he'd return to them when his tour was up. There was no permanency about their separation. It was just their oldest son going away to work before returning to the ranch.

Then Duncan put himself in his parents' shoes, recalling the day his brother Dallas left for the Middle East. Everyone thought Dallas was going off for a nine-month stint in Afghanistan. Everyone thought he was coming home afterwards. He didn't.

A chill ran over Duncan's body as he shook these thoughts out of his head. It was time for him to focus, as the next few hours would dictate whether he returned to the Armstrong Ranch alive, in a casket, or not at all.

"Hey, now that I can see, I think I know where we are," shouted Sook.

Duncan held onto the rail as he pulled the bumpers inside the boat. The water started to get choppy as they traveled south.

"Have you been this far south before?" he asked.

"Twice, two years ago," she replied. "Dear Leader ordered the fishermen to expand their fishing zones. The patrol boats escorted us into the Yellow Sea for five consecutive days. Our catch was very large, as were others from our village. We were rewarded with a larger share."

"Where are we now?"

Sook pointed toward an inlet that carved its way into Korea. "That is the Taedong River. It runs into Pyongyang."

"Shall we pay Dear Leader a visit?" said Duncan jokingly, still trying to make sense of whom he had assassinated a week ago. If it was a body double, he chuckled to himself, maybe he could ride into the city and finish the job.

"Oh, no," replied Sook, taking Duncan's question literally. "He does not make public speeches often. He must protect himself from bombs."

"And bullets," Duncan muttered under his breath.

The two rode along in silence as Sook focused on the increasingly choppy waters. A tackle box broke loose from its ropes, and Duncan crawled on all fours to tie it off. His rifle had been stashed under a compartment beneath a V-shaped seat at the front of the boat. The compartment also stored fishing nets, poles, and a tarp. Chae had insisted upon leaving the fishing gear on board in case the patrol boats boarded them. If Duncan could manage to hide, the fishing gear would provide Sook a cover story that she was helping her father fish for the day.

"We are thirty miles from the western tip of Hwanghaen-do. Twenty miles after that, we are in international waters, but not necessarily safe, as you know."

Duncan nodded. He helped Sook watch ahead and then found himself looking for things to do. He went to the back of the boat and checked their fuel levels. They were on the second can and, based upon his calculations, would be depleting the third can within the hour. At that point, they'd switch the fuel lines and begin to head into South Korea, *home free*.

He took a turn at the wheel for a while, following Sook's instructions to maintain a due south heading. She also checked the fuel levels and took a moment to survey their surroundings. As she returned to Duncan's side, she had a look of concern on her face.

"This choppy water is causing us to use too much fuel. We will have to stop sooner than Father predicted."

"What does that mean?" asked Duncan.

"We will have to turn southeast soon," she replied as she cupped her hands over her eyes to look to the east. The sun was getting brighter, bringing welcome warmth to their bodies, but it made it difficult to see the shoreline.

"Closer to shore and the patrol boats," added Duncan.

"Yes."

She took over the wheel, and Duncan made his way to the bow of the whaler. He checked his sidearm and his ammo levels. Then he retrieved the Barrett from the storage compartment and readied his rifle. If they encountered a patrol boat, he wanted to be ready.

CHAPTER 56

November 30
Near the Northern Limit Line
The Yellow Sea

The Evinrude motor began to sputter as the third fuel can was drained. Sook immediately turned off the ignition and worked with Duncan to switch over the cans. The small whaler rocked back and forth, throwing Sook off balance onto her back. They both had a good laugh as she struggled to right herself.

After Sook recovered from her fall and the laughter, she steadied the cans as Duncan attached the lines. She gave them a final check and began to stand when she immediately fell to her knees.

"Duncan, a boat is coming. Very fast."

"From the east?"

"Yes. I can't see it, but I hear it approaching."

Duncan raised his head over the fiberglass side of the whaler and listened. The low rumble of a boat could be heard, and it was growing louder. The sound was distinctive, not like the outboard engines that powered most of the fishing boats he'd seen at Sinmi-do.

"Sook, listen to me," he began giving instructions. "I want you to stand at the center console and pretend you're having trouble starting the engine."

"But they will board us!" she protested in response.

"We won't be able to outrun them or their radio. You have to talk to them. I'll get ready. Okay? Can you do it?"

She studied his eyes and then nodded. She hoisted herself up on the side rails and slowly walked to the console. She pulled her hat over her forehead and made sure her hair was hidden from view. At a distance, she looked like a young boy. Her disguise, however, would not pass closer scrutiny.

Duncan crawled along the deck, being careful to keep his back below the rail. The roar of the engine grew louder, and he realized he did not have much time. When he reached the bow, he began unloading fishing nets and pushed them toward the center console with his feet. He unfurled the tarp, grabbed his rifle, and positioned himself in the middle of the bow under the tarp.

Then he waited, unable to see what was happening.

Sook did a good job of flooding the motor and making it appear the Evinrude wouldn't turn over. Duncan sensed the patrol ship was getting closer as the driver of the boat throttled down and the wake pushed into the side of the whaler, causing it to rock severely from side to side.

The soldiers began yelling at Sook in their native Korean. The tone of their voices spoke volumes, even though Duncan couldn't understand them.

Although he barely knew Sook, Duncan sensed she was pretending to act frightened and innocent in her replies. She continued to stall, and Duncan began to break out in a sweat. For all he knew, she had turned on him in order to save herself. He really missed his partner and translator, Park, at this moment.

Duncan held fast, resisting the urge to spring into view. The whaler began to rock severely as the battleship gray patrol boat pulled alongside. The soldiers yelled orders to one another as the two vessels bounced off one another.

Duncan remained under the tarp, waiting and listening. He'd already removed his sidearm, opting for it instead of the bulkier Barrett rifle. He had to hold his position, even though his mind screamed to act now.

Then he heard tapping.

One, two, three.

The men were talking fast, giving each other instructions.

The tapping against the fiberglass of the whaler continued.

One, two, three.

Sook is signaling me! There are three soldiers on the patrol boat.

Duncan heard the sounds of boots hitting the deck of the whaler. The soles of his shoes squeaked as the man moved across the aft deck, causing the whaler to list to its right side. Another set of boots hit the deck, causing the boat to sway in the other direction.

That's two. Now!

Duncan threw the tarp off his body and fired his weapon as he sat up. His first two rounds were aimed at the soldiers' chests, catching each man once and forcing them off balance.

As the shots zipped by Sook, she crouched below the center console and then scrambled to put it between her body and the patrol boat.

Duncan directed his attention to the third soldier, who had lost his balance and fallen backwards into the boat's wheelhouse. The patrol boat was made of solid steel, and the man was well protected.

Duncan maneuvered onto his knees and quickly fired rounds into the soldiers' heads at the back of the whaler. With those threats eliminated, he could focus on the last soldier.

He fired several rounds through the door opening, shattering the glass windows on the other side. The soldier stuck his Type-88 rifle around the edge of the opening and fired wildly into the whaler, blasting holes in the hull and puncturing the gas cans. Fuel began to spill onto the aft deck, causing Sook to move closer to Duncan.

Duncan rose above the side of the boat and emptied the handgun's magazine, shooting out two porthole windows in the wheelhouse and sending bullets ricocheting inside.

Undeterred, or out of fear, the soldier fired back, this time destroying the half-windshield of the center console and imbedding two rounds in the Evinrude engine.

Duncan holstered his weapon and raised the Barrett, focusing his sights on the opening. With the steel protecting him, Duncan's only option was to shoot the rifle, or maybe even the shooter's hand on the trigger.

He took a deep breath and trained his weapon where the rifle barrel would appear. He waited and prepared to react. His opportunity came.

The weapon appeared, and just as it began to fire, Duncan let go of a burst of the powerful 7.62-millimeter rounds. The bullets tore into the barrel of the Type-88 and slung it out of the soldier's grasp. Without hesitation, Duncan leapt onto the side of the whaler and, with a second jump, landed on the deck of the patrol boat. His quickness shocked the soldier, who momentarily froze before Duncan riddled his body with five rounds *from stem to sternum*, as Dallas used to say. Duncan never asked where the stem was, but the visual was as gruesome as the phrase sounded. *Gutted like a fish* could have been just as appropriate.

"Sook, are you okay?"

She emerged from behind the center console of the whaler. "Wow!" she exclaimed. "You are Rambo."

Duncan laughed as he stuck his head into the wheelhouse and gave the interior of the patrol boat one last look to make sure they hadn't missed anyone.

"Not really. Rambo makes a lot more money than I do."

Sook gingerly walked across her father's destroyed whaler, careful to miss the mix of blood and gasoline that was accumulating on the deck. Duncan extended a hand to her and pulled her up onto the patrol boat.

"Welcome aboard," he said with a laugh.

She looked around the thirty-foot vessel. The bow held a large anchor and the aft deck held three propane tanks and life rings. From the boat's antenna, a vinyl rope was attached to a rod at the rear of the vessel. The soldiers were drying tee shirts and boxer shorts by hanging them on the rope.

She shook her head in disgust. "They are lazy and sloppy. You cannot win a war with men like these."

Duncan furrowed his brow and turned his head slightly. At first glance, he was impressed that Sook had not broken down into a basket case of fear. Yet her statement seemed odd under the circumstances. It was full of contempt and *disappointment.*

He handed her the Barrett and entered the wheelhouse. He'd torn up the soldier's body so much that blood and gore were splattered against the back seating area. He dragged the body out the aft side door and dumped it over the railing into the water.

When he returned to the other side, Sook had found a set of binoculars on the patrol boat's console and was studying the waters to their east. The sun was no longer an impediment to their visibility.

"I'm afraid the whaler is finished," started Duncan as he looked around the patrol boat with his hands on his hips. "I guess we'll ride this one into Incheon."

Sook shrugged and walked back to the men's laundry line. "I see no flag or markings. We could use these as a flag of surrender." She pulled down a pair of white boxer shorts.

Sook removed her hat and allowed her hair to flow in the breeze. She began waving the man's boxers over her head and laughed. "I surrender. I surrender."

Duncan laughed hysterically at the spectacle. This was probably the first time in her life that Sook could act silly without fear of retribution. She was truly embracing freedom. Duncan, however, knew there was still work to do.

CHAPTER 57

November 30
The Yellow Sea
International Waters
West of Incheon, South Korea

Duncan untied the two vessels and then fired several strategically placed rounds below the waterline of the whaler. Both of them agreed that the boat might be traced back to her father, so a resting spot several hundred feet below was deemed appropriate. The boat gradually filled with water, and as it sank farther, Duncan added more holes to ensure its demise.

He took the soldiers' weapons and ammunition and stored them in a compartment on the patrol boat. Once the whaler disappeared, he and Sook started their new ride and headed southeast toward the coast.

At the bow, a flag was erected on of a flagpole they found in the hold, and the boxer shorts were affixed with a string. The white flag was intended to signal any South Korean vessels they encountered that they were not hostiles.

Duncan and Sook rocked along at a steady pace. The steel-hulled patrol boat crashed through the surf better than the whaler, but the vessel was not the best in the North Korean's fleet. They'd traveled barely twenty miles toward the southeast when the boat began to vibrate.

Duncan checked the seventies-era instruments on the vessel, which appeared to be normal. The fuel gauge rested at a quarter of a tank. All indicators were positive, except for the boat's behavior.

"Do you know anything about boat engines?" asked Sook.

"Nothing. I guarantee you know more than I do. It doesn't appear we're running low on gas unless the gauge is wrong. We're definitely losing speed, and the engine appears to be failing."

Sook grabbed the binoculars and studied the shoreline. She could see freighters parked outside Incheon harbor, awaiting their turn to come to port. Airplanes were taking off from the airport, which was on a small island west of the city.

"We're only twenty miles from shore," she said as the boat gave one final groan and the engine died. Sook shook her head and shrugged. "I am a good swimmer."

"Forget it," said Duncan with a laugh. "Are we safe from the North's patrol boats?"

"Yes, absolutely. Soon, South Korean Navy will see us. We can wait until that happens."

Duncan muscled the boat's steering wheel to point the bow toward land, but the waves immediately steered them back toward the north. "They better find us soon, or the wind might blow us back to Pyongyang."

"No, maybe Haeju. Not possible to float to Pyongyang."

Duncan gently put his arm around Sook and laughed. Sometimes, the girl was a warrior. Sometimes she was incredibly literal and gullible. He liked both Sooks.

"Well, the sun is shining and it is warmer today. Why don't we sit on the bow and wait?"

"Okay. I found snack bars and cigarettes. Do you smoke?"

"No, but I used to chew—tobacco, that is."

Sook pulled the cigarette out of her mouth and studied it. "You chew this?"

Again, Duncan couldn't control himself as he laughed at her. He took her by the hand and led her up to the bow seating, which was cold steel. He went into the wheelhouse and found a blanket for them to sit on.

"Sook, do you know how to locate your family in the South?"

"I think so," she replied. "They settled in Seoul in the Bukchon Hanok Village many years ago. I will find someone there."

She lit her cigarette and Duncan tried a bite of the snack bar. His reaction was uncontrollable as his face turned sour and he spit the food out into the sea.

"That's awful," he said.

"Yes. The soldiers eat worse than the villagers sometimes. Would you like a cigarette instead?"

"No, thanks," he answered before continuing. "Sook, what if you don't find your family? What will you do?"

"Do not worry about me, Duncan. Korean people are very welcoming and friendly. As a defector, they will take me in as a hero. I will avoid the government, however."

"Why is that?"

"The government will use me as a propaganda tool. I will be a prized possession to aggravate Dear Leader. The soldiers will distribute my picture all over North Korea until they find my family. They will be publicly executed as a warning to all others against defecting."

"Makes sense," said Duncan as he lifted his binoculars. He thought he'd heard the faint sound of an approaching boat. "Sook, two, no, three fast boats are approaching from Incheon. We have to make them understand who we are. Let them know we are surrendering."

"Yes, I am anxious to speak with a South Korean. I have dreamt of this moment all my life."

CHAPTER 58

November 30
Near Boundary Creek
Northern Montana

Palmer and Cooper had studied the map, and the five riders rode east toward the St. Mary River, which flowed from St. Mary Lake into Montana. Boundary Creek was a small tributary known for traversing the U.S.-Canadian border. After they reached the river, they found a fresh, well-worn trail that meandered through the hills and over the border. Cooper was surprised that the refugees waiting at the border crossing didn't consider other crossing routes, but then again, people are like cattle, sometimes they lack the ability to think for themselves and apply alternative thinking to problem-solving. Instead, they opted for following the person in front of them, mindlessly moving along through life like the herd.

Since they'd left Calgary, their luck had gradually changed for the worse. Cooper thought the longer the apocalypse lasted, the more dangerous the world would become. Even the process of crossing the border had been complicated. And clearly, every town they approached would not welcome them with open arms.

Kind of like the old War World II stories Pops used to tell about Normandy and Iwo Jima, they were going to have to fight inch by inch and mile by mile to make it home. He, Riley, and Palmer were up to the task. It was becoming apparent Morales was not, and his loyal friend Pacheco would stay be the injured man's side.

As predicted, as the day went on, his fever worsened, and his condition deteriorated. Palmer was concerned that a bone might have been splintered or internal bleeding might be taking place. Bacterial organisms could invade a deep cut or wound, causing infection around nearby bones. If a bone was chipped or broken, the bacteria could invade the bone itself. He continued to have a fever and chills. The wound area was turning red and swollen. Overall, Morales was becoming irritable, insisting upon frequent stops.

While they were taking a break at mid-afternoon, Palmer studied the map with Cooper. They'd decided already to avoid major highways, and the route they were traveling along Highway 464 led them directly toward Great Falls.

They agreed not to rehash the multitude of threats they'd face as they entered a city of sixty thousand people. Everyone's concern was for Morales's well-being. Once they arrived on the outskirts of Great Falls, then they'd consider their options. In the meantime, they had to decide where to stop for the night.

Morales and Pacheco were pushing to stop now, although they still had a couple of hours of daylight. Cooper showed them the map and convinced them to travel two more hours so they could stop on the fringe of the Blackfeet Indian Reservation. In the morning, they'd get another early start and make their way to Valier, a small town about halfway to Great Falls. The area was sparsely populated and should be safe. The day after that, they'd get Morales some medical attention.

After some discussion, and complaining from Morales, the group saddled up and continued on their way. The day's ride was uneventful, and that actually gave the rodeo kids some welcome relief as well as hope.

The first four days of the apocalypse had given them plenty of excitement, including Riley's killing of a man. He showed no aftereffects of the shooting. He hadn't brought it up, and his demeanor seemed unchanged from his usual wise-cracking self. During quiet portions of their ride, Cooper tried to psychoanalyze his brother and finally gave up.

Riley was unpredictable, to be sure. He also wore his emotions on his sleeve. If he had been scolded by his parents, he'd brood for hours. If angered, he'd lash out without hesitation. There was no filter on Riley. Cooper decided that the killing didn't bother Riley in the least, as he showed no outward signs of being troubled.

Then the more he thought about it, the more he became concerned for his brother, who'd just killed a man and it didn't seem to impact him. Cooper wondered if he were forced to kill someone, would he have the same reaction.

He really wasn't sure.

CHAPTER 59

November 30
Red River Bridge at I-30
Oklahoma-Texas Border

Former Defense Secretary Montgomery Gregg, now a private citizen following his resignation from President Harman's cabinet several hours ago, flew with newly designated commander of the Texas National Guard, Kregg Deur, and Gregg's former aide-de-camp, Jackson Waller, to perform a border inspection where certain hot points had been identified.

"This is an incredible chopper," said Gregg as the newly commissioned Piasecki X-49 rocketed across North Dallas toward their destination. The SpeedHawk, as it had been nicknamed, was a four-blade, twin-engine helicopter capable of cruising at one hundred seventy miles per hour. Equipped with two lifting wings and a large round ducted propeller at the back of the aircraft, the SpeedHawk was designed for quick takeoffs and incredible thrusts as it set on its journey.

Deur finished a conversation he was having with the pilot as he laid out their course. This was more than a nickel tour. Deur needed to show Gregg and Waller the challenges he was facing with his small group of newly commissioned deputies turned guardsmen.

The clearly identifiable waterway came into view. The water, a muddy, brownish color, meandered slowly along the Texas-Oklahoma border until it reached Arkansas. In times of drought, the river left a muddy base that could act like quicksand. During the winter, when rain was more abundant, the river still flowed at a steady pace and became too deep to cross at most points.

There were several major interstate bridges leading into Texas, with Interstate 35 being the busiest of the north-south transportation routes. Over the past forty-eight hours, nearly ten thousand refugees had amassed at the border. From the helicopter's point of view, now hovering at two thousand feet, the mass of humanity pressing closer to the Red River resembled a large marathon beginning to start a race.

People were lined up along both sides of the interstate, engulfing the Border Casino and Truck Stop and the entire community of Thackerville, Oklahoma, a mile away.

"That's more than ten thousand people," said Gregg as he pressed his face against the window. "I'm amazed that you've been able to hold them back."

Deur explained his methods. "We learned a lot from the debacle at the I-10 bridge at the Louisiana border. I immediately ordered more concrete barriers for this bridge and a total of four water cannons from Dallas SWAT to fire upon the crowd if necessary. Tear gas has been deployed as well."

"And that combination has proven effective?" asked Waller.

"Yes, for the most part," said Deur. "Occasionally, a group will attempt to swim across the river and we'll fire warning shots to turn them back."

"Have they killed anyone yet?" asked Gregg.

Deur hesitated and grimaced. "No, but I'm afraid that's about to change."

"Why?" asked Gregg.

"After last night's speech by the president, the word apparently got out to the crowd. They've been unruly since. Plus, we're starting to take on sporadic gunfire."

"They're shooting at your men?" asked Waller.

"Yes, from a distance, at least so far. None of our people have been injured, but they're certainly unnerved. My concern is that as soon as one of these potshots finds their mark, our people will react and it will look like a slaughter. Many of our men are equipped with their own weapons, the majority of which are AR-15s."

"America's rifle," muttered Gregg. He took a deep breath and exhaled. "The incident in Beaumont was not witnessed by the media. That will change now. They're being flown in on charter aircraft from all over the world. All eyes are on Texas after secession was declared and the president drew a line in the sand. One misstep on our part, and world opinion will be clearly against our new republic."

Deur issued a suggestion. "I can beef up our men and issue rubber bullets to them. We could treat this as a riot-control situation."

"That won't stop them from shooting across the river," said Gregg. "We need to draw them away and shut off their access to the bridge." He continued. "Naturally, I'll have to clear this with the governor, but it's a twofold plan. First we'll create nonlethal chaos on the other side."

"What does that look like?" asked Deur.

"I'll call in a humanitarian airlift of food and water. We'll drop packages of emergency rations and bottled water about half a mile back toward the WinStar casino. This will draw them away from the bridge entrance. Any who remain, we'll blast with the water cannons."

"Then what, Monty? Won't they just come back?" asked Waller.

"There won't be anything to come back to. I'll call an airstrike on the interstate on the Oklahoma side, effectively obliterating their access to the bridge. When a true recovery starts, the highway can be rebuilt easier than the bridge itself. With the crowd pushed back onto terra firma, we can build fortified gunner stations to stop the swimmers from trying to cross without fear of our people being shot. Further, it will send a clear message to the crowd that we're prepared to use overwhelming force to secure our borders if need be."

"I like it," said Deur. "I believe the governor will sign off on it. She's going to want assurances that we've minimized loss of life."

"We'll do our best, but border conflicts have a history of brutal internecine warfare. By nature, the actions required to protect your country will be destructive to both sides. Our goal is to minimize the destruction to ours."

PART SEVEN

Thursday, December 1

CHAPTER 60

December 1
South Korean Naval Base
Incheon, South Korea

Duncan didn't expect the South Korean Navy to welcome them with open arms, a basket of fruit, and a bottle of wine. He just hoped they didn't gun them down while they stood on the bow of the North Korean patrol boat with their hands held high. Sook, on the other hand, was disappointed in their treatment. Unknown to the two escapees, there were larger forces at play, which prevented them from being as well received into the South as they'd hoped.

It was after midnight and the two were being held in adjoining holding cells at a South Korean Naval Base near the airport at Incheon. As they were en route to the base, they quickly concocted a story. They would claim to be married so they wouldn't be separated, and that Sook was now an American citizen by virtue of their marriage.

Further, they would tell the South Koreans they were on a United Nations' mission and a fishing boat they were riding on began to capsize. The North Korean patrol boat stopped to pick them up, but when they became hostile, Duncan defended his wife and threw the men overboard.

Duncan knew this concocted story wouldn't hold up under further scrutiny, but his continued insistence to speak to a member of the United States military or an American consulate representative bought them time from any interrogation.

Sook finally fell asleep on a concrete bench, but Duncan remained awake, trying to consider all of the possibilities as he waited for any representative of the United States government. It was two in the morning when the main door into the holding area opened with a loud clank. A uniformed naval officer carrying an iPad approached Duncan's cell, escorted by two South Korean soldiers.

"My name is Lieutenant Daniel Stallcup with the United States Embassy and Consulate. I apologize for the delay in my arrival. Your name, please, place of birth and social security number."

"Duncan Armstrong Junior. Borden County, Texas. 645-48-0887." Duncan chose not to volunteer any other information at this point.

The lieutenant typed in the data and then presented the iPad to Duncan. "Press your palm onto the screen, making sure that your fingertips are registered."

Duncan followed the instructions and waited for a reaction. The lieutenant typed in several fields on the iPad and then information began to appear on the screen, including Duncan's picture. After a moment of scrolling through the information provided to him, the lieutenant raised the iPad over his right shoulder so the South Korean soldier could read it.

Puzzled, Duncan studied the man. He raised his eyes to look at Duncan's bearded face, and then he glanced at the iPad once again.

"He's one of ours," the South Korean soldier said in perfect English without a dialect. "We'll take him to Yongsan for a debrief."

"What about the girl?" asked the lieutenant.

The South Korean soldier, who, Duncan now realized, was probably with the agency, asked, "What is this girl to you?"

"She's my wife," Duncan quickly replied.

"No, she's not. You're off to a bad start. What is this girl to you?"

"She's a defector who saved my life. She does not want to be used by the South for propaganda purposes because she fears for her family's safety."

The man walked over to the cell where Sook was now sitting upright and awake. He returned to Duncan.

"We'll cover for you and this bogus story, for now," he whispered through the cell. "There's a lot to talk about, Armstrong, and you better be truthful."

"Not a problem." Duncan was willing to say anything to move out of South Korean custody, but he certainly didn't appreciate this guy's attitude. Park had died and he'd risked his life for his country. He wasn't gonna put up with any crap.

The man stared Duncan down one last time and then nodded to the other soldier. "Tell them we'll take these two into our custody. Lieutenant, advise USFK command of this development. We should be at Yongsan Garrison within the hour."

Duncan thought to himself, *Saddle up, cowboy. Your ride is just beginning.*

CHAPTER 61

December 1
Raven Rock Mountain Complex
Liberty Township, Pennsylvania

"Any discussion of targeting North Korea with our nuclear arsenal is delusional and should be taken off the table," started DHS Secretary Pickering. "We've been warned by our allies and the DPRK's chief allies—China and Russia. The humanitarian, economic, and environmental consequences would be devastating, and not just within North Korea's borders. Our allies insist we'd be putting them at risk of nuclear fallout as well as a likely nuclear counterattack by Pyongyang."

President Harman was under tremendous pressure to craft a response to the EMP attack that had devastated the nation. The impact assessments continued to come into Raven Rock, and the news was not good. The supervisory control and data acquisition control systems, known as SCADA, used for utility systems' infrastructure and coordination, were permanently damaged. In addition to computers, SCADA was damaged due to fused power lines and lost data, requiring a complete replacement and reprogramming of the systems.

The EMP Commission had warned Congress that the costs from the detonation of an EMP over Washington, DC, would exceed seven hundred seventy billion dollars. The entire country was facing an infrastructure expenditure of hundreds of trillions of dollars.

The Federal Aviation Administration provided the president a death toll from the aircraft impacted by the EMP attack. Hundreds of flights fell from the sky, killing those on board and unsuspecting persons on the ground below.

Now, on the seventh day after the power grid's collapse, grocery stores and home improvement stores had been emptied either through purchases or looting. Health care had been reduced to its most rudimentary level, as medical personnel made do without their complex diagnostic equipment.

Transportation was nonexistent except for older automobiles that did not rely upon modern-day electronics to function. However, as society became more and more lawless, those fortunate Americans who owned one of these vehicles had to stay vigilant. With the total breakdown of the rule of law, an operating vehicle was an asset worth killing for.

Finally, law enforcement and first responders were completely overwhelmed, and most had opted for protecting their families rather than lose their lives for a lost cause. Gangs immediately began to form, tearing through communities like bands of marauders, virtually unopposed by police.

Fires were raging out of control across the nation, but more so in the northern states, where fires were being built inside structures to stay warm. Early warning devices, fire-control systems, and available first responders had all failed to meet the people's needs.

The estimated three hundred million plus weapons in the United States began to be put into use. Many weapons were used for hunting and self-defense. Others, especially in the big cities like Los Angeles, Chicago, New York, and Philadelphia, were used by thugs to take anything of value from their fellow man.

Turf wars broke out in the inner cities. Police no longer controlled the streets, and the president's Declaration of Martial Law did little to stem the tide of violence. Soon, military commanders within the FEMA regions declared certain areas as so inherently hostile as to be unsafe for their troops. Those who lived in the cities were on their own.

President Harman surmised that near-term recovery could prove difficult because of the nation's reliance on transportation and electricity-powered infrastructures such as the internet and telephone.

Against this backdrop of distracting domestic consequences of the EMP attack, the president realized it would be difficult for the U.S. to organize a coherent retaliatory strike against the DPRK and, based upon their best evidence, the Iranians.

President Harman took another sip of coffee and then addressed the chairman of the Joint Chiefs, who was overseeing the nation's military operations from Cheyenne Mountain in Colorado.

"Admiral, prior to Secretary Gregg's resignation, he assured me the military was ready to initiate a first strike against our aggressors. During our many cabinet meetings, Secretary Gregg continued to reassure me our defensive capabilities were second to none. I take it you'd agree with the former secretary's position."

"Yes, Madam President," said United States Navy Admiral Terrence *Top Gun* Dasanti. Admiral Dasanti was a highly decorated pilot, starting his career at the U.S. Naval Academy in Annapolis, Maryland. He'd earned his bona fides when he excelled in the U.S. Navy Strike Fighter Tactics program at Naval Air Station Fallon, an hour outside Reno, Nevada.

Admiral Dasanti continued his thought. "It would be game on if the DPRK were to fire a missile at us or any of our allies. This is a game of minutes, but our initial detection of a missile launch by the DPRK would occur in seconds. Our retaliatory strikes would be so swift that our missiles would pass theirs in mid-flight before our defensive capabilities would strike their ICBMs down. The entire flight time from North Korea to the U.S. mainland is less than forty-five minutes."

The president interrupted. "Admiral Dasanti, in 2017, one of my predecessors authorized his national security team to act immediately to defend us if a North Korean missile was headed toward Guam, Hawaii, or, of course, the U.S. mainland. President Billings rescinded that order on the day he was inaugurated. He thought the decision to retaliate should come directly from the Office of the President. I agreed with him at the time, but the situation is much more precarious now. Do you think I should turn over that authority to you and the personnel within Cheyenne Mountain?"

"I do, Madam President," replied Admiral Dasanti. "When any missile is launched from around the world, it produces a plume and heat signature that is quickly picked up by our satellite network. Within seconds, this information is transmitted to NORAD as well as USSTRATCOM. We quickly assess where the missile is going and whether it is a credible threat to our interests, allies, or military installations."

"Admiral, if I entrust this responsibility to you, I need to have total confidence in your abilities."

"Madam President, the system can and will defend the homeland if attacked. However, only you can order a retaliatory strike, in my opinion. Let me say this, a retaliatory strike in response to incoming missiles is about more than vengeance and punishment. The launch of our ICBMs will act to destroy both the offensive and defensive capabilities of the DPRK. For that reason, Madam President, and I say this out of complete honor and respect for the challenges you face, but the axiom *he who hesitates is lost* applies in this instance. If we delay our nuclear response, their second wave of missiles could take out our silos. As I said previously, this is a game of seconds."

"Understood," said the president. "I assure you, I will not hesitate to give the order. Major Patterson, who is carrying the nuclear football, is in the room with me now, and I'm sure he's tired of sleeping on the couch outside my quarters at Raven Rock. When the time comes, I'll be ready."

CHAPTER 62

December 1
United States Forces Korea
Yongsan Garrison, Seoul, South Korea

The United States Forces Korea was the primary command under the umbrella of the U.S. Pacific Command. USFK, as it was known, was headquartered at Yongsan Garrison, a suburban area of Seoul. Over forty thousand American soldiers were present in South Korea as part of their mission to keep the region stable and to protect the South from attack. USFK coordinated this military presence, but also performed an important intelligence function. As a result, as Duncan liked to say, *the place was crawling with spooks.*

It was dawn when Duncan and Sook were escorted into separate interrogation rooms at Yongsan Garrison. After being given a black coffee, a bottled water, and a cellophane-wrapped cheese Danish, he was visited by the man who had masqueraded as a South Korean soldier, together with a woman wearing a gray suit.

"Armstrong, we've reviewed your file. Decorated combat vet. Recruited by the agency. Performed admirably on assignments. Then poof, you disappeared. Yet here you sit with a tall tale of having visited the Hermit Kingdom, got married to a local, scooted off on a fishing honeymoon, and to top it off, single-handedly took out a North Korean patrol boat."

Gray-suit lady chuckled at her counterpart's sarcasm.

Duncan smiled. "Wow, sounds like a good book, doesn't it?"

The agency interrogator sat back in his chair and clasped his fingers across his stomach. "Why don't you fill in the gaps, Mr. Armstrong?"

Duncan studied his interrogators. Either they knew who he was and what his real mission entailed in North Korea, or they didn't and they were just fishing.

He smiled and replied, "I think you have all *you need to know*, wouldn't you agree?"

The interrogator slammed his fist on the table. "Armstrong, you better start talking real quick like or this is not going to go well for you. What were you doing in North Korea?"

"I met a nice girl, got married, and hope to live happily ever after," Duncan replied without breaking eye contact.

"Last chance, pal! Tell us what you know, or I will send your gal pal back through the DMZ."

Duncan clenched his lips together and curled them in slightly. He shook his head from side to side. "Sorry, that's all you're gonna get. Now, may I have my one phone call? Are there any American lawyers around here or—"

"Armstrong!" his interrogator shouted as he gripped the arms of his chair and began to stand.

Then the woman in the gray suit touched the interrogator's arm and softly spoke for the first time. "Would you excuse us, please?"

Smoke was still coming out of the man's ears when he spun and left the room. With his eyes, Duncan followed him out of the room and then slowly turned his attention to the woman. He wasn't going to fall for the good cop, bad cop routine.

"Mr. Armstrong, I am Lynn Sweeney, assistant chargé d'affaires for the U.S. Embassy and Consulate. Like my associate, I work for the Central Intelligence Agency; however, I report directly to Billy Yancey, head of the Political Action Group within the National Clandestine Service. I will state that I am unaware of the details and purpose of your mission in North Korea. Very few people are. The questioning by my associate was intended to determine if you are capable of keeping your mission's details secret. In my opinion, you've passed the test."

"Thank you," said Duncan, who still vowed to keep his mission, and its results, to himself.

"I am sure you're still hesitant to speak with me, so your handlers have provided me this code—08282018DRA."

Duncan raised his eyebrows in surprise. The alphanumeric code, meaningless to most people, was one that had been established by Duncan before he left Langley for the Middle East months ago. It was a combination of the date Dallas had been killed in action and his brother's initials.

"Okay," said Duncan hesitantly.

"Armstrong, what happened to Park?"

"He was killed, shot in the back by DPRK soldiers," said Duncan somewhat defiantly. He still was angry that he and Park had been abandoned on Sinmi-do by this person, or Billy Yancey, or someone higher up.

"Who is the girl?"

"A villager with basic medical training. She and her family found me and kept me alive. I promised to bring her to safety in return."

"Are you aware that Kim Jong-un is alive?"

Duncan grimaced. "I gathered that. Has it been confirmed without a doubt?"

"Oh, yes," she replied. The agency representative sat up in her chair. "Did you attempt to fulfill your mission?"

"We did fulfill it," Duncan shot back. "Let's just say we obviously received some bad intel at Langley or we were set up. Park and I did our job, and he died for his country."

"Armstrong, the logistics of your mission may be over, but the secrecy never is. Do you understand that?"

"I do."

The woman reached into her pocket and retrieved a cell phone. She began typing what appeared to be a text message and sat silently while she awaited a response. After several minutes, her phone notified her of a text message and she typed once again. This time, the response was almost immediate.

"Final question, then we need to have a discussion about your future," she began. "What does the girl know about your mission? Is she a security threat?"

"She knows nothing, nor did she ask," Duncan replied. "Washington needs to know there are more like her in North Korea. They want a better life. They have no use for their government or its military. We need to help them any way we can."

"Armstrong, that may all be moot soon," the woman began. "You need to listen and understand what I'm about to tell you. The world has changed drastically in the last seven days."

CHAPTER 63

December 1
Kingsbury Colony, Montana

Morales's condition was deteriorating rapidly. He was unable to hold the reins of his horse. Slumped over the horse's neck, Morales was covered in extra blankets while his close friend Pacheco rode alongside, periodically preventing the injured rider from falling off. The bleeding from his bullet wound was under control, but he was suffering from chills and a high fever. Infection was raging inside his body, and he'd likely die if he didn't get treatment soon.

The group's progress had slowed considerably, and any thought of reaching Great Falls and medical treatment were cast aside. They were easily two or three days away at this pace.

Cooper debated his next decision with Riley and Palmer. Palmer suggest that she ride ahead in search of a ranch or any home where Morales could rest in warm, comfortable surroundings. Cooper absolutely refused to let her go on her own, insisting that she and Riley ride together. Even then, their inability to communicate concerned him. Because they'd stayed together for most of the ride, they hadn't taken the time to recharge the Uniden radios from their get-home bags. It was a mistake they'd learned from. Either way, he didn't like splitting the group up.

In the end, it was Morales's suffering from uncontrollable shivering that forced a decision. Palmer and Riley were sent south toward Great Falls. They'd take the risk and approach the first house they found, hoping to enlist the help of a Good Samaritan.

It had been two hours since they'd left, and Cooper was already fraught with concern. He chastised himself for choosing the health and safety of a relative stranger over his own family. Granted, Morales and Pacheco had been loyal to the three Armstrongs; however, in a survival situation, hard choices had to be made, and generally, family concerns trumped those of others.

Another half hour passed, and the sun was beginning to approach the tall peaks of the Rockies to their west. They'd been very fortunate to avoid any additional snowfall since the day after the grid collapsed. Now, clear, cold skies dominated their surroundings.

"Coop, I see a wagon coming our way," said Pacheco. "Should we move off the road?"

"There's no cover out here," Cooper responded. He pulled his horse to a stop. "Whoa."

He pulled his rifle and dismounted. Pacheco did the same and brought the three horses to a highway sign that read *Kingsbury Colony, 6 Miles*, where he tied them off.

"It is what it is," mumbled Pacheco as he stood off to the side, forcing the approaching riders to choose a target.

"Hah!" could be heard from the driver of the two-horse wagon. Then a dog's barking grew louder—a deep, baritone woof.

Cooper could see three people in the seat behind the horses. "It's Riley and Palmer! Here comes the cavalry!"

He and Pacheco lowered their rifles and walked toward the wagon, waving their arms.

"Hey, Coop!" yelled Riley as he began to slow the wagon. "We've found our angel of mercy!"

The high-strung wagon horses rumbled to a stop just beyond the traffic sign, causing the three horses to spook slightly. Morales groaned and began to fall off his horse, but Pacheco scrambled to cradle the larger man in his arms. His knees began to buckle until he turned Morales to land on his feet. Cooper quickly jumped in to assist.

"Thank God, y'all. Morales is in real trouble."

Palmer and Riley jumped out of the wagon and helped down a

woman bundled up in a suede leather trench coat with a thick Sherpa collar. She wore a brown felt cowboy hat that revealed flowing red hair underneath.

Riley made the introductions. "Guys, this here is Fiorella Schlossmacher. She owns the ranch up a ways in Kingsbury Colony. She's a retired nurse practitioner and has supplies to help Morales."

"Wow, it's a pleasure to meet you, ma'am," said Cooper as he removed his hat and shook her hand.

"It's nice to meet you, young man," she replied. Fiorella showed no outward concerns at being around a group of strangers on the road. As she spoke with the group, there was an inner peace about her that Cooper couldn't quite put his finger on. In a way, he envied her casual, unexcited demeanor.

The dog began to bark again. "Oh yeah," said Palmer. "That's Winnie, Fiorella's English bulldog. She came along for the ride."

"Won't she get cold out here?" asked Cooper.

"Oh, no," replied Fiorella. "She has plenty of chub to keep her warm. Winnie is our baby. My husband and I adopted her as a rescue pup when we lived near Kansas City. Winnie is named after a French bulldog in a book series my husband really enjoyed from years ago. That dog was called Winnie the Frenchie. In a way, it was prophetic. Winnie the Frenchie endured a power outage caused by a cyber attack. Our Winnie has to live through a power outage too."

The group continued to make small talk as they carefully got Morales settled in the back of the wagon. Soon he was bundled up, and the group traveled the six miles to the small ranch owned by the Schlossmachers.

Kingsbury Colony was a Hutterite community near the small northwestern Montana town of Valier. Like the Amish and Mennonites, Hutterites traced their roots back to the Reformation period throughout Europe in the sixteenth century. Almost extinct as a religious group, they had fled Europe and moved into the upper Great Plains of Montana and Western Canada, where they thrived. Hutterites focused on small local colonies of ranchers and farmers, focusing on self-sufficiency for everything from clothing to food to medical care.

The entourage arrived at the limestone and log home, which sat alone in the middle of a large snow-covered field. Smoke rose out of chimneys constructed on both ends of the residence, and the warm glow of candlelight could be seen through the windows.

"Here we go, buddy," said Cooper as he and Pacheco hoisted up Morales and carried him through the front door.

"For now, place him on the settee in front of the fire," instructed Fiorella. "Palmer and I will step into the kitchen while you change him into these long handles. My husband is larger than this young man, but at least his clothes are dry. Also, please put these warm socks on him."

Fiorella, Palmer, and Winnie left the room while the guys stripped Morales of his wet clothes and dressed him. The warmth of the fire had a positive effect on their injured friend, as he tried to speak.

"Are we at the Motel 6?" he asked with a slight laugh before he coughed up bloody, mucus-filled fluids.

"Yeah, something like that," said Pacheco. "Why don't you leave the jokes to Riley and get some rest. We've got someone that can take care of you."

Morales nodded his head and curled up on the small two-person sofa. A wool-knit blanket was tucked around him, and he was asleep within minutes.

Fiorella asked Palmer to assist her in examining Morales while he slept. Riley and Pacheco went outside to secure the horses in the barn. Their rides were treated to a warm spot to sleep, fresh hay and water, and a roof to avoid the cold.

Cooper sat by the fire as Fiorella examined Morales's wound. She didn't make any comments, only occasionally uttering a *humpf* or an *oh*. Palmer provided her the first aid supplies as requested and focused on the procedures Fiorella employed to bandage the gunshot wound. For Palmer, everything was a learning experience.

Finally, the examination was over. She placed a small pillow under Morales's head and wrapped him in another blanket. She nodded her head toward the kitchen, indicating Palmer and Cooper to follow her.

"I wish I could give you some good news about your friend, but I can't," she started. "He has a very serious infection. I hated to wake him, albeit briefly, but I needed to give him the only antibiotics I have, Clavamox, which is left over from an infection Winnie had last summer. It is a form of amoxicillin that is identical to what humans take. Also, I have a few tramadol for the pain. English bulldogs are susceptible to hip dysplasia, and the tramadol provides her some relief."

"Won't the medication make him better?" asked Cooper.

"There must be bullet fragments inside his shoulder, which are causing the infection. Sometimes the medication works, but he may need to go for medical treatment."

"In Great Falls?" asked Palmer.

"Unfortunately, that's not a good idea," replied Fiorella. "The worst of our society has reared its ugly head in Great Falls. Some members of the Colony went there in search of a family member who hadn't returned. They came back with horrible reports of violence and looting. It's the same all over the country."

Cooper walked toward the living room and looked at Morales. With his back turned to the kitchen, he asked, "What do you suggest?"

"The best I can do is treat him with these antibiotics and change his bandages regularly. Only rest and the Good Lord will determine his fate after that."

Cooper turned his back to the women and stared at Morales sleeping. "How long?"

"A week to ten days, to be sure. Infections fester even though the mind and body disagree. The trauma his body is suffering is not to be trifled with."

Cooper took a deep breath. Each day that passed, society fell deeper into the abyss of collapse. They had been isolated from the carnage that even small cities like Great Falls was experiencing. A seven- to ten-day delay in returning to Texas could be the difference in their survival.

The front door opened, breaking Cooper out of his thoughts.

Pacheco and Riley reported on the horses and a discovery in the barn.

"You'll never believe the sweet ride we found in one of the horse stalls," started Riley. "It's incredible."

Fiorella started to laugh. "You boys must've discovered my husband's favorite toy—Red Rover."

CHAPTER 64

December 1
Lubbock, Texas

"I'm not real thrilled with leaving the ranch right now, especially after what happened last night," Lucy said as she glanced to the pickup truck bed where the two men were chained together and huddled behind the cab to stay warm. She'd refused to allow the dead girl to be buried on the ranch, so Preacher had found a large tarp and rolled her up in it. Her body was in the back with the two trespassers.

"Thank you for patching the whiner up," said Major with a chuckle. "I knew I was too far away to kill him with the shotgun, but I did manage to tear up his arm pretty good."

"The only reason I treated him was so he'd stop his squallin'. Even then, I can hear him behind us. *It's cold. They're inhuman.* Crybaby. Shut up already!"

Major laughed at his wife's feistiness. If Miss Lucy had a vote, she and Preacher would've definitely been in the *hang 'em from the tallest tree* column.

"I agree, Lubbock is an hour from home, but the meat will be ready, and we can pick up another cooler full of dry ice. We can drop these two clowns off at the sheriff's office on the way."

Lucy looked around the town of two hundred and thirty and saw only three people standing on a street corner. Stores were closed, and the Exxon station's pole sign read *out of gas.*

Major had filled up the truck with fuel from their farm diesel tanks at the ranch. He doubted any law enforcement officers would care that he was running red diesel in his truck rather than the street legal and heavily taxed green diesel.

After arriving at the sheriff's office, they spent a few moments discussing the matter with a deputy, who promptly locked the two men up. The sheriff was out on patrol. There had been several other reports from the western parts of the county of break-ins and petty thefts.

Major and Lucy didn't spend a lot of time chitchatting with the lone deputy on duty. They weren't sure what to expect in Lubbock and certainly wanted to get their business done and back home around dark.

After a forty-five-minute, uneventful drive, they arrived at the outskirts of Lubbock. Just before they entered town, they passed through the small bedroom community of Woodrow on the side of the city. At a traffic signal, they were stopped by a City of Woodrow patrol car.

When the officer approached them, Major provided his license as well as his Texas Ranger identification card as issued by the Department of Public Safety. This was the first time he'd been approached by law enforcement since his retirement from Company C years ago.

"Good afternoon, Officer," Major started cordially after handing the two forms of identification to the young man.

"Good afternoon, sir, ma'am," he said, tipping his hat to Lucy. "This is a courtesy stop only, Major Armstrong. I need to advise you there has been some unrest on the west side of town along Route 114 toward the New Mexico state line. Apparently, a large group of people had gathered at the checkpoint near Farwell, which is northwest of here. They began moving southward until they found a section of the border that was undermanned. They killed three Bailey County deputies and rushed into the state."

"How many?" asked Lucy.

"Several hundred, ma'am," the officer replied. "Maybe more. Lubbock County sent a large contingent of officers to stop the flow of people coming in, but that left the patrols of the city undermanned. While our department is trying to help out, there are dozens who slipped through the cracks. They're looting homes and assaulting the elderly. It's pretty bad on the west side, so I was gonna warn you not to head that way."

"Thank you, Officer," said Major, who reached out his window to retrieve his ID cards. "We're headed straight ahead to Plain Meats on Avenue G."

"Okay, but the interstate is closed to local traffic. Under the circumstances, the county judge has ordered the primary roads crisscrossing town to be used by military and emergency personnel only. Your two best options are up Avenue P to our west or MLK Boulevard to our east."

Major nodded and was about to roll up the window when he asked one additional question. "You mentioned military traffic. Is the military being used in Lubbock?"

"Not in the town per se. They have a staging area at the South Plains Fairgrounds on the other side of I-27 from where you're goin'. I've heard the governor has divided the state, um, I mean the republic into large geographic regions, each with their own military contingent."

"Whose military? United States?" asked Lucy.

"No, ma'am. I mean, it's complicated. I'm not really high on the need-to-know list. I've heard rumors that the military installations within the state have joined Texas, under the command of General Gregg, who resigned as Secretary of Defense. Now, listen, please don't repeat this. I've based all of this on chatter back at the station. The only thing I know is Texas isn't a state anymore, and there's an army gathering at the fairgrounds."

Major nodded and thanked the young man for providing him a heads-up on the events around the city. He turned left at the next intersection and found Avenue P, where they discussed what they'd learned.

"Lucy, they can't keep this border sealed forever, especially around the Panhandle," started Major. "It's too deserted and wide open around here. Frankly, it's the same problem we have at the ranch, which allowed those scoundrels to break into Jose's home. The ranch is too big. We're fenced, but that doesn't mean anything unless we've got several armed men greeting anyone attempting to cross it. The same thing applies to Texas. The natural borders like the Red River and even the Gulf of Mexico help protect the state from intrusions. But up here, you've got to build a fence with razor wire, like a prison. Then you have to patrol it with trained soldiers or law enforcement personnel."

"Do you think that's why the army is here?" asked Lucy.

"I assume so," he replied as he made another right turn to work his way over to Avenue G, where the slaughterhouse was located. "Look around us. Cars aren't going anywhere, but neither are people. Folks seem to be content to stay home, waiting to see what happens next. Lubbock is a pretty good-sized city. If it had lost power, there would be chaos in the streets. Instead, folks seem to be pretty calm."

Lucy studied the docile surroundings as they slowly made their way to pick up the food intended to sustain them for at least four to six months. During her lifetime, her gut had warned her about situations when her surroundings appeared to be too quiet. This was one of those moments.

"Yeah," Lucy mumbled as she rested her elbow on the door and stared at Interstate 27 above them, which was devoid of traffic. "Maybe they're waiting to see what happens next."

CHAPTER 65

December 1
United States Forces Korea
Yongsan Garrison, Seoul, South Korea

"They are letting me go," said Sook as she embraced Duncan. The two had been reunited for the first time in ten hours since their arrival at Yongsan Garrison. "They asked me many questions, mostly about you and your friend. I was truthful with them. I know very little."

"That's good news, Sook," said a demoralized Duncan. After his conversation with the CIA official, he'd become somewhat depressed. "I have something to tell you. Let's sit down."

"I have something to tell you, also. Duncan, being apart from you the last ten hours has been horrible. I ached to be by your side. I think—I know—I've fallen in love with you."

She immediately hugged him and buried her face in his chest. Duncan could feel the tears of relief soak through his shirt. He closed his eyes, seeking guidance from above, unsure of what to say. He'd begun to feel the same way, but what he wanted was impossible.

He pulled away and wiped her tears with his fingers. "Sook, listen to me. Something bad has happened."

"What? What is it?"

"America was attacked by two nuclear explosions. Our country has lost its electric power. The nation is in chaos."

"Oh no. Duncan, your family, are they okay?"

"Sook, I don't know. It's impossible for me to call the States. The power is off, so the telephone lines don't work. There is some good news."

"What? Please tell me," she insisted.

"My state of Texas is safe. They still have power where my parents live."

"This is great! Duncan, please take me with you. Take me to Texas. I can learn more better English. I will help your family. I'm smart and I can cook, too."

He put his arm around her and pulled her head to his shoulder. It felt good.

But it was impossible.

He had one chance to catch a military transport to Guam and connect on another one to San Diego. From there, he was on his own.

"Sook, it's complicated. You see, my state, Texas, has left the United States. The government formed its own country. I can't fly back to Texas, only to California. I must find my own way home."

"We can do it," she pleaded. "We work well together. I am a fighter, too. Remember? I will not be a burden to you."

Duncan had never fallen in love before. His life was devoted to serving his country. In his mind, he couldn't adequately do his duty and leave the love of his life at home wondering if he'd return in one piece.

But things had changed. His days of undertaking black ops missions were over. Now, his life was dedicated to taking care of his family. He did love Sook, and they could make a life together in Texas far better than the one she'd lead in Seoul with hundreds of missiles pointed at her from the North.

He thought of the practical aspects. First, she was a North Korean with no passport and no identifying documents. Would that matter at the Armstrong Ranch? His parents had taken in many illegals from Mexico over the years. They'd taught them how to live like Americans and helped them gain their citizenship.

Was Sook any different from the Mexicans who worked on the ranch? Well, she was Korean, and this brought back the history Duncan had studied in high school. After Pearl Harbor was attacked, Japanese living in America were more than shunned. Many were gathered up and put into internment camps in the name of national security. Would that happen now with respect to North Koreans? Maybe not, especially if he kept Sook tucked away at the ranch, away from prying eyes.

But he had to get there first. She might be verbally abused from Seoul to Guam to San Diego. He would have to shield her from that. Then there was the trip from San Diego to Texas. It had to be a thousand miles, he didn't know. Was she up for that? Heck, was he up for that?

Duncan took a deep breath and looked down to Sook's hopeful face. "Are you sure you love me?"

"Yes, I love you, Duncan."

"You know what, that's all that matters. I love you too. Sook, this will be very difficult and dangerous. We could be hurt or even killed. Are you sure you want to be with me?"

"I would rather die than be without you."

The door opened suddenly, and the woman CIA officer arrived with two U.S. Army personnel.

"Armstrong, these gentlemen will drive you to the airfield."

They stepped into the room and handed Duncan his Barrett rifle and a travel bag that was heavy enough to hold his ammo. He was also handed his travel credentials and identification.

Duncan studied the documents, which were standard-issue alternative passports to be used temporarily until he arrived stateside.

"Thank you, but I need one more thing. I need you to print another set of these for Park."

She replied, "For what purpose? He's—"

"I know that. It's for my purposes. My country owes me this favor. Please, make it happen."

The agency woman's eyes darted back and forth between Duncan and Sook. A slight smile crossed her face as she nodded.

"I'll adjust the gender designation as well. Thank you for your service, Armstrong. Good luck upon your arrival in San Diego."

CHAPTER 66

December 1
Korean Peninsula

Korean Air flight 765, a Boeing 747 wide-body quad jet, took off from New Chitose airport just south of Sapporo, Japan. The flight carried the South Korean Winter Olympics team, which had been practicing at some of the twelve venues still in operation from the 1972 winter games in Sapporo. After South Korea had successfully hosted the games in PyeongChang in 2018, popularity for winter sports grew, and the team had reached out to Japan to share their Sapporo facilities. Their two-week-long training session was cut short due to concerns over the EMP attack upon America and possible retaliation resulting in a regional war with the North. The Japanese government had encouraged foreign citizens to return home for their safety in the event hostilities broke out.

The flight was a routine one, as evidenced by the lighthearted attitude of the two pilots in the cockpit. Both the captain and first officer were seasoned pilots with Korean Air and had flown this route many times. After they were airborne and reached a cruising speed of five hundred eighty miles per hour, the captain left the cockpit to have a conversation with a flight attendant he'd become intimate with the night before.

The two had a flirtatious conversation in the galley while the first officer manned the cockpit, periodically looking around the flight deck just out of habit. With everything in hand, he elected to greet the passengers on the flight.

"Good morning from the flight deck. This is First Officer Ju Ji-hoon, and it is my pleasure to assist Captain Lee Hyun-woo as we escort you to Seoul via our beautiful Korean Air 747-400 aircraft."

First Officer Ju stopped his address to the passengers as he received a message from Seoul's air traffic control center.

"Roger, Seoul Center. This is Korean Air seven-six-five. Go ahead."

"Korean Air seven-six-five, weather system has stalled in your route. Aircraft in region are experiencing violent turbulence at all altitudes. Suggest you alter course to a heading westward of your current flight path."

"Roger that, Seoul Center," said First Officer Ju, who finished sending a text to his wife. The buzzer rang on the entry door to the flight deck, and he unbuckled his harness and confirmed it was the captain.

"Come in, Captain," said First Officer Ju as the captain pushed his way in with a flight attendant in tow.

"You won't mind if I take care of a little business in the latrine, do you?" he said with a laugh. The flight attendant was draped all over the older man and looked at First Officer Ju with a shy, flirty look.

"No, of course not, enjoy," replied First Officer Ju.

He returned to his seat and strapped himself in again. He tried to tune out the sounds coming from the small bathroom on the flight deck. He was about to continue addressing the passengers when he remembered he needed to adjust the flight path to avoid the inclement weather.

The first officer quickly made changes in the computer, and the plane could be felt making a gentle turn toward the west. Proud of his efforts to provide a more pleasant flight for the passengers, he took to the intercom again.

Had he been a prankster, he'd relocate the microphone for the intercom system next to the latrine door and treat the rest of the passengers on Korean Air 765 to the audio from his captain's tryst in the latrine. But First Officer Ju was all business.

*****

The Korean People's Army Air Force spent considerable resources on their air defenses. North Korea shared borders with the Chinese and Russians, both deemed allies, and South Korea, with whom they'd maintained a closely watched truce along the 38th parallel and the DMZ.

Along their coastline at the Sea of Japan, hundreds of bunkers had been built for the purpose of defending against possible air attacks from Japan and the United States. After the attempt on Kim Jong-un's life, their military had been placed on its highest alert status. Once the EMP attack was initiated, the Korean generals allowed these Air Defense units carte blanche on repelling any air attacks. Nervous, tired soldiers manned the bunkers, which stretched from the DMZ to Sonbong County in the extreme northeastern part of the country.

At first, an airman manning his station thought his monitors were malfunctioning. He quickly made several keystrokes in an effort to confirm the findings. In a panic, he raised his hand in the air and shouted for his superior.

Seconds later, other hands were raised within the bunkers on Hwadae peninsula, the easternmost part of North Korea, which jutted out into the Sea of Japan. Their conclusions were confirmed. An aircraft was approaching at nearly six hundred miles per hour.

*****

First Officer Ju took to the airwaves and addressed the passengers. "We have received word from Seoul operations that a low-pressure system has stalled over the Sea of Japan, causing a significant amount of turbulence. We have adjusted our flight path to avoid the bad weather and to insure you enjoy the most pleasant of rides back to Seoul. Also, I would like to take a moment to welcome the South Korean Winter Olympics squad on board with us today. They've been training in Sapporo and are returning home. I, too, am a skier, and one of my favorite phrases is *it's all downhill from here!*"

First Officer Ju would have been pleased to hear the laughter of the passengers. But for the heavy security door, he would have. Then again, if he'd keyed his mic for one last thought, the passengers would have heard him scream in terror as he saw the six KN-06 surface-to-air missiles streaking toward the nose of Korean Air 765.

CHAPTER 67

December 1
Kingsbury Colony, Montana

While Palmer and Pacheco remained inside to discuss Morales's condition, Riley showed Cooper the 1982 Land Rover Defender in the barn. Painted in apple red with a white roof, the vintage diesel truck was in pristine condition.

"Check it out, Coop," started Riley. "It's right-hand drive like over in England. That's where it's made, see." Riley pointed to the license plates, which were the original United Kingdom-issued plates, and the Land Rover emblem for the UK dealership.

Cooper walked around the vehicle and kicked the tires mounted on the white rims. He opened the driver's side door on the right side of the truck and looked in.

"Check it out," Riley continued as he gushed over Red Rover. "There are no electronics on this thing. Everything works on toggle switches. There are only a couple of gauges for speed and fuel. Simple as pie."

"This is amazing, Riley," said Cooper.

Fiorella approached from behind. "Start him up. Because its cold, he'll be a little stubborn. You can use that shifter at the passenger's feet to increase the idle. Seriously, go ahead."

Riley didn't hesitate and bounced into the driver's seat, turned the key to allow the diesel motor to ready itself, and then turned the key.

While he went through the motions, Fiorella pulled Cooper aside. "Your friend Pacheco is going to insist you go forward without them," she started. "He is a very unselfish young man and loyal to his best friend."

"Then we should stay as well," said Cooper.

Fiorella shook her head. "Cooper, you are a grown man, and all of your companions look to you for guidance. They trust you to make the right decisions. You must decide what is best for your family. Do you understand me?"

Cooper frowned and shook his head. He'd already reached this conclusion, but he felt obligated to speak with Palmer and Riley about it. "I feel I'd be disloyal to leave them behind."

"You must consider your family, Cooper," Fiorella insisted. "My husband was in Kansas when this happened. I know that he is trying to return home to me at all costs. As his wife, I take comfort in knowing he is trying to put me first above all others. You must do the same for your brother, sister, and parents."

"Okay, I'll talk to them. Fiorella, thank you so much for taking care of Morales and allowing us into your home. God bless you."

"Oh, young man, He has. Make no mistake about that. Now, I will send Palmer out to speak with you while Pacheco and I prepare dinner to be cooked in the outdoor kitchen my husband built years ago. The sky is crystal clear tonight, and we should rejoice in the blessings we've all been given."

Cooper gave Fiorella a hug as Riley started Red Rover. The diesel engine puffed out some black smoke but roared to life.

"Thank you so much. I'll talk to them now."

Fiorella added one more thing. "My husband would be honored to give you fine young people his beloved Red Rover to expedite your journey home. He would not hesitate to make the sacrifice if he were standing next to me right now."

"But we couldn't," protested Cooper. "This is an operating vehicle, a valuable asset to travel around in. You may need it to go—"

Fiorella held up her hand and interrupted Cooper. "To go nowhere. We have everything we need right here in Kingsbury Colony. My husband simply returned to Kansas to retrieve his sister and brother-in-law for the move west. They have a place set aside for them down the road to join us."

"Fiorella, are you sure? This is so generous."

"It is yours if you wish," she replied. "Now, let me retrieve your sister, and we'll meet you around the side of the house for supper."

Cooper looked skyward and smiled. Despite Red Rover's age, it appeared to be reliable. Even at thirty or forty miles per hour, their trip home was cut short from many weeks to a matter of days. As was typical of Cooper's thought processes, he did the math quickly in his head.

Fifteen hundred miles. Forty miles an hour. Less than forty hours of travel time. Works for me.

"Hey, I wanna see it too!" exclaimed Palmer as she trotted through the crunchy snow toward the barn.

Riley turned off the ignition and joined his siblings. "I love this ride, guys! Can you believe it? A truck that runs after what's happened."

Cooper hugged them both around the shoulders and walked them into the barn. They had some decisions to make.

For the next ten minutes, they agreed to leave Pacheco and Morales with Fiorella. There were many reasons for their decision. First and foremost, to give Morales a chance to live. Taking him on the road was out of the question. Second, the Brazilians could help Fiorella protect the ranch until her husband returned, or at least until Morales could ride again. Third, and it was an unspoken understanding between them from the moment they'd left Calgary, they wouldn't have to be put into a difficult situation in which they'd have to choose between their own safety and their friends.

With the decision to pull out in the morning made, the mode of transportation was debated. Riley was one hundred percent for taking Red Rover. His arguments stemmed around the usefulness of an operating vehicle that ran on diesel fuel, which could be obtained at any farm or ranch.

Palmer lamented the loss of her horse. She'd handpicked it as a foal from Governor Burnett's Four Sixes Ranch. The two had competed in many barrel-racing competitions. In the end, she was willing to leave her horse behind for a chance to reunite with her parents in a matter of days rather than months or not at all.

Cooper raised a few negatives, including the fact they'd have one of the only operating vehicles on the road. Red Rover, while beautiful, was a bright, shiny candy apple red. It wasn't gonna sneak up on anyone. As a result, they could find themselves fighting to defend their Defender, only to lose it and be without transportation when the battle was over.

Riley and Palmer agreed with Cooper's concerns, but they offered a variety of measures to avoid hostile contact. It might slow their trip down, but it was a huge difference over riding the horses. In essence, they could travel an hour in Red Rover the same distance they covered in a day on horseback.

The rodeo kids fist-bumped to memorialize their unanimous vote. They'd pull out of Kingsbury Colony, Montana, in the morning, with Red Rover delivering them home.

Pacheco broke up the subdued celebration as he shouted at them from the outdoor kitchen. "Hey, guys! We've got homemade brats, ranch-style beans, and cornbread."

Fiorella and Pacheco stood around the warm fire and the cast-iron cookware emitting heavenly smells of down-home cookin'. As the group toasted cups of apple cider and said a quick prayer thanking God for their good fortunes, a growing rumble began to fill the air from a distance.

Everyone turned to the east, searching for the cause of the now roaring, grumbling sound. It grew louder, causing them to look in all directions as the Rocky Mountains echoed the noise back toward them.

The grumbling changed to a loud, intense crackling like someone was shaking a giant piece of sheet metal. Then a wind accompanied the noise, which came at the group like a wave. Cooper could almost see the wave in the previously still night air. The winds accompanying the wave hit them, pushing them backward, causing Fiorella to lose her balance and fall against a chair.

The crackling was relentless, like fireworks erupting over and over, closer and faster until the pressure was squeezing Cooper's chest. And then he looked up.

Across the horizon, from Canada to Colorado, the sky was alit with the red glow of the solid rocket boosters of more than a dozen intercontinental ballistic missiles lifting off in perfect coordination, rising high over their heads and tilting toward the west.

"My God," said a gasping Fiorella.

Cooper muttered the words from Revelation, "*And he gathered them together into a place called in the Hebrew tongue, Armageddon.*"

Palmer followed with the words from the next verse. "*It is done.*"

THANK YOU FOR READING BEYOND BORDERS!

If you enjoyed it, I'd be grateful if you'd take a moment to write a short review (just a few words are needed) and post it on Amazon. Amazon uses complicated algorithms to determine what books are recommended to readers. Sales are, of course, a factor, but so are the quantities of reviews my books get. By taking a few seconds to leave a review, you help me out, and also help new readers learn about my work.

And before you go…

SIGN UP to Bobby Akart's mailing list to receive special offers, bonus content, and you'll be the first to receive news about new releases in The Lone Star Series, The Pandemic series, The Blackout series, The Boston Brahmin series and The Prepping for Tomorrow series—which includes sixteen Amazon #1 Bestsellers in thirty-nine fiction and non-fiction genres. Visit Bobby Akart's website for informative blog entries on preparedness, writing, and his latest contribution to the American Preppers Network.

www.BobbyAkart.com

29724630R00192

Made in the USA
Lexington, KY
02 February 2019